And The Young Gods Killed Themselves

:::::

TOWNS

Thank you
To everyone who shares with me this life
To Cris, for helping my words make sense
And to Katie, for her unending support

And The Young Gods Killed Themselves

The sky bleeds colors
Dripping down from my own veins
As lights in the distance
In the middle of my eyes
Remind me
That I'm alone

The wind blows cold
Across the skin of everything
Wet metal beneath my feet
As I slowly slip away

Falling with the rain
I watch as the lights don't move
And everything within me
Inside these eyes eternal
Collides against itself
Against the pain

And so the end
Was the beginning
And the beginning
Was the end

I

I was the last one of us to awaken here.

Though I don't remember where I was before this life.

What it was like when they existed.

And I didn't.

I try to push myself into the past, but there's this endless sort of wall just sitting there in my mind. It goes on in every direction, blocking me from every path. I touch its vague surface, and it flows within my hands. Its endless shadows move across my body, through my mind. I dig myself deeper while the darkness gets thicker and its shape gets harder, and before I know it I'm stuck in just a single point in time.

I see a blue sky.

The silhouette of a child standing in front of a sun.

I feel water sitting wet on my back.

My naked body lying on stone.

I hear an endless expanse condensed into a single point.

"Were you the one making that awfully strange sound?" the child asks me.

I understand the words that move into my ears.

I understand that I am here and that I am me and this is that and that is this and everything is something or nothing or both.

But what I don't know is how I know these things.

"You probably can't hear a thing after such a loud noise as that," the child says to me as she moves closer to my face.

Or is it a he?

"What sound?" I ask.

"So you can hear!" he yells moving even closer.

Or is it a she?

"It appears so," I say.

"But can you see?" it asks. "Or taste or smell or touch?"

"I can see and I can touch," I reply, "but there's not much here to smell or taste."

The child turns and looks away from me.

"Oh, there's plenty to smell and taste here," it says, "but I'm guessing you won't need to eat. At least if you're like the others you won't."

I sit myself up, but can't see much. Tall slabs of concrete lie around my body. Amongst the walls they form are cascades of water falling slow from brightly colored pieces of metal. Small patches of green plants grow around the places where the water gently flows.

"Others?" I ask the child.

"Yes, others," the child replies.

He, or she, turns back around and walks to a spot close to me. I can see the child clearer now, though I still can't tell if it's a boy or a girl. Messy white hair sits atop a soft white face, a face whose only feature is its innocence in form. Rings of soft gray float in the child's eyes, where they surround large black pupils that stare openly into this world.

She smiles.

Or he.

"I can't feel a thing," the child tells me in an empty sort of way.

"Not a thing?" I ask.

She falls down through the concrete and then he floats back up through the puddle of water surrounding my body.

"I was walking along in the rain," the child tells me, looking into my eyes. "I wasn't cold, and I wasn't wet. Water doesn't touch me. Nothing does, besides the ghosts. So I guess I wasn't really walking. I was pretending to walk, and I was pretending I felt the rain. I heard a noise that I thought was thunder. But it was different. It was quiet, yet it was somehow louder than any sound that I could hear. It grew and it grew until it was the only thing that could be heard. Such a loud, loud hum! It sounded so near. Almost inside of me. Then the clouds began to open up in the distance, and I could tell that the noise was coming from where the sunlight started to shine in. It kept getting louder and louder and brighter and brighter until it was all too much. I couldn't just sit there and listen and stare, so I pretended to run. And when I came upon you lying here naked in this puddle, the noise stopped. You opened your eyes. One is blue by the way. And the other is green. I asked you if you made that awfully strange sound, and then before we knew it we were here."

I look down at my naked body. I don't feel ashamed even though I do feel as if I should be for some reason or other. I look into the puddle and see a blurred reflection of what must be my face.

It doesn't look familiar.

It doesn't look like anything special at all.

Just a face being pushed around by the waves in its reflection.

"This doesn't make sense," I say out loud to both the child and myself. She smiles.

"How do you know?" he asks.

The darkness pulls me back into a place a little closer to now.

I try to stay put, but I've got nothing to hold on to.

She's perfect.

And I know it before I even see her.

I can tell she is by the way that I feel before I meet her for the first time.

Sam pretends to hold my hand as we walk along a hill made of rusted metal. It scrapes against the bottoms of my feet, yet the pain seems to only whisper into my mind. Long white flowers blow gently in the wind, moving in ways that echo my thoughts.

I feel I'm moving closer towards myself.

Towards being whole.

As we reach the top I see her.

And I fall back further into my mind.

"Do you have a name?" I ask standing up.

"I haven't got one," the child replies, "but I like to call myself Sam. And I suppose the others do too. So I guess you could say my name is Sam. But I don't suppose I have it. If anything it has me. I'd ask you for your name but I already know the answer. No one comes here with one."

I think about myself. I think about my name. I think about where I am and try to think about where I was. It all leads to nothing.

But how can I think without ever having thought before?

How can I know without ever having known?

"You're the youngest one here now," Sam tells me, "although I'm not sure who's the oldest. Vin seems to know the most, or tries to know the most, but Indiana feels to me like she's the wisest. Actually, they never have told me how long they've been here. Of course I was the youngest until you showed up. Vin and Indiana found me pretending to sleep. I'm not sure what I was doing before that, but I don't really think I need to know. After all, I'm not there anymore. I'm here."

"Vin?" I ask Sam. "And Indiana? They're the others?"

Sam nods yes while floating up to be level with my eyes.

I look around at the world that I'm in. It's definitely real, whatever real means. The sound of water dripping upon metal sends little tings into my ears. My feet feel cold in the puddle below. I now see the reflection of my entire body, with a few small white clouds floating past behind. I look ahead to the corner that leads away from these concrete walls.

"I'll take you to Indiana," Sam tells me. "She'll let you know more. Or at least let you know that there's nothing more to know."

The child motions for me to follow.

And I do.

Walking forward, I leave this place behind.

As I turn around the corner, the entirety of this new world flows into my sight. Endless objects exist all around me as far as I can see. Fragments of metal and concrete float by in the sky. Islands made of stone sit balanced upon single beams of rust. Waterfalls, which begin much higher than I can see, pour down from eternity and descend into eternity. Little planets covered in the greenest grass sit statically in the air.

My eyes take it all in, but my mind sits blind and confused as to what it is that I see.

Is this a place that really exists?

Am I really here?

This doesn't make any sense.

But why?

I know of no other life than this.

I know of no reasons for this world to seem strange.

"The others say that this place is indescribable," Sam tells me, "although they can't say why. They seem to find that funny."

"It is," I reply.

"Funny?" Sam asks. "Or indescribable?"

Again, I slide back closer to the present.

Again, I see her for the first time.

She's holding out her hands, moving them about in graceful motions with her palms always facing down towards the ground. Small drops of color appear out of nowhere just beneath her movements. She turns her eyes to me, and my mind collapses into countless thoughts of her and only her. Her soft brown eyes that stare at me with openness. Her short, dark hair that ends just as it graces her slender neck. Her smooth white skin, which wraps its radiance around the gentle curves of her body. Her perfect lips, which seem to say everything without saying anything at all.

A smile crosses her face.

"Would you like some clothes?" she asks me. "Or would you prefer staying the way you are?"

I'm standing naked thinking only of the way she said the words she said, not the meaning behind them. She laughs and walks closer.

"I suppose it doesn't matter here does it?" she says. "Perhaps it's just some old habit we got from somewhere else." She holds out her hand, and I see the muscles in her arm just barely move as tiny threads dance out of nowhere above her palm. Strings of fiber tie themselves and grow into strands of cloth that multiply until seconds later a neatly folded stack of clothes rests upon her hand.

"For you," she says.

I take them without saying a word.

Because I don't know what to say.

Because I know nothing at all.

I dress myself and look up into her eyes.

"Looks good," she tells me.

"Thanks," I reply.

I look down at the given clothes.

A shirt with sleeves too long.

Pants with legs too short.

"Uhm," I stutter, "could I have a pair of shoes?"

She nods and almost instantly creates a pair that lie on the ground in front of my feet. I put them on.

They fit perfectly.

"He's kind of weird," Sam tells her quietly, "but he seems to be nice."

I keep staring at her.

I keep thinking of her.

How does she create something out of nothing?

Why is this so strange?

"How long have you been here?" she asks me.

I think about the answer.

How long have I been here?

I'm being pushed and pulled around until I fall down violently into a place that holds me tight.

"There doesn't seem to be any answers," he tells me, "for any of the questions that come to mind. All you get are more and more mysteries as to what and why and when and how."

His fingers trace along the dark gray marble wall.

They leave behind empty valleys in the stone.

"You can't stop asking though," he says turning to me, "because what else do we have besides our reason? What else do we have besides our minds?"

He looks back to the wall.

I watch him as his fingers move in circular motions with no apparent pattern, digging emptiness into the stone, his eyes always keeping powerfully aware of his movement. Rough, dark hair grows upon his face, though he doesn't appear to be old. He lifts his finger and spreads out his hand, hovering it beside the wall. His muscles violently tense as a massive hollow forms in the stone. Cracks shoot rapidly outward from the crater, and a thunderous noise echoes through the long hallway that we stand in.

Sunlight shines off of the facets of his creation.

Or better yet, his destruction.

"What is it?" I ask him.

He turns his hand towards his face

As his eyes glare at his palm.

"Nothing," he replies.

She pulls me back, through the shadows in my mind, to where all I knew was her.

"We don't know why we're here," she says. "We're not even sure what here is. All we know is that it's where we are."

She walks back to the place she was standing before Sam and I arrived. I follow close behind her, turning my head to look at her creation upon the ground. Streaks of color flow across a white cloth shining gold from the sun. The colors move about the canvas with intricate detail, yet no image of an object is made.

"Vincent is the one to go to if you want to figure out what all this is about," she tells me. "He never stops thinking of it, never stops asking questions. I told him that he needs to try letting go of it all. That the answer is in living life, not in thinking about it. But he says that he can't stop, that all he can do is ask why."

I turn my eyes upon her as she stares into her painting.

"We're here," she says. "That's all we'll ever know."

"What is it?" I ask her, looking back down.

She stands silent for a moment.

"Something," she replies.

It's almost now.

Almost, for still the past holds me tight within a former place and time, as the present sits close nearby, ready to pull me back into its endless flowing movement, its ceaseless drift towards the future.

He gives me a look that burns deep into my soul.

Soul?

What is a soul?

Is it me?

Or am I it?

Does it even exist at all?

Or is it just a word within my head?

In front of me he stands naked.

Just as I was.

He looks as if he were a mirror of myself.

Yet somehow also my opposite.

His hair is blonde, almost white.

His skin is light.

His eyes are a deep, rusted brown.

"Who are you?" he asks me.

"Cyan," I reply. "And you?"

"How long have you been here?" he asks, ignoring my question.

"I'm not sure," I tell him. "I suppose not very long."

"Strange," he says, continuing to stare me down, "I've never seen another living being here before, and I've been here a long, long time."

"Who are you?" I ask him again. "Do you have a name?"

He turns and walks off a bit into the distance, where he stares at an island hovering by in the air. His hands move upwards toward the large chunk of concrete floating by. Its surface is covered with patches of dead grass and rusted metal. Bit by bit the island rips apart, with each piece floating steadily in the air.

He turns towards me and grins.

It's a grin that bleeds hate.

His arms violently swing towards me as the mass of concrete and metal flies at my body. I jump back and fall upon the ground.

I stare up at the heavy fragments floating above me.

"Morgan," he says.

I can hear the present mixing with the past as a single, dying moment slips quietly back into my mind. I'm in two places at once.

I'm here.

And I'm there.

She takes my hand in hers.

I feel safe.

I feel the opposite of alone.

"I'm guessing you don't have a name?" she asks me.

"I don't believe so," I reply. "I don't really know anything about myself."

"You're not alone," she tells me. "None of us know much about ourselves, or really anything at all."

She pulls my hand, and I move closer.

"Those eyes are something," she whispers as we stare deeply into each other.

And I wonder what exists within her mind.

"Sam," she says, breaking our connection, "how about you give him a name? Something to do with those eyes of his."

She turns to look at the child, who floats slowly around the both of us. Suddenly, Sam moves in front of me and looks into my eyes. We stay silent, and motionless, for some time.

"Cyan," the child says excitedly, turning to Indiana.

She smiles and looks to me.

"Cyan?" she asks staring into my eyes.

I'm pushed into now.
The wall is solid and complete.
Its surface smooth and strong.
I'm again within a single point in time
As my feet hang over the edge of grass
And I stare at the Myriad below.
I listen to its disordered sounds.
The ceaseless noise of a drifting chaos.
Of metal grinding forever against itself.
The low rumble of endless heavy objects moving slowly past.
Distant cries of countless things being torn apart.
I watch it.
Moving, never moving.
A little yellow car drifting atop the disarray.
A bright red door fixed upon a dark green building.
Lawn chairs, crumpled into round balls of plastic and aluminum, rolling atop hills of black metal.
Thousands of sheets of white paper flying past, rustling through the wind.
It all seems so familiar.
But how?
I've never known a thing but what I've experienced here.

I've never lived a life where these objects have existed as I feel they were supposed to exist.

Yet I know what they are.

And I know what they're for.

Indiana, seeming to appear out of nowhere, sits beside me on the soft ledge of grass.

"It flows as if it were water," she says to me while staring out at the Myriad. "It seems to always be near us, always pushing us along. The places that we are, that we live upon, are just fragments of it. Or at least that's what they seem to be."

"None of this makes any sense," I tell her.

She remains quiet, staring at the Myriad.

"It's as if we're within some mistake," I add.

"I remember a place called Indiana," she tells me. "I don't know why I do, or if I even really do, but it sits there in my mind and it sounds like home. So that's what I call myself. I don't suppose that it's much proof of anything, but maybe it's a sign that there was something, some life, before this. And if that's so, then maybe there's a reason we're here, a cause for all of this."

She holds out her hand, and in the air surrounding she creates little balls of metal and glass that drop down into the endless mass of things below. We listen to the sound of their collisions, and it makes me feel alone.

"How is it you do that?" I ask.

"I'm not quite sure," she tells me without stopping her creations. "I've always been able to. At least I've always been able to while I've been here, which to me is always. I know it seems illogical, for some reason, that I can create matter. It's as if I were a god, whatever a god is. But it feels natural, like I was meant to have this power."

I hold my hand in front of me and try to do the same.

But nothing happens.

Nothing.

I feel a repulsion towards everything, including myself.

"You've got something hidden there within you," she tells me. "We all do. You'll find it."

She stands up and walks to the other side of the small strip of land we're on. I feel detached from everything around me.

"Meet me somewhere in a little while," she tells me.

"Where?" I ask.

She turns back to me.

The wind blows her dark hair across her face.

"It doesn't matter where," she says. "I'll be there."

Walking away, she leaves me to my thoughts.

Thoughts that I don't wish to be near.

I'm walking down a concrete tunnel.

Large holes scar its sides, letting in the bright sunlight. Just a hint of golden color dances amongst the light, which I assume means that the day is nearly done. I was told that the days last long here. Longer than what, I do not know. I was also told that if night comes I should not be alone, for something called the ghosts show up more often then.

In the distance I see Sam pretending to walk upside down upon the ceiling.

"Hello!" she yells.

Or he.

I wave and walk forward.

"How is it that we always find each other?" Sam asks.

"I was getting ready to ask you the same thing," I reply.

"How is it that we always find each other?" a voice asks in repeat from outside the tunnel.

Morgan slips in through one of the holes in the wall, floating gracefully amongst the broken pieces of concrete.

"And just what are you?" he asks as he flies face to face with Sam. "A boy or a girl? Because for the life of me I can't tell!"

Sam's eyes show a hint of pain, but it's quickly followed by what seems forgiveness.

"I am neither," Sam replies. "Or I'm both."

"So you're an it!" Morgan laughs back. "You're just an object in this place. Just another piece of stuff."

He flies through Sam and out of another hole in the wall while laughing along the way.

"He's something different," Sam says to me while staring out of the hole, "much like you."

"Like me?" I ask.

"Yes, like you," Sam replies.

"I have no powers," I say. "And I'd like to think I'm much nicer than him."

The child gives me a smile showing teeth that match the pale white skin upon her face.

Or his.

"You're much nicer," Sam tells me, "but you do have something special about you. I can feel it, and it feels just like what's inside him."

I stare out of the hole that Morgan left through and attempt to fly as he did. Nothing happens, yet again.

I look down to see that Sam is gone.

Again I am alone.

The light becomes more golden as I walk along the scarred corridor of a place I do not know. Green vines begin to grown upon the walls, wrapping themselves around the pieces of broken metal that protrude from the concrete. I glimpse upon the ground small drops of dried red paint.

Is this from Indiana?

I follow the trail of red until it climbs up the wall and begins to form a familiar shape. Words are cast upon the wall in bright red colors. They sit amongst the holes that shine inward a glowing light.

ARE YOU AWAKE?

I understand it more than I understand myself.

Am I awake?

Is this just a dream?

Is this all within my head?

Or is this real?

A loud rumble shoots out of the distance to my right, collapsing away my questions. I can feel my feet begin to tremor as the ground starts to shake.

Falling.

Something is falling.

I can see it now.

And I'm running as the tunnel collapses behind me.

It matches my speed.

Never catching up, but always at my heels.

And I'm jumping over concrete slabs that block my path.
I'm climbing over walls that try to keep me where I am.
And the sensation, the touch, of the world around me
It feels so real, so alive, that I know this is no dream.
The noise of it all falling apart burns in my ears.
Sweat pours down upon my face.
Running.
My muscles begin to ache.
Jumping.
My movements begin to slow.
Climbing.
My foot slips, and I'm down.
And there's air beneath my back as I spin.
The Myriad is in my vision.
I'm just another piece of trash
Falling into this mess.
It all gets closer.
And closer.
Until someone grabs me.
Someone stops my fall.
It's Morgan.
His rust colored eyes stare into mine
As we fly through the falling concrete.
It happens too fast for me to think.
He drops me onto solid ground.
"You're welcome," he says, and shoots out of sight.

She's standing there with Vincent as I walk into the hollowed out space within the massive wall of stone. The sunlight shines a golden-orange color upon their skin. Their hands are held together. Their lips so near one another's. She moves and whispers into his ear. He turns and stares towards me without an expression on his face.

"It's almost night," he says, "and even though this place seems peaceful, nothing is safe or certain."

They let go of each other, and Indiana begins to walk towards the center of the hollow. She gets down upon her knees and puts her hands flat on the ground. I stare at her body as she bends herself into a curved position. Her legs fit tight into smooth black pants. Her soft white skin shows just slightly out of the bottom of her dark red shirt, which hangs loosely on her body.

From deep within my mind, my body, my everything, I feel a passion grow. I want her. I want everything about her.

I watch, as her muscles begin to tense.

Her back arches inward as flakes of black form on the ground around her hands. More and more an object appears beneath her palms. A dark gray, almost black rectangle sits below her hands. It grows higher and higher until she's sitting nearly straight up. Her hands fall over the edge, as she can no longer touch the top. Still, it grows higher, her hands sliding along its side. Her head is fallen backwards, her short hair hanging down.

It stops.

And silence.

Small beads of sweat dripping down her face are the only things that move.

She opens her eyes and smiles.

"It's done," she tells us as she stands up gracefully showing no sign of exhaustion.

"My turn?" Vincent asks.

She nods as she walks next to me.

"You need something to protect yourself," she tells me with a serious tone. "You haven't even seen what this place can be like."

"The ghosts?" I ask. "Are they violent?"

"Not all of them," Vincent replies while walking to the large, slate obelisk. "Some are kind. Some don't even seem to notice us. But many of them are quite vicious."

He puts his hands upon the slab of strange material and closes his eyes. He stands there silent and motionless.

"What it is that they are," Indiana says, "we have no clue. All that we know is that they're different from us. They don't seem to be here, yet here is where they are. And they always seem to follow us."

"Or maybe it's us who follow them," Vincent says.

He pulls his hands violently off of the slab as it dissolves into the air. Its shape becomes ambiguous as its contours melt away into an ever-evolving form. Vincent stands, with his eyes still closed, near the swirling mass of vanishing substance.

Out of the destruction I see what is created.

24

Standing straight upon its end, a rod of dark gray glows in the golden light of a dying sun.

"It's yours," Indiana tells me.

I walk up to the staff near Vincent.

He wraps his hand around the top of it and begins to push with force. After what appears to be a great effort, the rod begins to heavily fall. It crashes upon the ground, shooting fissures outward from where it lands. Dust floats up from the impact and into our eyes.

I step back and stare at what is supposed to be mine.

"You want me to carry that?" I ask the both of them in confusion.

"It's just for you," Indiana tells me. "Go ahead. You can lift it."

I walk across the shattered ground and stand above the weapon designed for me. I kneel down and wrap my hands around the staff. With ease I lift it up.

"Only you can carry it," Vincent tells me.

I hold it in front of my body and awkwardly swing it around.

"She can make extraordinary things," he says looking at Indiana.

"But it's you who gives them shape," she tells him with a look of affection in her eyes.

"How can I lift it so easily?" I ask her.

"Because it's made just for you," she replies. "And that's as much of an answer you will get in a place like this. When I want to create something, I just think of what it is that I want to make, and with my body and my mind I force it into this world. I thought of something just for you. Something only you could use."

"And you?" I ask Vincent.

"The opposite," he tells me. "Or maybe the same. I think of what it is that I want to take away. I see it dissolving in my mind. I feel this sensation flow throughout my body, and it rips away at what exists until what exists is no longer there."

"And what do I get?" a voice asks us from behind.

We turn to see Morgan as he walks up to us with a smirk upon his face.

"Do you always have to appear out of nowhere?" Indiana asks him. "And with some witty little remark to say?"

"Actually, yes, I do," he replies as he walks over to the hollowed-out shape in the ground where the staff had landed.

"I gave you the clothes you're wearing," she tells him. "Maybe if you're a little bit nicer you'll get more."

"He saved me earlier," I say.

"From what?" Vincent asks.

"The ground began to fall beneath my feet," I tell them, "and I couldn't escape. I slipped and fell and almost became a part of the Myriad. He flew by and grabbed me."

"Well maybe that proves you're not evil," Indiana says to Morgan, who's seemingly lost interest in us and has begun to levitate small bits of stone off the ground. "But you could at least be a little less cruel about the way you act."

"It's almost night," Vincent says to all of us, stopping Morgan as he starts to utter a reply to Indiana. "We should get ready."

"Where's Sam?" I ask.

"Somewhere close by," Indiana replies. "Sam never seems to go far away. Especially when night begins to come."

The sky has turned into a vibrant violet color.

The few clouds that flow by shine brightly orange.

"How long does night last?" I ask.

"As long as it wants," Indiana answers.

"How long did the day last?" Vincent asks me.

How long did it last?

I can't say.

There isn't really time here.

Yet somehow we move along.

Sam quickly slides up out of the ground.

Morgan and I jump back in surprise.

"They're here," Sam whispers playfully, yet with a small amount of fear in the words.

"There," Vincent says pointing towards a moon that seems to have appeared out of nowhere.

Behind the bright circle of white, which hangs in the now dark indigo sky, little wisps of silver begin to fly outward and around into the atmosphere. Even though they come from behind the distant moon, they fly around our bodies as if the vast expanse did not exist.

"They seem different this time," Sam says while pretending to stand next to Vincent, "but I can't say how."

26

The streaks of silver begin to become more complex, forming long tails that shoot outward from round bodies. One of them floats past, just barely grazing my skin.

It feels cold.

Empty.

And somehow alive.

"Lets go," Vincent says to the group. "We should keep moving."

"Why?" Morgan asks.

"If you remain in one spot too long," Vincent replies, "they become more attracted to you. And that attraction isn't always friendly."

Some of the wisps now have large sets of teeth on the front of their bodies. Others have just a single, large eye. Strange sounds begin to buzz from the insides of their bodies. Vincent makes a motion towards a path along the edge of the hollow, and we begin to move.

I think to myself, as we walk along the ledge that wraps around a tall column of stone, about the graffiti I saw earlier on the wall of the tunnel. I think of asking Indiana about it, but she and Vincent are talking quietly to each other up ahead.

The question sits heavy in my mind.

Am I awake?

And I realize that I've haven't slept.

That I'm not even tired.

"So do we ever need to sleep?" I ask Sam, who pretends to walk alongside me.

"Nope," the child replies. "You'll never get hungry either. Although we can't quite decide what hunger or sleep are, since neither seem to occur. How do you think we know about them if we never have to eat or sleep?"

I throw the question around in my head, and just as Vincent told me would happen, I get nothing but more questions.

"Maybe the great goddess Indiana could make us a nice meal?" Morgan says as he turns around and walks backwards up the ledge ahead of us.

The silver ghosts, who have been following us since they arrived, now have arms and legs that flail about their floating bodies. A small group of them begins to collect around Sam, nudging the child's soft skin. They become more and more aggressive with him until they begin to push her around.

"Get away!" Sam shouts at them while floating ahead to be next to Vincent and Indiana.

The ghosts lose interest and begin to nudge each other instead. Two of them wrap around into a knot and squeeze until their bodies become one. More and more of them join together in this way until behind us walks a lumbering white body with no details other than its long limbs and one large eye upon its head.

It awkwardly hums a somehow familiar song, which makes me pause for a moment. I almost get shoved off the cliff by the large ghost as it continues to walk past me.

Why does its song sound so familiar?

"Please don't die," Indiana says to me while turning back in my direction. "That is, if you can die here. And I'd rather not like to found out right now."

I quickly walk between the ghost's legs and catch back up with the group.

"They like to play tricks on you," she tells me. "They somehow know what's in your mind. In fact they seem to know what's in there more than you do."

She holds out her hands towards the large ghost as a wall of stone forms across the path.

"I'm sorry but you'll have to go another way," she says to the giant, who in return confusedly turns around and walks away as if there was somewhere more important to be.

We continue to walk along the spiraling path, as the sky grows darker. Morgan floats beside me, seeming to be lost in thought.

"You said that you'd been here a long time," I say to him, "and that I was the first living thing you'd met. So you never saw any ghosts before?"

"Are the ghosts alive?" he asks back.

"That's beside the point," I reply. "You never saw them before?"

"Not once," he answers, floating forward and ending our conversation. After some time, we reach the top of the stone column. In the distance, across the vast gap of darkness, we can make out a large, floating island with lights strewn about it. Indiana steps slowly towards the edge to peer into the distance.

"That's where we will go," Vincent says.

"But we don't know what's there," I say. "And we lack a way to get there."

Suddenly, without waiting for a further decision, Indiana walks forward into the air. With each step, she creates a stone platform beneath her feet. We follow her, walking along the bridge she forms, with the endless night surrounding us.

Faint white stars blink in and out of existence within the strange night sky. Stray ghosts float around our bodies and disappear down into the depths below.

Morgan leisurely glides by my side.

A smirk sits on his lips.

"I'll let you know what's ahead," he says to the group.

"You should probably stay with us," Vincent says back.

"What could happen to me?" Morgan replies before shooting off quickly into the distance.

And so we walk along in silence.

No one speaking a word.

The faint whispers of ghosts are all we hear.

I stare down at my feet as my legs stride along beneath me.

I feel my body collide with the world that I am in.

That Indiana creates beneath our feet.

And only one thought comes to mind.

Why?

II

Little footprints dance in and out of existence, leaving a barely visible trace of the steps they take about the surface of a dimly lit bulb. I reach up to touch them. The little shadowy tracks scatter away from my finger and wander about on the opposite side of the light that hangs upon the broken lamppost I lean upon.

I hear Vincent and Indiana talking quietly in the distance.

Are they arguing?

Or speaking words of love?

The footsteps gather up the courage to return to this side of the light. I listen hard to the conversation that happens across the space from here to there, and instead of words I can almost make out little clicks and clacks of steps in the air.

"Inside is a strange place," Sam says.

I look to my right and see the child floating halfway through the wall of a long, brick building.

"What is it?" I ask.

Sam floats back into the building, leaving only a small white hand visible outside of the wall. It slowly floats along, and I follow it in curiosity. Two large glass doors sit at the entrance of the building. Darkness lies behind them.

"How can you see?" I yell in at the child.

"You don't need to," Sam replies. "Come inside."

I wrap my hand around the cold metal handle of one of the doors, and opening it wide, I slowly walk into the darkness.

"Here!" Sam yells down what I think is a hallway.

I walk clumsily down the pitch-black corridor until I hear it.

People talking.

People screaming.

People laughing, crying, moaning, singing.

Whispering.

I can hear the whispers more than anything.

I can almost make out the words.

Almost.

"I should be scared," Sam says, "but I'm not. The words don't belong here. They're just a shadow of another place. Of other people. People who are confused. People alone, together."

"Like us?" I ask.

"No," Sam replies. "We're together, alone."

We listen to the voices as they flow about us.

"Where are we?" I ask Sam.

"If you mean this world we're in," the child says, "I don't know. But right here, in this room, I think we're in a very sad place. Something bad is happening. Something that shouldn't, yet it must."

"What's happening?" I ask.

Talking.

Screaming.

Laughing.

"Someone is dying," Sam says.

Crying.

Moaning.

Singing.

"Someone is being born."

Whispers.

Small hints of color begin to melt into the dark atmosphere.

I sit, watching the changing sky.

We had been walking about this abandoned cluster of flat buildings, doing nothing but listening to the echoes of voices that flow about this place. We stopped and gathered around a group of streetlights and broken down benches. Indiana sat at the fringe of the light, trying to make fire out of nothing. All that would appear would be a small flash of light and ashes that fell to her feet.

Morgan levitated about small chunks of brick that lay scattered along ground. He would spin them around his body and send them hurling off into the darkness, waiting to hear the crackle of it breaking against something solid.

Vincent sat beside Sam as they talked about the ghosts and why they seemed to be so miserable.

"Why do you think they're here?" Sam asked.

"Why do you think we are?" Vincent replied.

"Don't answer me with a question, Vin," Sam said with an irritated tone while floating into position in front of Vincent's face.

"They seem to want something," Vincent answered. "But it's something they can never have. What that is, I don't know."

I sat alone in the middle of the light, clutching the staff that was given to me in my hands.

Would I ever use it?

The question shot more questions through my mind.

How long will I be here?

How long until I die?

Forever?

Or tomorrow?

Or today?

I stood up and began to swing the staff around my body. It somehow felt natural for me to spin it about in my hands. I felt a little bit stronger as it revolved around me.

"You want some practice?" Morgan asked.

"What do you mean?" I asked back.

He lifted his hands, and out of the darkness shot a shattered brick towards my body. Before I could stop it, it hit me in the gut and sent me to the ground.

It was the first time I had felt pain.

Yet it was a familiar sensation, like something I've felt forever in the past and something I will feel forever in the future.

"Stop it!" Indiana yelled, breaking her attempt at making fire.

"No," Vincent said firmly. "Go ahead."

I sat with my hands upon the ground, feeling the pain in my stomach. I could hear Indiana utter something under her breath as I stood up and grabbed the staff that sat beside me on the concrete. She again continued to send sparks into the air and ashes onto the ground.

"Again?" Morgan asked.

"Again," I said back.

With a swing of his arm another brick came rushing in from the darkness. This time it did not hit me, yet neither did I hit it. Instead, I twisted my body about as the brick flew past in the air beside my head. Before I could stable myself he sent another one flying. As my foot hit the ground, my muscles pulled tightly across my body and swung the staff quickly in front of me, smashing the brick into small pieces.

"That's it!" Vincent yelled while clapping his hands in approval.

Morgan and I continued through the night. My body ached, yet my mind felt so alive. I was becoming something stronger than before. Morgan seemed to enjoy it as well, but mostly when I would fail, as a brick would painfully hit my body, sending me to the ground.

Now I rest beside Indiana, watching the sky slowly regain its color. She's given up on her fire. Around her lies a layer of ash that gently blows into the wind.

"We need to move soon," she tells me. "We can never seem to stay in one place for very long. You can stop, and you can start to feel as if you're becoming familiar with what's around you, but slowly things begin to change. Before you know it there's a wall where there wasn't one before. There's a this where you could have sworn there was a that. There's nothing where there certainly was something. You look around and it doesn't seem so familiar anymore. And then there are the ghosts. They find you and the gather about you, more and more. Some aren't so bad. But most have nothing good about them. And so you avoid them. And you avoid everything. Always moving."

She holds out her hand, with her palm up, in front of my face.

I can just barely see it.

A small fire appears and floats in the air above her skin.

"But we can still live," she says. "And we can learn. And maybe someday we will find a home. A place where we won't have to keep moving."

A small wind blows out the flame, and with it comes a sudden rush of sunlight from in front of us.

The night has ended.

"You're fucking stupid!" he screams.

The other makes no reply.

He just stands there rocking his body back and forth.

Back and forth.

"You're fucking stupid!" he screams in repeat. "Stupid!"

Back and forth.

Back and forth.

He points his long, white finger at the other man.

"You're fucking stupid!" he screams again even though he lacks a mouth, or any facial features for that matter.

They do this over and over again.

Back and forth.

Back and forth.

"Why do they do it?" Indiana asks.

"Because they're both fucking stupid," Morgan says back.

Across the concrete street there are more of them.

Some sit on the ground staring straight into the sun as their faces burn in the heat, yet they don't move.

I can smell them as their white flesh melts.

It burns as it flows up my nose and into my senses.

Like melted plastic.

Others touch themselves and send out moans that drone through the air. Some of them touch each other and together they sigh in a dissonant chorus.

On a street corner sits a fat one with a mouth that stretches around his entire head. He has no legs and just one arm.

He's gnawing at his single hand.

I stop and stare at him, yet he doesn't seem to notice.

None of them do.

Vincent walks ahead of us as if he knows where he is going.

All around us are the ghosts.

"I thought they came out at night?" I ask Indiana.

"They mostly do," she replies, "but a few stay out in the light. I've never seen this many though."

"I don't like this place," Sam quietly utters, floating close to Indiana's body.

She pretends to caress the child's head.

Sam pretends to feel the comfort that it would give.

Long stretches of concrete lay out in front of us, with lengthy, flat buildings strewn about.

The sun sits above, sending heat down upon our bodies.

All of us sweat except Sam.

"We should find a place to rest," Vincent says to us all.

"I'm quite fine," Morgan says back. "I think I'll go have some fun."

"What do you mean?" Indiana asks him.

He doesn't answer as he flies off down a street that leads to somewhere.

"Over there," Vincent says pointing to a shaded area beneath some sort of pavilion of white stone. "We can rest for a moment."

The shadows cool our bodies as we sit staring out at our surroundings. In all directions we see the same thing.

Concrete.

And buildings.

Stones and bricks and scattered ponds of warm water glistening in the sun.

There's no point in moving.

It's all the same.

Yet we can't stay here.

Already I feel confused.

As the walls around me seem to move every time I look away.

"What's that?" Indiana asks.

"What?" Vincent replies.

She sits staring in the distance.

"Listen," she says quietly.

Nothing.

Just the sound of the warm wind blowing past.

No.

Something.

A voice?

A scream.

And it gets louder.

And closer.

"There," Vincent says, pointing behind me.

I turn and see him.

One of the ghosts, white and faceless with a large mouth right in the middle of its stomach, is running directly for us. His hands are up in the air and his legs stride along the ground awkwardly, yet fast. I stand up and hold tight to the staff in my hands.

Indiana walks in front of me and lifts her left arm straight out in front of her body. Shooting upwards and downwards from her hand, a smooth bow forms. Its polished, dark wood is intricately carved with a design that flows across its entirety. Instantly, a string forms from the top to the bottom. She holds her right hand in position, and out of the air a long white arrow becomes created in her grip. I watch the muscles in her arm draw the bow as her back just slightly arches inward. I look into her eyes, which stare straight down the arrow towards her target.

She lets go, and time seems to freeze as the arrow sits in the air beside her. I see her face. I see her thoughts. I see nothing but her.

A flash and again time moves forward.

The arrow pierces right through the head of the ghost, sending him flying backwards to the ground. The sound of his screaming doesn't stop though. In fact, it multiplies, growing louder.

Though, it isn't his scream.

It's theirs.

More of them.

Running from around the buildings.

They're reaching for us.

Closer and closer.

"We've got to go," Vincent says while standing up.

He pulls his arm behind his body and grinds his feet against the ground. With a loud scream he rips his body around, tearing out a wide circle in the ground around us.

Sam pretends to grab onto my leg.

"Stop them," the child says shakily.

"Float up high and be safe," I tell Sam. "Don't stay here."

"No," Sam replies. "I have to stay close to you and Vin and Indiana. I can't be alone. I won't be alone."

The ghosts reach the gap around us but don't stop running.

They fall into the opening, arms reached out for us.

They keep coming.

Keep falling.

Vincent points to the rooftop of a nearby building, and without delay Indiana begins to form steps beneath her feet as she walks up into the sky.

"Follow her," Vincent says.

Sam still pretends to hold tight to me as we move to the stairs. Just as my foot touches the first step, I hear a scream much closer than any before. I spin and see it lunge across the gap, reaching for Sam with the mouth upon its stomach opened wide. Its gums ooze thick spit, and its large white teeth shine bright and sharp.

It grabs Sam's body and pulls the child down, causing Sam to shriek in terror. The ghost spreads its mouth even wider, and its spit drips down upon Sam's body, hitting the soft white skin and sliding down to the ground.

Vincent dashes directly to the ghost and rips it away before it can engulf the child. Holding the ghost by the back of its head, he slams its skull down upon the solid concrete, sending white splatters of blood shooting across the ground.

"Go, damnit!" Vincent yells to Sam, who is lying paralyzed in fear. The child shakes awake and quickly floats upwards to Indiana, who has now reached the roof of the building. She pretends to hold the whimpering child in her arms and stares down at Vincent and me.

Her eyes widen.

Her muscles tense.

"Vincent!" she yells towards us.

We spin around and see three of them jumping clear over the gap. Two of them head for me and one for Vincent. I pull the staff to my side and spin it around my body, hitting one of them and sending it flying into the gap. The second one trips over the dead body of the headless ghost and falls beneath my swing. It grabs my ankles and pulls me down. To my right I can see Vincent grappled against the other ghost, whose mouth is violently chomping through the air, sending spit across his body.

I push my staff down hard against the head of the ghost at my ankles, yet its grip doesn't release.

Harder

I push.

Harder

It grabs.

I scream out in fear.

And in hope of pulling more strength from my body.

Vincent tumbles down to the ground with the other ghost in his grip. A rush and a thud and a large white arrow sits lodged in the body of the ghost at my feet.

Still, it pulls hard at my ankles.

Still, I push down on its head.

A crunch, and the staff bursts through.

With its skull broken open, its grip finally loosens.

I stand and see Vincent still wrestling with the ghost. Both of them roll upon the ground. Indiana can't get in a shot. She can't risk hitting Vincent. I lift the staff high above my head and send it down towards the ghost, but before it collides I'm pulled to the ground.

Another one had cleared the gap.

Its arms squeeze tight around my neck.

Its body sits heavy on my back.

My face grinds against the concrete.

My throat gets tighter.

And the air gets less and less.

I see the blue sky colliding with the gray horizon, as edges start to blur and the darkness around my vision begins to creep inward.

Blue.

Gray.

Black.

Black.

Black.

Release.

And air painfully fills my lungs.

The darkness slides away.

And the blue and the gray separate.

I lift my face from the concrete as a strong hand pulls me up from the waist.

"You okay?" Vincent asks.

Am I okay?

"Yea," I reply. "I think."

I look out past the gap.

A few ghosts remain.

They move slower and less angry, but far down below I can hear the screams of the ones who still want to tear us apart. Vincent and I wearily walk up the steps created by Indiana. He destroys them behind us as we go higher, until they're completely gone upon our reaching the top.

"Why didn't you just erase them, the ghosts?" I ask him.

He shakes his head.

"It doesn't work on living things," he replies, "which is proof the ghosts are at least somewhat alive I suppose."

"You were right," Sam says to Vincent. "They do want something, and it's us. I could feel it in the way its hands squeezed hard into my skin. The way its fingers dug deep. It wanted to be a part of me. It wanted to devour me whole."

"Morgan," Indiana says. "Where do you think he is?"

"He's fine," replies Vincent. "I'm sure he can take care of himself."

We walk about the rooftop, looking out into the distance in hopes of seeing anything worth seeing. Far off in one direction we make out the edge of the large island we're upon. Stretching out endlessly, a tall, stone wall blocks our path to the edge.

"I suppose that's where we'll go," I say as the sun sits high above us, still throwing its heat upon our bodies. Silently we stare in the direction we will travel, breathing in the warm air of this static moment.

He's holding the pale head of a dead ghost in his hands.

Its white blood drips down into a puddle below, where it swirls about like oil in water.

"The damn thing tried to fuck me," Morgan says, dropping the head into the water.

I somehow know what it means to fuck someone.

I somehow know it even though I never have.

"At least it didn't try to devour you whole," Indiana says.

"Well it didn't," Morgan replies, "but the other's did after I killed this one. They rushed out of nowhere with their damn mouths wide open and screaming like mad. It was easy to get rid of them. In fact, I think I enjoyed it."

"We'll I'm glad you had fun," Indiana tells him.

"So did our training come in handy?" Morgan asks turning to me. I nod yes in reply.

"Good," he says while floating upwards to look into the distance.

"We're heading towards the wall," Vincent tells him.

"Oh, we are?" Morgan replies mockingly.

"Yes, we are," Vincent says back. "You can come if you want, but if you do you're going to help us with that power of yours."

Morgan gives a snicker and floats back down.

"Why wouldn't I help?" he says shrugging his shoulders.

The buildings become fewer as we walk closer to the edge, closer to the wall. We're now surrounded by nothing but flat concrete.

The sun has disappeared behind a sheet of white clouds that hang across the sky.

We reach a final stray building before the long distance of nothing in front of the wall.

"Let's rest here," Indiana says as we walk up to the doors of the building.

"All right, but we can't stay long," says Vincent. "Cyan, come with me to check the inside."

Morgan and Indiana sit upon the steps outside of the entrance.

Sam pretends to sit next to them.

The building is long and gray. The doors, of which there are at least six, are made of a dark wood that has begun to rot at the corners. Vincent pulls open one of the middle doors, and from behind it floods out a river of water that pours down the steps.

Indiana and Morgan move out of the water's path, but Sam sits unaffected in the middle of the stream of water.

"Go ahead," Vincent says to me, almost smiling.

We walk down a marble hallway as our feet become soaked in the water that flows from the walls.

"Where does it come from?" I ask Vincent.

"It doesn't have to come from anywhere," he tells me. "Nothing here has to have a reason for what it does. I don't know why, but it just doesn't seem right. There has to be a reason, a cause for everything. How can anything exist without a reason?"

He puts his hand into a small stream of water that trickles down a broken piece of stone. The water bends around his fingers and flows down his arm, stopping before it reaches his elbow to drip down to the ground.

"Why is it that we never sleep, yet we know what it means to sleep?" he asks me. "And we know that it's strange that we don't? It doesn't make any sense. Nothing does. But what does it mean to not make sense when you don't know what making sense would be?"

He opens a door to our left, and instead of water pouring out, the water from the hallway pours in. The room is mostly dark. The only light comes from a small window high upon the wall, where a bright beam shoots down to the ground and collides with the smooth marble floor.

Vincent walks into the light and turns to face me.

"Why are we here?" he asks.

"I don't know," I reply.

"No," he says back. "Why are we here?"

I think about it for a moment and come up with nothing.

"I don't know why we're here," I answer. "Nothing here has to have a reason. Remember?"

He closes his eyes and lets the light shine down on his face.

"Why are we here?" he asks with his eyes still closed.

I don't know what to say, so I say nothing at all.

The sound of water dripping throughout the building echoes into my head. Vincent opens his eyes.

"There has to be a reason," he says strongly. "Nothing can exist without a reason. Now cannot be without a before. Effect cannot happen without a cause. And existence cannot exist without a reason."

He throws his arm to his right and lets out a scream as his muscles violently tense. Sunlight rushes into the room as the wall beside us dissolves into nothing with a loud crack. I shield my eyes to let them adjust to brightly burning light. Vincent stands with his arm still held to his right.

"How can I do that?" he asks between heavy breaths. "There has to be a reason. And I won't stop asking until I find out why."

I barely notice Sam float into the room through the gaping hole that's taken place of the wall. The pale white skin of the child blends in with white sky outside.

"Is everything okay?" asks Sam. "Vin?"

He turns his face to the child.

"It's fine," he answers.

Sam floats farther into the room and drifts in the air beside Vincent's head.

"Indiana wants you," the child tells him.

He nods and turns to me.

"We have to leave soon," he says. "Get some rest while you can." I nod back to him as he walks out of the hole that he created. Sam floats in place, staring at the room we're in. The walls are made of pale green stone. The sunlight shines off of them and reflects green light into the puddles that scatter the ground.

"Indiana says that Vin asks too many questions," Sam tells me, hovering in place, "and that if he ever did find an answer he wouldn't even recognize it. He would just think it was another question, another reason to ask why. But really there are just too many whys to keep asking questions. Sure there's always an answer, but behind every answer is another little why just waiting to be asked."

"Indiana," I ask Sam, "has she ever said anything about me?"

"About you?" Sam says spinning upside down. "She says you're nice. She says you're different. But she says that everyone and everything is different. She told me that I was different because nothing touches me besides the things that matter."

"And what's that?" I ask.

"Love," the child says spinning in circles. "That's the most important. And the light that shows me the world. And the sounds that play in my ears. And the thoughts in my head that tell me who I am and where I am and what it is that's going on."

The child stops spinning and drifts in place upside down.

"She seemed to forget the ghosts though," Sam says staring blankly into the air. "It's the only time I really touch the world, and it makes me feel so alive that I can sense death in every little bit of my skin. I see how fragile I am. And when they let go... When they let go I'm set out adrift into nothing. Again I'm not alive or dead. I just am."

I walk up to Sam and move my hand into the middle of the child's body. I don't feel a thing.

Sam seems to move, however, as if something was felt.

"What is it?" I ask.

And we stay there motionless.

The sound of water in my ears.

The bright white light shining off the child's gray eyes.

The touch of stale air against my skin.

"I don't know," Sam says. "I feel nothing."

"You always feel nothing," I say.

"No," Sam replies. "The nothing exists inside me, where you are. I can feel it."

I pull my hand away.

The child looks down at its own small, white hands, and then stares back up into my eyes.

"Is it me or is it you?" Sam asks. "Which one of us is here?"

Morgan floats above our heads, looking out at the long wall that stretches on forever to our left and right.

"What's the point if nothing ever happens besides this?" I ask. "If all there is to do is to keep moving?"

"What point would you like there to be?" Indiana asks back.

I sit and think about her question.

Vincent walks around us, staring up at Morgan and waiting for him to tell us what he sees.

"Truth," I answer back to Indiana's question. "I'd like to know the truth about everything. Why we're here and why anything exists at all. That's my reason."

"What if the truth was that there is no point?" she asks.

"Then at least I could relax a little, knowing that nothing really matters," I say.

She smiles and shakes her head.

"Just because there isn't a point," she says, "doesn't mean that nothing matters."

"It goes on forever," Morgan says floating down to the ground next to us. "And on the other side is nothing."

"Well," Vincent says, "anywhere is better than here, including nowhere. The ghosts could soon show up again. Either I can clear through the wall or Indiana can take us over it."

With no reason to stay any longer, we head out towards the wall. The walk is long, as the sky continues to burn, through thin white clouds, on our backs and in our eyes.

We move on for some time.

There's no way to tell for how long.

Eventually we reach the wall, where again we find the ghosts.

But here they're different.

They're small and transparent.

Their movements are slow.

Morgan kneels down to stare closely at one.

"There's nothing in there," he says, pushing it on the head with his finger. It falls over to the ground and lies there motionless. Drool pours out of its mouth and its eyes sit blank.

Another one, who sits nearby, turns its head and walks over to the ghost lying upon the ground. It bends over and lets out a grunt while it grabs the other's head and rips it away.

"Damn!" Morgan yells standing up.

The ghost shoves the head into its mouth and continues to eat at the rest of the body. With each bite it grows fatter and slower. With the last limb of the ghost, the obese devourer slows down to a standstill.

"There's hundreds of them," Vincent says scanning around us.

Some of them are piled up in slow-motion orgies that slump about as if they were one entity. Others scream quietly at each other in high-pitched gibberish, pulling at each other until their limbs rip off.

"There's more than that," Indiana says staring closely at the wall that lies in front of us. We walk next to her and see that the wall is not made of stone. It's made of them. It's made of little ghosts who fuck and fight and scream and die. Little ghosts who eat and eat and eat until they're eaten themselves.

Some of them are as small as a fingernail.

Some as big as a hand.

"Well it looks like I won't be able to tear a hole in this thing," says Vincent.

"I'll take us over it," Indiana tells us as she looks up at the top of the wall.

"Please do," Sam says shakily while staring at the wall from a distance.

"What's that sound?" Morgan asks.

We listen.

We hear it.

A low rumble radiates from the wall.

"It's getting louder," Sam shrieks stepping back.

Louder.

And louder.

Then silence.

For just an instant.

Then it's everywhere.

Exploding.

The roaring of orgies all around us, flying through the air.

Something brushes past me.

Its rough, long fur cuts my skin.

I can feel the heat of its body.

I can smell its stench.

The ghosts have all fallen.

I'm standing alone, staring at a massive boar that grunts and kicks its feet at the ground. The others are scattered about, thrown apart from the bursting wall.

The piles of ghosts on the ground are growing.

Growing upwards.

Fast.

And faster.

The sky is gone.

The ground is gone.

We're surrounded by them.

Light shines in through the shifting gaps that move amongst the walls of ghosts. The boar groans a deep, loud noise. The others are beginning to stand up in confusion.

"What the hell was that?" Morgan yells out.

I see its face.

No.

Not a face.

A mask.

A large, white mask upon the boar's dark brown body.

Its shape is angular.

Its edges sharp.

There are no eyes.

Just shallow cavities that project shadows down upon its smile.

An evil smile, with large fangs that shoot downward from the sides of its mouth.

Above its ears are two massive horns.

And in the center of its forehead, above its eyeless gaze and its wicked grin and its sharp fangs, below the two large horns that glisten in the rays of sunlight that break through into our cavern, sits another, smaller mask.

It's almost the same.

Almost as evil.

But the grin is not so foul.

The horns are not so large.

The fangs are not so sharp.

But its eyes.

Its eyes are just as empty.

The beast lets out a grunt and turns its body about.

"Move!" Indiana yells at me.

The boar whips its head in my direction and begins to run.

White arrows strike the side of its body as it rushes at me.

It doesn't seem to notice.

It doesn't seem to feel them at all.

The nearer it gets the more I feel the ground rumble.

Before it reaches me I dash out of its path.

My leg hits the mask and I'm spun down to the ground.

I feel the rumble upon my back.

I hear a scream.

It's Sam.

"No!" Indiana yells.

I see arrows fly past me as I sit up.

I see Sam's eyes.

Alone.

The child stands against the wall of ghosts.

The wall that pushes against soft white skin.

Skin that feels the pain of being alive.

Of death.

I see it happen.

I see the child flinch.

The eyes that close in fear.

I see the pain Sam feels as the boar smashes the small, fragile body against the wall of ghosts who endlessly fuck and fight and devour each other.

I see the blood that drips down the large mask that smiles at its murder.

I feel the unbelievable sadness that sits in my chest.

That sits in the chest of Indiana as she cries out.

And I feel the anger within Vincent.

I hear it in his scream.

He couldn't do a thing.

And now Sam is dead.

And now Sam drips down from the long, sharp fangs of the boar's mask.

The beast scrapes its feet on the ground.

"You've got to do something, Indiana!" Vincent yells, but she's lost inside her pain.

"Morgan," Vincent says quickly. "Do something. Move him."

"I," Morgan stutters, "I can't. I can't move what's alive."

"Damnit!" Vincent yells.

The boar faces me.

Hot air shoots out from behind its mask as it grunts in my direction. I stand up and pull out the staff that hangs upon my back, not knowing what else to do.

I'm dead.

We're all dead.

"Indiana!" Vincent screams again and again.

The beast is running.

I again feel the rumble against my body.

Again, I see Sam.

Dead against the wall.

No.

The beast gets closer.

No.

The rumble gets stronger.

No.

I can feel the heat of its massive body.

No.

Its heavy breaths.

No.

It's here.

No.

And it's now.

No.

And the grin is inches from my face.

The hollowed-out eyes cast their shadow on my body.

No.

I'm gone.

But I'm not.

I'm here.

But I'm there.

And I'm everywhere.

Nothing moves.

Besides me.

Nothing is really here.

Besides me.

And I'm above the huge beast

As it's getting ready to tear my body apart.

But my body isn't there.

I feel something pulling me in all directions.
Yet something pushing me back to the place where I was.
Where I would be slaughtered
Like Sam
Bleeding dead against the wall.
A pain builds in my mind.
A weakness grows in my movements.
But what is it that's moving?
My thoughts begin to crumble.
My thoughts
Begin
To die.

I feel the release.
My mind snaps back.
The air forces outward from my body as I fall down upon the beast. My staff is pulled back above my head. I want to question how I got here, but don't have time. I swing down at the boar, at the blood-covered mask. It cracks into pieces, and the beast lets out a loud roar that echoes around and painfully into my ears.

There is no face behind the mask.

There's not a thing inside the huge boar.

Just emptiness.

And the roar of pain that pours out of the gaping hole where the mask used to lie.

The beast's thick hair melts away into the ground.

The rough skin beneath burns away into nothing.

The shattered mask turns to dust that lifts off the ground and blows into my left eye, making it burn hot.

But I don't think about the pain.

I'm too lost within this moment.

All that remains of the beast is the smaller mask piece that sat lodged into its forehead. It lies alone upon the ground.

"What was that?" Morgan asks flying over to me. "What the hell did you do?"

What did I do?

Where did I go?

"I was here," I answer. "But I was nowhere."

"It was instant," Vincent says to me. "You were there in front of the damn thing and then you were above it. The air around you vibrated. I saw it shoot out from your skin. How did you do it?"

Indiana is sitting on the ground staring at me.

Tears are pouring down across her face.

And I remember.

Sam is dead.

One by one the ghosts begin to fall to the ground like dead leaves. Moaning and crying, they dissolve into nothing.

Their disappearance reveals a sky that shines pure blue.

I walk to Indiana.

She stands up and looks me in the eyes.

Her perfect eyes are buried in sadness.

Her perfect lips are shaped by sorrow.

I almost say something to her, but can't gather the strength to touch the grief in her heart. She walks to Vincent, burrowing her head into his chest. He wraps his arms around her and whispers something into her ear.

"How did you do it?" Morgan asks me.

I want to hold her.

I want to be the one she needs.

"Hey," Morgan asks pulling at my arm and grabbing my attention. "How did you do that?"

I think about the moment that I disappeared.

I think about the fear of death.

"I didn't want to be where I was," I answer while staring at Indiana. "I wanted to escape. And I guess that I did."

She lets go of Vincent.

She stares at the ground.

"Well I suppose you can do something after all," Morgan says.

Behind her I can see it move.

It's jumping about across the ground.

The small white mask, the only remainder of the boar, is alive.

"It's moving," I say to the others.

Vincent turns his head to the lifelike movements of the mask.

He puts his hand upon Indiana's shoulder.

I imagine my hand upon her, in place of his.

She turns around.

"What is it doing?" Morgan asks.

It's dashing along the ground, looking for something.

But there's nothing there.

"We should go," Vincent says.

"But what is it?" I ask him. "What is it doing?"

"It doesn't matter," he replies.

Indiana steps slowly apart from us and to the mask.

Vincent tries to stop her, but she pulls away.

"It's just another damn ghost," Vincent tells her.

She reaches the mask, which stops moving upon her approach. She stares down at it as it lies still on the ground. Both the mask and Indiana motionlessly gaze at each other. After a long moment, she bends down and picks up the small piece of white stone. She traces her hand along its contours. She tilts her head and studies its shape.

It moves.

Just a little.

Her eyes seem to understand.

Understand what?

She holds it with one hand straight out in front of her.

Her muscles pull.

Her eyes close.

From behind the white mask, black droplets of thick liquid begin to drip down in slow-motion. Before they can reach the ground, however, they seem to get caught in some hidden form, splashing black across an invisible shape, as if the dark drips were filling up a mold created in her mind.

Her beautiful mind.

Her perfect mind.

Her lonely mind.

Dripping down.

Slowly.

A body takes shape.

Beads of glistening black liquid trace the shape of a hand.

An arm.

A chest.

A neck.

A head.

The body is complete.

It hangs lifeless from the mask.

Its limbs long and its skin smooth and gleaming.

Indiana stands still, holding both the mask and body in place.

Her eyes stare curiously at them both.

First a finger.

And then a hand.

And then a foot.

And a leg.

They move, wildly reaching for anything.

Indiana doesn't let go.

She just stares as the limbs of her creation flail about.

The hands reach up and stretch their long, black fingers around the mask. They slide across its shape. They touch Indiana and all movement across its body stops.

I realize that there is silence.

No one is saying a word as we stand in this concrete desert, entranced by what we see in front of us.

"I was nowhere," a hazy voice says, breaking the silence, "and now I am somewhere. How did you know? How did you bring me here?"

Indiana drops the mask, and with it the body.

Its feet touch the ground and it balances itself firmly.

"You seemed lost," Indiana says, "but you weren't looking for a place. You were looking for yourself."

The new being stretches its long muscular arms above its body, sending out a rubbery sound from beneath its skin.

"This feels," the voice says. "I've never felt before."

Its words seem to come from behind the mask, yet they are born not within this place. It's as if they leak through from another world. Their hoarse tone vibrates through some hidden membrane, shooting an obscure voice into this realm.

"Who are you?" asks Vincent.

The shadowy man turns his vision towards us.

"Who am I?" he asks back.

Morgan slowly floats up to him and circles around his body, examining the man up and down.

"What do you call yourself?" Vincent asks him.

"We have had many names," he replies, "but everyone one of them has died."

"We?" Morgan asks him, still floating around his body.

"I am just a part of them," the man says. "Just as they are a part of myself."

"Who?" Morgan asks violently.

The man turns his head to face Morgan.

"The dead," he says.

Morgan floats back with an irritated look in his eyes.

"The dead?" asks Vincent.

Indiana is staring at the ground again.

I know what she is thinking.

Sam is dead.

"We were alone," the man says. "Endless minds floating about through nowhere. But we felt this place exist. And we became I. And I became this. And this became I."

"He doesn't make any damn sense," Morgan spits out. "Just like everything else in the fucking place."

A teardrop

Falling lonely from her eyes.

She lifts her head up and wipes her face.

"If you were the dead," says Indiana, "then you were Sam, even if for just a moment. If you really were the dead, then a part of you is Sam now."

"No," the man says shaking his head. "We were not Sam. We were not anyone. We were dead and that was all. And now I am this. Now I am alive."

She turns her head and walks away to be alone.

I want to follow her.

I want to hold her.

Why don't I?

Why can't I bring myself to?

Because her sadness is too much to embrace.

Because her mysteries are too perfect to discover.

"You," the man says to me. "Who are you?"

"Cyan," I reply.

He walks closer and stares at me with the shallow eyes of the mask. It shoots a remembrance of the massive beast sitting inches from my body as I disappeared.

"You seem so familiar," he says tilting his head to the side.

"So what should we call you?" asks Vincent.

The man ignores him and continues to stare me down.

"Have you ever been dead?" he asks me.

"As far as I know I haven't" I answer in confusion, "but I don't know much."

Vincent grabs him by the shoulder to get his attention.

"I'm sorry?" the man says.

"Would you like to have a name?" Vincent asks him. "Or should we just call you the dead?"

The mask seems to be lost in thought, even though it can't change its expression.

"Do you have a name?" he asks back. "You seem to be quite attached to the idea of having one."

"My name," Vincent replies, "is Vincent. And this place is impossible enough without the confusion of not knowing each other."

The man hums a tone to himself while feeling the mask upon his head. His fingers move along the tall horns. He touches the shallow eyes. He strokes the fangs that hang from either side of his grinning mouth.

"Morgan seems to sound right," the man says.

"What did you say!?" Morgan screams.

"Morgan would be a good name for me," he answers back.

Morgan flies at him, stopping just before the two of them collide.

"My name is Morgan," he says. "Why the fuck did you call yourself that?"

"Oh," the man replies, "It just felt right. How strange? Well, I'm sorry. I'll choose another, since that one seems to be taken."

Morgan spins around angrily and flies into the distance.

I watch as Indiana sits upon the ground with her legs crossed. She's staring up into the sky.

I want to caress the thoughts that move through her mind.

"Les," the man says. "You can call me Les."

Vincent nods in agreement to him and turns to Morgan, who continues to float angrily about in the distance.

"Go talk to him," Vincent says to me. "Calm him down. He's vicious enough as it is. I'll talk to Indiana. Les, do you know anything about this place?"

"It seems to be here," Les replies. "And that is all that I know of it."

"Well that's all we seem to know as well," Vincent says back.

I walk in the direction of Morgan, who is throwing stones high into the air without ever touching them. I pass Sam's dead body lying upon the ground. The child's pale skin is splattered with bright red blood. I quickly turn away, unable to take the pain of seeing death. The memory of seeing Sam's silhouette ricochets across my thoughts, leaving sadness wherever it crosses. Every moment I spent with the child rushes inward, until I'm pushed back into staring at the small, dead body. I force myself to move forward towards Morgan.

"What do you want?" he says to me.

"Why do you think he knew your name?" I ask him.

"Why do you think he asked if you had ever been dead?" he asks back. The question shakes my mind as I think about death.

I see Sam lying lifeless against the wall.

Blood dripping down from long, sharp fangs.

Have I died before?

Just as Sam is dead now?

"We're both already dead," Morgan tells me as he floats down to the ground. "There's no life in this place. It's all pointless. It's all a meaningless joke."

"We should go," I tell him.

"Yea, yea," he says back as he flies past me, brushing against my shoulder.

I look to my right and see where the wall of ghosts used to stand. In its place is an impression into the concrete.

Something red catches my eye.

Splashed upon the ground in eccentric shapes is flaking, red paint. I try to decipher its meaning, but its form upon the vanished wall's impression is too large to clearly see from here.

But there's something behind these shapes.

They were put here.

And I have to know why.

Higher.

I've got to get higher.

Can I do it again?

I look up into the endless blue.

I close my eyes and stare into the red blood that moves through my eyelids. I feel my body existing where it is. I think about disappearing. I think about being there, not here. I think about seeing myself from above.

I think.
And I think.
And I think too much.
Still, I'm standing upon the concrete.
I try to stop thinking.
I try to move myself to where I want to be.
But the thoughts keep coming back.
I try to end them.
But they never stop.
So instead of pushing them away
I let them flow through.
I let them live.
And I let them die.
Until there's just one thought.
Death.
And I'm gone.

In every direction.
I'm pushed.
And I'm pulled.
Away.
From where I was.
And back.
To where I was.
So I force myself up.
But is it really up?
My thoughts.
Watch.
Yet it's all too vague.
Just shapes that flow like water.
But never really move.
Never.
Really.
Move.

I'm falling.
And I see it.
And I can read it.

TO OPEN YOUR EYES
THEY MUST FIRST BE CLOSED.

I don't have time to think about the words.
Or anything at all.
I'm falling fast. And faster.
The concrete is getting close. And closer.
I'm going to die.
If I don't disappear.
I'm going to die.
And I disappear.

I'm pushed with a weight that crushes my mind.
That pulls me down deep into the ground.
Against it I move.
Rising up.
But it pulls stronger.
So I push even harder.
And my thoughts begin to weaken
With every movement I make
Until the pressure fades
And everything
Stops.

III

"Red," she says as pain pulses through my left eye.
Through my brain.
And through my body.
"Just a little ring of red around the inside," she tells me.
And then the pain disappears.
"When did it start?" she asks.
I think back.
When did it start?
Far back.
When did it start?
The mask.
As it flew into my eyes.
And I think too far back.
To Sam.
Dead and bloody against the wall.
"Yesterday," I tell Indiana.
Yesterday seems so far away.
And it is.
We left the concrete island. We walked out into the sky.
And we traveled on for what seemed forever, moving through nothing at all, as Indiana led us forward upon the stone path she created. Surrounding us was an endless blue expanse scattered with slowly drifting white clouds. Their bulbous, misty bodies would caress our path, forcing us to move through their fog in blindness until we could find ourselves out of their grasp, surrounded again by the bright blue sky.

We never spoke; however, through the silence we seemed to share our thoughts, thoughts that danced between our sorrow for the past and our curiosity for the future.

We went on like this until the Myriad found us.

"It always finds us," Vincent said.

Its clinks and its clanks and its never ending rumble called out to us. Its red and its blue and its green and its orange came rushing in below us. With its arrival came a strange new manifestation.

"There," Indiana said pointing to it.

A large droplet of dark green water sat static in the air.

As we moved closer

It moved closer.

And the Myriad watched us from below

As the water's surface became clearer.

"Can you see what's inside?" I asked Vincent as he stared closely into the bluish green liquid wall.

"No," he replied, "but there's something."

"Maybe we should go," Indiana suggested. "Maybe its something that we don't want to find."

"Where would we go?" Morgan answered her while scanning the surface. "Back out into nowhere?"

"You're always somewhere," Les corrected him. "When you're alive at least."

Vincent's hands hovered above the surface of the water.

"Well then we must be nowhere," Morgan said.

And Vincent's hands touched the water.

And the water no longer had a surface.

Suddenly, it was everywhere.

We were thrown apart, sent floating through flooded city streets. My hands grasped for anything, but nothing would stay in my grip. It all slipped away as I flowed swiftly with the water's current, watching the vague shapes of the city flying past until above me I could make out the surface sinking closer.

I saw the tops of buildings as their image became bent upon the water's surface. Reaching upwards, I felt the air with my hands. My body began to slow along with the disappearing water until I was tossed upon the ground. After lying on the wet concrete, breathing in the air my lungs desperately needed, I stood up and looked about the place that I was in.

A jungle.

Within a city.

Or a city within a jungle.

Rusted signs that said nothing were bent upon street corners. Broken down cars, with missing doors and shattered windows, were strewn about the roads, as thick green bushes grew out of their bodies. Long vines hung down from the buildings surrounding me, as moss and grass grew upwards along concrete walls. Inside the windows of the buildings were mannequins dressed in wet, moldy clothing. Behind them were thick, dark growths of plants that led back endlessly into depths too dense and shadowed to see.

The air was hot and moist in my lungs and against my skin.

My clothing, soaked from the flood, clung to my body.

I yelled out for the others.

But no one replied.

So I walked alone through the wild jungle streets.

Through the wreckage of an abandoned city.

I moved amongst lakes of clear water that scattered the area. Signs were hanging everywhere, upon walls and windows and flooded street corners, but no words were found on them. Just an emptiness where a meaning should have been. It was as if no one had ever been there, as if the city had always been forsaken.

"Cyan," a voice spoke behind me.

A voice that I knew.

I turned around to see Les walking slowly towards me, not noticing the puddles of mud that he walked through.

"This is a strange place," he told me.

"Yes it is," I replied. "We should try and find the others."

He nodded in agreement.

As we began to walk together, the color of the sky and its reflections in the water and the windows of the buildings turned from deep blue to saffron.

We hiked in the direction that we thought we flowed outward from, where the water became everything around us. The air was thick as it slowly moved in and out my lungs. My movements became exhausting as we trekked our way through the dense streets. I could see less and less as the light began to escape us.

"We need to find someplace safe," I said.

"What is there here to harm us?" Les asked.

"The ghosts," I replied.

"The ghosts?" he asked.

"They exist in this place," I said to him, "just as we do. Or almost as we do. Their minds seem to be separate from this world, yet they desire nothing other than to be attached. You came from one yourself. That mask, which from what I can tell is you, was a part of the ghost that killed Sam."

"I was nothing before she pulled me into this place," he replied. "I had nothing to do with killing the one you call Sam."

"That may be," I said back.

"It is the truth," he answered.

"Either way," I said, "the ghosts are dangerous. And we need to find someplace safe, if someplace safe exists at all."

We continued on, searching about until we found a small clearing between two buildings. The night had almost fully taken over and we could only see as far as our hands could reach.

"We wont even be able to see ourselves soon," I said.

"Then we must talk," Les said, "as the dead do."

"So you really were dead?" I asked him.

"We were dead," he replied. "Not I. There is only an I in life and death. Once dead, that is, once through the journey of life and past the barrier of death, there is no self. However, it seems to me that I may still be dead, even though I am now this self. There's not much of a difference between being dead and alive, other than there is no you. And when I say you, I mean the you that only thinks its you. Not the you that really is you. That's the part that keeps on living through death."

"And just who is the real you?" I asked him.

"The real you," he said, "doesn't exist."

"You contradict yourself," I told him, but he made no reply.

And so we sat in silence.

In shadowed air.

I wasn't even sure he was still there.

I thought that maybe he had left.

That maybe I was the only thing that existed.

In the quiet, empty darkness.

And I sat there within myself.

Until myself was gone.

Until being was the only thing that was.

"You contradict yourself," he finally said, snapping me back into where I was before and shattering the sensation of nothingness.

"So since death is not the end," I said to him, "I suppose there's really nothing to fear."

"The pain," he said with a pause. "The pain is what you should fear. The dead feel endless pain."

"But there's no one there to feel pain?" I asked.

"We all feel pain in the realm of the dead," he answered. "A pain stronger than any other. It's the pain of not existing. The agony of wanting what you don't have. Of wanting what you did have. Of wanting what you will never have again. I remember. We felt it forever. And we wanted it so bad. Until we had to have it. Until we couldn't take it anymore. But we had to. There was nothing else besides the pain of desire. And then we began to desire the pain. Until the pain became real. Until we became I. And I became this."

"So there really is no I?" I asked him. "It's just our desire?"

"All there is," he said, "is I."

"You contradict yourself," I told him.

And again we sat in silence.

Until forever ended.

And the light slowly returned.

The black became violet.

The violet became blue.

And the blue became clear and bright.

"When the mask flew into my eye," I tell Indiana, "when I killed that thing."

I see her eyes flinch slightly.

Her lips just barely move.

Her thoughts think of loss.

"I'm sorry," I say to her. "I'm sorry we couldn't save Sam."

She stares emptily at nothing, as if she wasn't even there behind the hazel eyes that reveal the world to her soul and her soul to the world. I want to touch her. I want to make her feel okay.

Why don't I?

Why the hell can't I?'

She puts her hands down to the grass that we sit upon and closes her eyes. The muscles in her arms begin to pull just slightly. I stare at her smooth skin. I think of moving my hand across hers, then sliding it up her arm and down her back and around her body and through her hair.

Colors begin to flow upwards
From the bottoms of the blades of grass.
Green turns to blue.
To red.
To yellow.
To purple.
And orange.
To colors that don't have a name.
Until we're surrounded by endless hues of grass that sway faintly in the breeze.

I look up and see a single teardrop fall from her eye.

It lands upon a yellow blade of grass, washing the color away and turning it green again.

"Your eye," she asks, "is it okay?"

I want to tell her that it doesn't matter.

That she's the only thing that does.

My pain means nothing compared to what she feels.

"It comes and it goes," I say. "But yes, it's alright."

She reaches her hand out and touches the side of my face. I collapse into pieces and the only part of me that still exists is the skin that feels her soft hand.

"Take care of yourself," she says to me before letting her hand go, sending me back into the person that I was before.

I can hear footsteps coming closer to us, and I turn my head to see Vincent approaching.

"We can head in that direction," he says pointing down a long, wide street.

"Why?" she asks him standing up. "Why can't we stay here while its peaceful?"

"Because it never stays peaceful," he replies. "You know that."

"And why do you think it will be safer down the road?" she asks him. "What if it's worse?"

"What do you want us to do, Indiana?" he asks in frustration. "Stay here and do nothing until the ghosts come to tear us apart?"

She throws her hands down fast, and all the color in the grass gets covered in a layer of rigid dark gray. Her face shows anger. Or is it love?

"Indiana," Vincent says reaching out to her, but she stands up and walks away. He follows her, leaving me alone upon the ground, surrounded by solid, gray blades of grass.

I watch the two of them walk into the distance until they vanish around a corner. I feel a jealousy sit within my chest.

Why?

Because I want her anger.

Because I want her love.

Because I want her to feel anything at all towards me.

It burns in my chest until it burns itself out.

I sit empty in the rough, gray grass.

And I let myself go.

Let it all go.

Through.

In every direction.

Inwards.

And outwards.

I can't stay here.

But I can't go there.

Only somewhere in between.

My mind.

And my mind?

I try to stay put.

But my thoughts

Break apart.

And so I try to go far.

But the distance

Tears me into pieces.

Until I'm stuck in the middle

Of there and there.

Or here and here.

Or there and here and here and there.

And it's too much.

And it's everything.

And it is.

My body appears a small distance behind where I was before. My mind feels weak and tired. This movement or not-movement or whatever it really is seems to drain away at something deep inside myself. It burns a hole in my thoughts that pulls at me physically, sucking strength from my body.

I walk across the hill of grass that sits against the ledge of the roof that I'm on. It's a long, low building, much different from the towering skyscrapers that sit everywhere else in the city. Half of the building is engulfed in green grass that grows upon its roof and over its sides, leading down to the street below.

I'm alone with my thoughts.

Thoughts that push me backwards to the morning when Les and I were searching for the others.

The humidity never left us.

The air was still heavy in my lungs.

Heavy on my skin.

But we walked on.

Looking.

Until we saw Morgan in the sky, ripping buildings apart and floating the pieces around his body. The chunks amassed into a sphere of concrete and glass and metal, which surrounded his floating body.

"What is he doing?" Les asked from the otherworldly voice box inside himself.

Then suddenly everything came shooting.

Flying outwards from Morgan's body.

Thick pieces of concrete tore apart cars. Holes were dug deep into walls. Glass shattered as fragments collided. Les and I took cover behind a corner until we heard the blast stop, until the only sound was Morgan's laughter.

I yelled out to him, and he turned to face us from high above.

"Well there you are," he said back, just barely loud enough for us to hear.

"What are you doing?" I asked him.

"Whatever I want," he said floating down to us. "What else is there to do?"

"Do you know where the others are?" I asked him.

"I imagine they're somewhere around here," he said. "We unfortunately never seem to get too separated."

"That's a foolish thing to say," Les told him.

Morgan snickered back at him.

"I'm a fool?" he asked. "For wanting to be alone in a place where nothing matters? In a place where the only joy you can find is doing whatever the fuck you want to do?"

"We need to find Indiana," I said before the argument could continue, "and Vincent."

"They'll show up," Morgan replied. "Just as I did to you and you did to me."

"Well then let's go," I told him.

"Whatever," he replied.

And so we hiked along the streets, with Morgan floating by easily above us. My feet were damp from the water. My skin was moist from the humid air and the sweat that poured out from every part of my body. The sun seemed to stop in the middle of the clear blue sky. The light shined down upon us, making the warm dampness of the air on my skin and in my lungs even worse.

There was nothing else to do but to keep moving.

So we kept on moving.

Over long, torn apart buses lying in pieces on the ground, as winding trees grew out of their insides and wrapped around their rusted metal bodies. Over fallen streetlights with dark green vines growing in spirals all around them. Over bridges made from the tops of cars that sat rusting away in lakes.

Lakes that went on for blocks at a time.

Countless little waterfalls, splashing against the concrete ground and the scattered water in the streets, fell from the windows of tall buildings.

Les had slowed down, straggling behind.

Morgan drifted listlessly by in the air, not far behind Les.

And so I led us along.

Led us through nowhere.

And then I saw her.

Her skin shining in the sunlight.

Her shirt torn off just below her breasts.

Her pants cut off high upon her legs.

Her.

I only saw her.

I wanted every inch of her body.

Every inch of her mind.

And then I saw him.

Him.

He walked up beside her.

And he touched her.

And he held her.

And he whispered

Into her ear

As his hands slid down her side.

And then one hand slid back up

And around her body.

Squeezing her.

While the other touched her more and more.

Slowly

Moving

Beneath her clothes.

She tilted her head upwards as she reached back and touched him. A smile crossed her lips. I felt her hands touch my body as if I were Vincent. I felt her smooth skin as if I were Vincent. I kissed her lips as if I were Vincent. And my fingers slid inside her as if I were Vincent.

I could hear the others approaching behind me, so I kicked a stone across the ground to let the lovers know they were not alone. I pretended to be looking in the other direction. And I pretended not to notice that she was his.

"Cyan!" I heard her yell.

And I faked my surprise.

"Cyan!" she screamed again.

She waved an innocent wave.

As if they were there waiting for us.

Not touching.

Not loving.

Just waiting.

For me.

I waved back to her

As we moved closer.

And we were together again.

In the city.

In the jungle.

And the present brings me back
To the grass upon the rooftop.
But I want something else.
Not this.
Not that.
But nothing.
I want nothing.
And lots of it.
I pull myself in.
And I push myself out.
Again.
I'm gone.

Again.
I'm nowhere.
Being pulled everywhere.
And I can't stay still.
But I can't move far.
So I focus.
On what it feels like.
On what it is.
On what I am.
On being.

Back where I was
For just a few moments
As I catch my breath
As I catch my thoughts
And throw them all away.

Into the emptiness
That sits inside of everything.
I push myself forward.
Against everything.
Or with it?
Until I can't push anymore.

And I'm back, but I'm flying.

Forward.
And fast.
My feet graze the ground.
And I fall, spinning headfirst.
Colliding hard against the rooftop.
I'm going to die.
My body skids over the edge.
And I shoot off the end of the building.
I'm falling through the air, towards the building ahead.
I force my thoughts to separate.
From my movement.
From my body.
From everything.
And I let myself go.

Into the pain.
But why?
There's no body to feel it.
No nerves to scream out.
Just thoughts that I have to swim against.
The agonizing pressure of movement.
And the buildings sway like water.
In my mind?
I move.
Against it all.
And I learn.
That I can't.
Stay.
Here.

And I'm back on the roof
Or above it
As I fall, but don't catch myself.
I'm too tired to even move.
I just lay there.
In the green grass.
Staring at the blue sky.
A white cloud floats by.
Slowly by.

Its shadow covers my body
And the heat fades away.
I close my eyes.
And I let myself go.
But I don't disappear.
I stay here.
Empty.
Then the pain begins to burn in my left eye.
Slowly growing.
Radiating across my face.
And I can no longer relax
As the sun returns from behind the cloud.
The cloud that keeps on floating.
And moving.
Reaching.
And grabbing.
At a tall building to my right.

I forget the pain in my eye and look more closely at the billow of white above as a plump arm reaches out from its misty body and wraps its grip around the top of the building.

It's not a cloud at all.

It's a ghost.

And it opens wide a mouth that lies hidden beneath the white, foggy skin of its body. It has no teeth. There's just a massive dark hole in its middle. And it pulls at the building until it tears it apart, shoving the top of it into its mouth. Its chewing sends loud rumbles out across the streets.

And it grabs again.

And it eats again.

And there are more of them slowly floating by in the distance.

I stand just as Vincent and Indiana come walking up to me.

Did you touch her?

Or did she touch you?

"They're here," Vincent says to me.

Bits of the building crumble to the ground.

"We should go," Indiana says, staring up at the large ghost above. We move to the street we were planning to head down. There we find Morgan floating about, tossing bits of metal into the windows of the cars that line the street. Les is there as well, staring at his reflection in the glass window of a building. His long black hands passionately caress the white mask upon his head. He doesn't seem to notice us at first.

"So they're here," Morgan says. "At least there's something to do now."

"Yes," Vincent replies to him. "We can leave this place right now." Morgan replies with a laugh that says fuck you, yet doesn't fight back against Vincent's orders. At the sound of Morgan's laughter, Les snaps out of his gaze and joins the group without saying a word.

We move down the street that leads to nowhere.

But all the streets lead to nowhere.

So we walk along anyway.

The ghosts begin to appear near us.

They sit inside the buildings that line the street.

They sit eating handfuls of trash and gravel and rotten bits of plants. Their bodies are large and round and seem to almost burst with every bite that they take. But instead of bursting they grow and they grow and they continue to eat as they continue to grow. And as we move along they become more crowded, piling out of the buildings and into the streets. More and more of them float by above, chewing up the buildings and sending bits of concrete down around us. We have to avoid the sidewalks because there are too many of them. Each one of them takes up the space of the five of us combined.

And as we walk down the middle of the street, we begin to hear their sounds. Their chewing. And their talking. Or something similar to talking. It's a sad gurgling sound that has only one meaning.

More.

Give me more.

And they get more.

Some of them sit high upon concrete ledges. They have baskets of things that the others want.

Rotting green things that send painful smells into my nose.

And the ghosts below on the crowded streets rip apart their bodies and throw themselves at the ones with the food. They tear apart every piece of themselves just for more.

Just for another bite.

As long as they have their mouths

As long as they can eat

They cry out for more.

And so the ghosts turn to fat balls of blubber.

No arms. No legs.

And the ones up above grow richer with every limb that they get. They sprawl out against the buildings like spiders.

Fat, white spiders.

And fat globs with mouths.

Everywhere.

And they push at our sides

And it becomes hard to move.

"We've got to get out of here," Indiana says from somewhere up ahead. "They're going to crush us."

We try to move faster

But they surround us.

Eating.

And eating.

And eating.

Until the sky is white with them.

And the buildings are white with them.

And the streets are white with them.

And everything is white.

"I can't move," someone says up ahead.

"We've got to!" someone else screams.

And the air is unbreathable

From the heat and the stench.

I no longer move.

And I have to escape.

Away from here.

Into myself.

Floating up
Through the white
Crammed
Insides of ghosts.
And I stop.
Within nothing.
I'm there.

Landing on top of one of the ghosts who sits motionless on top of another, I balance myself and look for the others. Morgan floats above, yelling at an obese ghost who stares blankly back at him. Indiana and Les sit balanced upon a platform made by Indiana.

Vincent is nowhere to be seen.

I pull myself in.

And push myself out.

I appear upon the platform with Indiana and Les.

"Where's Vincent?" I ask.

Indiana shakes her head.

"He told us to go ahead," says Les. "He was in front of us, but we couldn't see him."

"He's okay," Indiana says seemingly to assure herself. "He can take care of himself."

Morgan keeps yelling.

Keeps screaming at all of them.

"It's pointless," I say to the others. "They can't understand us. Or at least they don't want to."

And suddenly a rumble comes from the building ahead.

A building that isn't yet covered in the ghosts.

And a large hole appears in it side, dissolving away the concrete and glass.

"There," Indiana says, standing up.

"Vincent?" Les says.

Indiana runs toward the opening, creating a path beneath her feet. We follow close behind her and find Vincent waiting at the entrance of a tunnel that cuts through the building.

"These damn things!" he says angrily, pulling at clumps of white stuck to his body.

"What are we going to do now?" Indiana asks.

"Ahead," Morgan says to us as he quickly floats down from above, "There's something stopping them, but I can't tell what."

We move in the directions that he tells us and find that he is right. The ghosts stop suddenly against an invisible barrier that lines the street. We move down to the ground and stare at the plump wall that sways back and forth, its form made from the ghosts' fat, white bodies.

"Fucking ridiculous," Morgan says. "Everything here is fucking ridiculous."

"Why did they stop?" I ask stepping back from the wall, not trusting the hidden barricade that holds them in place.

"I don't know," Vincent says, "and probably never will. We should move while we can."

The streets are clear again.

In fact, more clear than before.

The sun shines bright against the light gray concrete.

There are no broken down vehicles.

No torn apart signs or rusting streetlamps.

Just tall buildings.

And long waterfalls, which splash down upon the flora growing green out of the sidewalks. Something red sits vaguely in the distance. We move closer and discover that it's an archway. It's tall and made of wood painted deep red. I touch its surface with my hand and feel small marks carved into it. I trace the carving with my finger, but can't make out any meaning.

"What is this place?" Indiana asks.

But no one replies, for no one knows the answer.

Not far ahead we see another arch.

And behind it lies more.

And more.

They go on far into the distance.

We walk beneath them, waiting for something.

But we don't know what.

"They have to lead somewhere," I say to the others.

"Nothing has to happen here," Vincent says. "Nothing has to do anything."

The archways become so frequent that the gaps between them disappear. We no longer walk in the sunlight, but instead through a dark red tunnel. Far ahead we can see an end.

A small bright light, like a single star in a crimson night sky.

The light grows brighter the closer we get.

Until the tunnel is gone.

And we're standing in the open again, staring at the beautiful surroundings. A vast cerulean waterfall cascades down the side of an infinitely tall building. The water plummets to the ground behind a massive stone statue.

"It's a toad," Morgan says unenthused.

"It's amazing," Indiana says walking up to it.

It sits there beneath the waterfall with a blank look upon its face. It's made of rough, gray stone that shines in the sunlight.

Indiana puts her hands upon its surface.

"It has to have a reason for being here," she says.

I walk up to the statue and put my hands beside hers.

We both slowly feel the rough texture of the stone.

"Do you think someone made it?" I ask her, turning my head to stare into her eyes, which gaze in wonder at the toad.

"It's a monument," she answers, but saying it seemingly to the statue and not me, "to something. But what?"

Her hands pull off of the surface as she looks upwards to the enormous face of the toad. Its bulging eyes sit atop its head, though they appear to be closed. Its long, straight mouth stretches across its face, drooping down just slightly at its ends, giving it a solemn expression.

I walk around to the back of the statue, where I find a large golden door attached to the building behind the toad. As the waterfall loudly collides against the ground, a shallow stream forms that flows into the crack that sits beneath the door.

I walk into the water and stare at the golden entrance.

Upon its surface is bright red paint splashed into a single word.

MORE?

The sound of rushing water masks out the rest of the world, leaving me alone with the word upon the door.

I have to know what lies beyond.

I want to know what exists there.

I want what I don't have, but must have.

I do want more.

I want it all.

Everything.

I reach forward, gripping my fingers around the cool, wet metal of the handles in the center of the golden door. I pull and it opens wide in the middle.

Darkness.

Complete darkness.

But something is there.

Something terrible.

Yet, I want it.

Reaching forward, my hand disappears behind the thick wall of black. A quiet buzzing sound begins to grow from within the shadows.

And I'm terrified.

Yet, still I move.

Farther into the darkness.

My mind is horrified.

At what I'm doing.

At what I want.

Which is this.

Buzzing.

Louder.

Buzzing.

Darker.

Buzzing.

Until I'm nothing but the shadows.

Nothing but the loud and painful noise in my ears.

And I want more.

But there's no more to get.

But I need more.

Buzzing. Buzzing. Buzzing.

I want it.

And something hits me solid in the chest.

It sends me flying backwards, out into the light.

And all the pain collects itself in my left eye.

Burning hot.

And I forget what it is that I wanted.

But I still want it.

So I'm stuck there in the pain of needing something but not knowing what. And the buzzing is unbearable.

And the buzzing is everywhere.

Buzzing.

Buzzing.

Buzzing.

And I can't stand it anymore.

So I scream.

Buzzing.

Screaming.

Buzzing.
Then they're everywhere.
Flying against the walls.
Scraping across my skin.
Killing me.
Buzzing.
Screaming.
Killing.
I can't.
Buzzing.
I can't.
Buzzing.
I disappear.

Backwards.
Through the stone.
Through flesh?
Through life?
And again through stone.
Past Indiana.
Past nothing.
Until I'm there.
And I'm here.

They swarm about in the air.

Torsos of men with wide hollow mouths, moist holes sitting in rotting flesh. Countless eyes look outward upon their heads, seeing in every direction. Upon their backs, large wings move too fast to be seen.

Their arms are long and narrow.

And their legs are nonexistent.

There's just a gaping pit that lies beneath their stomachs, dripping murky insides across the ground.

And the buzzing.

The buzzing.

Buzzing.

Never stops.

"Shit!" Morgan screams over and over again.

Vincent is running.

Running to Indiana, who sits beneath the large belly of the stone toad. I hear Les make a strange sound that cuts through the noise. I turn to see him grappled against one of the gruesome things. I begin to move to him, but one of the creatures shoots past and hits me in the face, sending me to the ground. As I rise to my knees, I look upwards to see the insides of one of them as it flies above me. Before I know what to do, I'm covered in the filth that seeps from its torso.

The buzzing, the stench, and the rotten chunks of something on my skin make my insides spill out of my mouth. And I can't stop vomiting across the ground, even though there's nothing in there to vomit out.

Buzzing.

Buzzing.

Buzzing.

The.

Fucking.

Buzzing.

Won't.

Stop.

I force my insides to stay where they belong.

And I look up to see bits of rock falling from the top of the statue. As the stone crumbles away, his eyes open wide. In the middle of the yellow spheres sit black slits darker than the shadows that gripped my senses earlier. His heavy eyelids blink as more and more of his stone shell falls apart. The large chunks fall to the ground, sending Vincent and Indiana running out into the swarm of flying, vile things.

The huge moist body of the green toad reveals itself.

His mouth opens wide and stretches apart as if it hasn't been opened in ages, or ever at all. Strings of spit hang in front of a long red tongue that sits coiled in his mouth. The tongue unravels itself and almost instantly shoots out at the swarm of creatures in the sky, grabbing two of them and pulling them into his mouth. He gulps the foul things down and sends out his tongue for more.

And the buzzing.

The buzzing.

Buzzing.

It doesn't stop because there's more and more of them. They keep flying out of the open door. Out of the shadows.

"We've got to get out of here!" Indiana yells through the noise that surrounds us.

And I see it.

In those large, golden eyes.

I see that he sees me.

That he wants me.

And before I know it happens it already happens.

I'm wrapped up in the hot, wet tongue of the toad. It squeezes me and makes my flesh burn and my bones feel like snapping and no air enters my lungs and no light enters my eyes and it squeezes me so hard I don't even hear the buzzing.

I just feel the movement.

The movement towards his insides.

I try to disappear.

I try.

But can't.

My thoughts are too hectic.

And the fear of death, the fear that first made me disappear, isn't there. Do I want to die?

Because I will if I don't move.

His tongue lets go, sending me flying back against his throat. I slide down his moist flesh, glimpsing for a second what lies outside his open mouth. His jaws close, and I'm surrounded by darkness.

And buzzing.

Buzzing.

Buzzing of the things in his stomach.

The stomach that I am heading to.

The acid and the things and the death and the buzzing.

It all shakes my mind apart.

And I feel one of them at my feet.

I feel the warmth of the insides all around me.

And for a second I see a light above as the toad opens wide for another bite. I see his red throat shine in the sunlight.

Buzzing.

Buzzing.

Buzzing.

A white arrow.

And another.

Flying into his mouth and striking against his throat.

And the thing beneath me grabs at my body.
Its half melted flesh slithers along my skin.
Burning.
Buzzing.
Again the light.
Again the arrows.
Indiana.
I see her.
In my mind.
She takes over my thoughts.
Until she's the only thing I know.
Until she's the only thing that's left.
Her eyes tell me to let go.
And I do.

Cut.
Cut.
Out.
I get out of there and here and everywhere.
Away from the buzzing.
Away from myself.
And to her
I move.
Only.
Her.

The air releases around my body.
No.
Not the air.
One of them.
I feel him split into pieces as my mind awakens to where I am.
"Shit!" yells Vincent, staring at me as I appear next to them.

Indiana is standing to my right, shooting arrows at the massive toad. Morgan is swinging his arms about, throwing pieces of whatever he can find at the things that fly around us. Les is fighting against one on the ground, punching it over and over again in the large ball of eyes upon its face.

"You smell awful," Indiana says to me while keeping her eyes on the toad and the arrows that fly at its body.

"Either these damn things will kill us," Vincent says, "or the toad will."

He looks around us in confusion.

"Where's the tunnel?" he asks. "Where did it go?"

I look around and see that the entrance is gone.

Surrounding us are tall buildings covered in the swarms of repulsive creatures that fly about. The only exit is a street that lies at the opposite end of the large enclosure we're in.

Indiana throws down her bow and faces the way out.

"Are you ready?" she asks.

Before anyone answers she runs forward, forcefully pulling her arms up from the ground and creating a wall that shoots forward to the street that leads away from here.

"You're amazing!" Vincent yells out to her.

You're more than amazing I want to tell her.

You're more than any word could describe.

But instead I run.

We all do.

Besides Morgan, who shoots past us and into the street ahead.

"They're following us!" Les yells as the creatures fly in our direction. I pull out the staff that hangs upon my back. The sensation of it in my hands reminds of the last time that I used it.

It reminds me of death.

We run down the streets, not knowing where to go.

Indiana keeps putting up walls behind us, yet the creatures keep multiplying as if behind the golden door were an infinite amount of them.

The ground shakes beneath us.

And suddenly there's a crash high upon the building to our right as the toad lands heavily upon the structure, sticking to its side and cracking its surface. His long crimson tongue whips about, catching more of the things that fly throughout everywhere.

"What the hell are we going to do?" Morgan yells out.

Vincent stops and braces his feet against the ground. Letting out a scream, he thrusts his arms upwards and dissolves away the chunk of building where the toad sits, sending the massive creature falling to the ground.

The crash of it landing throws dust high into the air.

Morgan shoots forward and sends the cloud swirling into violent shapes that storm down at the toad, cutting open its skin and splattering its blood across the street. The huge beast quickly jumps towards us, crashing into a nearby building and almost collapsing the entire structure. Indiana again builds a wall behind us as we run down the street ahead.

Still the buzzing.

Buzzing.

Buzzing continues.

And a shadow passes over us as the toad jumps high through the air above and lands with a crash against the ground ahead.

"Damn!" Vincent shouts.

And the toad's mouth, it almost smiles.

Do you have us?

Is that what you think?

His red tongue flies out and touches Indiana.

Touches her just barely.

Because before it can grab her.

Before it can rub its hot spit against her skin.

I'm gone.

And the red flows by.

Like a river.

Like a string.

Tying together here and there.

The here where I was.

And the there where I am.

Gazing deep into the black depths that sit inside his eye.

I exist in the liquid nothing

Of the place that I am in.

The place that I leave behind.

And I swing down hard at the golden eye.

And my staff digs deep into the radiant sphere.

Yellow blood seeps out, dripping down the staff and onto my hands. The toad shakes violently, sending me flying off its head. As I fall, I stare below at the bright red tongue lying limp on the ground. With all my weight I land and send my staff down, smashing the tongue into the concrete.

I pull back and swing.
Again.
And again.
And again.
My eye burns more with every strike.
Buzzing.
Again.
Buzzing.
Again.
Buzzing.
And again.
I swing.
And there, lying ripped into two, is the creature's tongue.
I look to my right and see the toad gasping for air.
And then it lets out a sound that overwhelms everything.
Not with its volume, but with the misery behind its vibrations.
Not even the buzzing can exist.
Just the sound of death.
Of the toad.
Of the creatures in the sky.
Of something deep inside myself.
I turn to look at Indiana.
I had to look at Indiana.
She stands at the end of the long, dead tongue.
Her eyes stare straight into mine.
And I can make out her lips.
As they say just a single word.
Red.

IV

The concrete beneath our feet turns to dirt. The hot air of the city, of the jungle, gives way to a coolness that soothes my body and calms my mind. Buildings disappear. Sunlight fades away.

The world around us changes.

We walk along a dusty path, winding amongst dark green hills.

Yet slowly the hills disappear too.

And all that's left is flat.

The sky burns its dying colors, and in the distance, far in the distance, we make out the silhouette of a forest sitting dark against the fading rays of sunlight left lingering in the sky.

The calmness in the air lets memories of my past dissolve, shooting echoes of what has happened into the places they belong. New soft clothing, which Indiana again created for me to replace the mess that had covered my body, sits gently against my skin.

Skin cleansed beneath the final waterfalls of the city.

"How far does our path go on?" Indiana asks no one in particular. "How long will we be in this place?"

"And why?" Morgan adds. "Why go on at all?"

"Because," Vincent answers without adding more.

The breeze caresses against my skin

As the violet sky swims amongst our shapes.

"Because," I say, "is the only answer. The only reason why. It all leads back to because. With every question we move further away. Further from the beginningless beginning. Yet, we're always tied to it as we drift apart. No matter how far we travel, we can always make out that vague reason echoing throughout everything. Because. Because. Because."

"Or maybe," Morgan says floating by, "you're wrong. Maybe because is just a lie. Perhaps the past is a mistake within our confusing little heads. And the present is its fucked up child. Empty and alone, with no reason why in sight."

I watch as Indiana's lips begin to speak, yet before her words are born she stops herself. What thoughts drift inside her beautiful mind? What can she not seem to say? The hazel eyes that lead into her soul show nothing but reflections of the world she sees.

The forest's silhouette grows larger, yet the waning of the sunlight has caused its edges to blur into the sky.

What lies within the shadows ahead of us?

More strings that tie us back to the beginning?

Back to because?

Endless waves that forever push us forward?

Always moving with the aimless drift?

Either way we're here.

Constantly going there.

And the question of where that is

Is impossible to answer.

So I stare down at my feet moving through the darkness, as the calmness in my mind returns. My thoughts begin to drift away.

Until the movements are all that I am.

"Where do they go?" Vincent asks, resting his hand upon the dark wood beside him. "And why do they exist? There's no one here to use them."

"Maybe they made themselves," Indiana answers.

"So you're saying telephone poles just grew right up out of the ground?" Morgan asks.

"No," she replies. "I'm saying that maybe they and everything else in this place creates itself. And the self that is created, that did the creating, is us."

"Not everyone can make whatever they want appear in front of them," Morgan says back to her.

She ignores him and turns her vision upwards to the vast amount of telephone poles that sit around us.

The forest was not a forest.

Or at least not one with trees.

Endless, tall telephone poles grow out of the ground.

Their wires connect in tangles with one another, leading off to somewhere unknown. The night sky behind them is scattered with countless stars that shine gracefully into our world, casting delicate light upon the dark wood of the poles. Everything glows with a faint cream-colored light.

"Has anyone even seen a telephone before?" I ask.

"Not here," Vincent replies.

"If not here," I say, "then where?"

A silence sits amongst us as we think about the answer.

"I," Vincent stutters, "I don't know. I just know that these are telephone poles. And that telephone poles connect to telephones. And telephones connect to people."

"What people?" Morgan angrily asks. "Who the hell is there to call? And what the fuck would you have to say?"

"Do you know?" Indiana steps in to ask Morgan.

"No," he answers, "I don't. So to hell with calling these telephone poles. There's no damn reason to if I can't seem to say why I should call them that."

"If you can't believe yourself," Les tells him, "what can you believe?"

Morgan ignores him and flies quickly off into the shadows.

"These questions get us nowhere," Indiana says.

"So lets continue on," Vincent replies.

We keep moving deeper into the shadows.

Following the wires that lead to nowhere.

And as the dirt at our feet becomes replaced with sand, we begin to realize that the poles are less frequent the farther we go. The wires that hang above, amongst the stars, are becoming less tangled. And the forest slowly turns to scattered poles sitting against drifts of sand. Through the strewn about shapes of the posts, I can make out in the distance a horizon. Yet, it confuses me. The sky appears to be below. The stars shine bright upon the ground, while above is solid darkness.

We walk onward through the sand until we stand upon a shore that stretches out to our left and right. The remaining telephone poles scatter the coast and lead out into the sea ahead, delving into the water's endless depths. The stars indeed no longer shine above us, but sit deep within the sea.

"The world has inverted itself," Indiana says walking towards the glowing water.

I stop and listen to the sound of waves slowly breaking against the shore. In and out of my mind, the soft noise graces lonely, shattered pieces of my thoughts, caressing me into a melded unity with everything around.

I pull off my shoes and walk forward into the shallow waters that drift onto the coast. I feel the cool water rush against my feet. I feel each grain of sand become a part of the sea and flow across my skin and through my toes. Indiana is kneeled down beside me, staring sharply into the glittering water.

"The stars have fallen," she says scooping up a handful of water. She stands and lifts her hands into my vision. Her palms sparkle in the darkness. The shimmer of her skin glows soft ivory and pale green. She smiles as she wipes her palms against her shirt, leaving behind streaks of glitter.

I reach down into the water and lift up a handful of the glistening particles. I stare closely at the light that reflects off of my skin and catch myself fading into a blissful state of nothing. Gathering my thoughts back together, I give a small laugh at the beauty of the place that I am in. Rubbing with my fingers, I create two streaks of light that cross the length of my face just below my eyes. I look back up to Indiana, who I see shares the same thoughts. Shooting upwards from in between her eyes, a glistening fountain of shapes curl about her forehead in elegant contours. Just below her right eye sits three glowing dots the same shape and size as her fingertips.

She smiles.

At me.

At us.

At this.

And even the glow of the water disappears.

As everything but this connection

Between me

And her

Dies.

"Well what now?" Morgan asks floating out from behind the group of telephone poles sitting beside us. "Are we going for a swim?"

And instantly it's gone.

The moment between us.
It disappears into the endless past.
But something remains.
Like an impression on the deepest part of myself.
It's her.
Her eyes and her thoughts.
Carved into my soul.
My soul?
Just what is my soul again?
It's the way she smiles.
And it's the water at my feet.
It's the sound in my ears.
And the cool wind across my skin.
It's everything
Flowing through my life.
Vincent walks up to us, as does Les.

"We can walk along the coast until we find something," says Vincent. "It's night, and ghosts could be near. We have to keep moving."

I see a sadness move over Indiana's expression. Her thoughts are easy to see, which contradicts her normal mystery. Why do we have to go? Why must we always change? Can't we stay here? Live here? Be here? All these questions escape her thoughts and send a melancholy across her face.

I want to tell her that we can stay here.
That we can live here.
That we can be here.
Always here.
But the only real answer.
She already knows.
Why do we have to go?
Why?
Because.

The night remains as we walk along the shore. We pass nothing but the countless telephone poles stranded in the sand and the vast glowing sea lying out to our left. I get the feeling that it's not just repetition that makes this place seem familiar.

"I think we're going in circles," I say to the group.

"I think you're right," Indiana replies.

Vincent stops and looks around as if in deep thought.

"Maybe some of us could stay here," Les says, "while the others continue walking. If we meet up again then we know we're getting nowhere."

"We know the forest that we came out of," says Vincent. "It was no island."

"But we also know that this place never stays the same," Morgan replies.

"He's right," Indiana says as she looks back down the path that we've walked.

Vincent reluctantly nods in agreement.

"Cyan," he says, "you go with Morgan and Les. Indiana and I will stay here."

You would stay here, wouldn't you?

With her.

Alone.

Will you touch her?

Or will she touch you?

"But what if we're wrong?" I reply. "What if we just become separated?"

"Here," Indiana says holding out her hand.

Appearing above her palm, a bright red string dances through the air and forms the shape of a ball. She pulls at the end of the string and tosses the rest to me.

"Take this," she says, "and we wont become separated."

Do you want to be alone with him?

Do you want him to touch you?

"Okay," Morgan says, grabbing my shoulder. "Let's go."

And so we leave them behind.

And walk down the shore.

Going somewhere unknown.

Or maybe somewhere we've already been.

"I know you're obsessed with her," he says as he floats backwards facing me.

"Who?" I ask.

"Who?" he laughs back. "Don't play stupid. The only fucking woman here."

"Why do you think I want Indiana?" I ask him.

"I can see it on your face," he tells me. "Not when you look at her. No. When you look at him. I see the way you hate it. The way they love each other."

"She is quite beautiful," Les says, stopping me before I could reply to Morgan.

"Oh, so you like her too?" Morgan says laughing.

"No," Les quickly replies. "No. Just stating a fact."

"I don't hate what it is that they share," I finally reply to Morgan. "Indiana can do whatever she wants."

"Whatever she wants," Morgan says while quickly flying up to me and floating near my face, "is Vincent."

And I see them.

Together.

"There it is!" Morgan yells floating away from me with a grin on his face.

"Just keep going," I tell him.

"Whatever," he mumbles, floating back around to face the direction that we head in. String slowly moves through my fingers as I walk along the sand. As we pass by places we may or may not have already been, I think of her and I think of him.

He cuts the red string with a flick of his wrist, releasing it from the ball of red within my hands. She ties our two pieces, or one piece rather, together in a knot.

"So here we are," she says, dropping the string to the ground.

"What should we do?" I ask.

"There's only one way to go," she replies looking up to the sea. We all stare out at the vast ocean that glows with the brilliance of the fallen night sky.

"Through the stars," Les says.

"To the unknown," Vincent adds.

"Can you give us a way sweet goddess of creation?" Morgan asks Indiana. She tilts her head just slightly to the side, as the edges of her mouth faintly give a smile.

"Of course," she replies walking towards the water.

And so she begins with nothing.

As we watch from the distance.

With the flowing water at her feet, she seems to be caught somewhere deep within her mind.

What is it that she sees?

What is that she will make?

Breaking the stillness, her arms begin to slowly move about her body. Her legs join in as she dances in slow motion through the water. Out of the air comes a nebulous shape that matches the color of the wood posts stuck in the sand. Her body drifts in circles as her creation begins to envelop her. The sparkling light of the glitter upon her face seems to float through the air as if it were a glowing piece of cloth dancing in the wind.

She disappears behind the wall of dark rust colored wood that surrounds her body. The shape of her construction begins to become something more tangible. We watch in amazement as the large boat becomes complete and sits against the shore.

"Is she done?" Morgan asks.

We don't answer.

We just wait.

And suddenly we see her appear on the deck.

"Well are you going to come?" she yells to us.

A smile crosses my face as I think of her beautiful mind.

She is a goddess.

Of creation.

Of everything.

We walk down the beach towards the ship.

It sits lightly swaying in the water's waves. Its form is solid, yet its edges gracefully shaped. At the head of it is a carved dragon staring clear out across the sea. The light that shines up from the water below makes the figure's wide mouth glow with a strange sense of understanding.

Indiana tosses down a ladder over the edge of the ship. Even Morgan climbs up it, stunned from her abilities and forgetting he could easily reach the deck himself.

As we stand upon the ship, staring at its details, Indiana disappears through a doorway that leads below. Above us a large white sail flutters in the wind, making quick flapping sounds that drift into my ears. The ship seems to leave the shore on its own accord, pushing us out into the sea. We follow Indiana down below, where a large room sits within the boat. Its walls curve with the contours of the vessel. The floor is made of clear glass, showing us the sparkling waters that flow beneath it. The sea's light illuminates the room with a serene glow.

"How do you do it?" Les asks. "How do you make such things?"

"I can't really describe it," Indiana says while walking to the center of the room. "I just see what I want in my mind, and I think about nothing other than it existing here in this world. Then it fades out of my thoughts and into being."

She holds her hands out in front of her.

"No," she says. "Not fades. It's more than that."

Her muscles begin to tense.

"I pull it out from within my mind," she says, stressing the word pull. A black cloth takes shape in the air.

"I grab the thought of it," she tells us as the cloth falls to the ground, "and force it into reality."

She stands still with her arms hanging down along her sides.

"But its drains me," she adds. "It takes away from something inside of me. And my body and my thoughts become weak."

"It's the same with me," Vincent says. "When I dissolve things, my energy fades along with whatever I make disappear. Not just physically, but in my thoughts too."

"It's like a part of me melts away," I add, "whenever I come and go. It returns after some time. But it's exhausting."

"How about you?" Indiana asks Morgan, who stands staring at the water below the glass.

"Yes," he replies. "It drains me too. I can feel something flowing out of me and into the objects that I move. Even when I levitate myself it disappears. But it's not much. And the more that I do it, the less that it depletes me."

"It appears," says Les, "that you are similar to each other. I, however, have no such powers. But that is because I am not like you. I don't come from this strange place. I come from outside of it."

"We don't come from here either," Vincent says to him. "How else do we know of the things that we know? Of telephone poles? And cars? And of a reality that's more fixed than this one?"

"Just because you have these thoughts," Les replies, "doesn't mean that you aren't of this world. This place creates itself. And it creates whatever it wants. So perhaps it created you and your ideas of what should be. The only proof that you're not from here would be a memory of what was before. And that you don't have, but I do."

"Even a memory," I say, "like the ones that you have, could be created by this place. Just as our ideas could be."

A low hum comes from the strange voice of Les as he tilts his head to the side in thought.

"Perhaps," he utters, but adds nothing else.

"We can stay here and second-guess ourselves forever," Indiana says, "but we should probably be moving on."

"Onward to nowhere," says Morgan, floating out of the room.

We walk onto the deck and stare out at the sea that lies in front of us. A faint glow shines across the horizon.

Where will these waters take us?

Where will the stars that shine below guide us?

"There," Indiana says pointing out at nothing as if she were answering my thoughts.

"Where?" I ask her.

"There," she says again.

And I know what she's trying to say.

And I know that there is the only way to go.

Because there is not here.

And here we cannot stay.

The wind pushes us along towards places we don't know.

But then again, do we know anywhere at all?

The water glows brighter the farther we sail.

The stars are multiplying, illuminating us more and more.

"Are we moving slower?" Les asks me as I stand staring out at the sea, at the glistening waters that float across eternity.

"Maybe," I reply.

The ocean's glow entrances me.

Its radiance soothes my mind.

My thoughts become heavy.

So I cast them over the edge.

And let the lights carry them away.

Les says something.

Something.

"Hello?" he says, breaking through.

"Maybe," I say, "we are moving slower."

The ship sways gently as I step down to face Les.

"The others said the same," he tells me. "And in the same way." I look down the ship to see Vincent and Morgan standing beside the ledge. Their gaze is fixed out towards the waters that move slowly past.

"Where do you think we're going?" Les asks me.

"I have no idea," I tell him.

"What if we get nowhere?" he asks. "What if we're stuck out here forever?"

"Then at least we can relax," I reply.

He makes a sound that shows his irritation as he turns away and walks down into the ship. I move to the spot where Morgan and Vincent stand staring at the sea. Their eyes remained fixed outward, not noticing me as I walk up to them.

"Do you think that we'll find land?" Morgan asks no one in particular. And no one in particular answers him.

"I wonder," Vincent says, "if we really know anything."

The sea continues to grow brighter.

As the ship sways and the sails flutter in the wind.

"Where are we?" I ask.

"I wonder," Vincent says.

And I think of Indiana.

"Where is Indiana?" I ask, turning to Vincent.

"Down below," he says, turning to me.

"Down below?" Morgan asks.

"Down below," Vincent says.

"Do you think that we'll find land?" Morgan asks.

"Where are we again?" I ask.

"I wonder," Vincent says.

And I think of Indiana.

"Where is Indiana?" I ask.

"Down below," Morgan and Vincent say in unison.

"Right," I answer.

"Right," Vincent stutters back.

"Just what exactly do you think this place is?" I ask him.

He turns his eyes back out to the gleaming water.

"Is it heaven?" he asks seemingly to the sea.

"What is heaven?" Morgan asks.

"It's where you go when you die, I think," Vincent says. "Or is that hell? Either way, it seems that we're alive. So it must be neither."

"Les would be the one to ask," I tell him.

"Les," Morgan says, "knows nothing. He only thinks he knows the truth."

And with his words the ship sways a little slower.

And the wind blows a little softer.

And the lights grow just a little brighter.

Sluggishly Morgan hangs over the edge and gazes at the water.

His long white hair hangs down across his face.

"The truth," he adds, "is just a lie."

Indiana, sitting with her legs crossed, gazes with a dazed look in her eyes at the radiant water that flows beneath the glass floor. Her body slowly sways left and right, as if mirroring thoughts that moved in the same languid motion. The light from the water shines upwards, illuminating her and every other part of the room from below. The glow swims from pale green to white to almost gold, and then back again to the hazy light green.

I sit down across from Indiana.

She doesn't notice me.

She just keeps swaying and staring.

Lost somewhere within her mind.

Or outside of it.

"What is it that you're thinking?" I ask her.

She slowly, very slowly, lifts her eyes up to look into mine. I see only emptiness behind them as they gaze into my own.

She says nothing to me, just stares with the vacuum inside of her mind. And I begin to feel a burning pain faintly sting in the center of my vision. It grows, spreading outward across my entire left eye.

Indiana puts her finger upon the glass floor and smiles.

It's not the kind of smile she usually shows.

It's not the kind of smile that shatters me into pieces and puts me back together in a way that makes me more complete.

It's a smile that tells me that nothing at all.

Or perhaps

It tells me just one thing.

That this is all I need

To make the pain leave

To make my thoughts relax.

And I realize that I'm not even staring at her smile.

I'm gazing at the glass floor

As it shoots brilliant light into my eyes.

Endless depths of nothing

Illuminated.

By endless shimmering lights

Swimming about the void.

Colliding.

Multiplying.

Dancing on for infinity.

And the pain

Is gone.

And everything

Is gone.

How wonderful it is.

The way it exists.

The way it exists just like that.

Perfectly.

And everything.

It exists.

Just like that.

Someone is talking.

To whom?

No one is here.

"Move."

Why?

"Wake up."
Who?
Someone is touching.
Touching whom?
Me?
Who is me?
Yelling.
"Get up!"
Who is that?
It's no one.
Just go back.
Just stay here.
Just be this.
Just relax.
But who?
Who should stay here?
Me?
And where could I go?
This is everything.
Everywhere.
"Wake up!"
From what?
Sleep?
"Wake up!"
Yes.
Someone is here.
And someone is there.
Sitting across from me.
"Cyan."
Me.
And her.
And them.
And him.
He tells me.
"Wake up, Cyan."
And I'm ripped away.
"You've got to get up," he tells me.
Yes, me.
I am me.

But it hurts to exist.
And it feels too much.
So what's the point?
"No. You've got to get up."
And again, I'm ripped away.
"Cyan," he tells me, "we have leave here."
And the light glows so bright that I can barely see.
"Where am I?" I ask him.
"The same place you were before," he tells me.
And my muscles barely work as I stand up.
As.
I.
Stand.
Up.
And Les grabs both sides of my face.
Shaking me awake.
He stares into me with his shallow eyes.
And I remember where I am.
Where I was.
It was perfect.
No pain.
No thoughts.
And I want to go back.
Why shouldn't I?
"You have to stay awake," he tells me.
Who is he again?
And who am I?
"Stay awake," he says.
Awake.
I'm awake.
"Why?" I ask.
"Because," he answers, "otherwise you'll sleep away
forever here. Just look."
He spins me around and I see them.
Them?
Yes them.
Indiana.
Morgan.
Vincent.

Sitting with empty eyes.

Staring at what lies below.

What lies below?

No thoughts.

No pain.

"No!" Les yells, spinning me around.

He pulls me by my arm and drags me somewhere dark.

My mind comes rushing in.

As does the pain of my burning eye.

But I remember that I am here.

And I remember what I felt.

"It was perfect," I tell Les.

"I'm sure you think it was," he replies, "but you were stuck there just like them. And the ship doesn't even move anymore."

"How long have we been here?" I ask.

"It's been some time," he replies. "The three of you have been sitting there in a daze, staring at nothing but the light. I tried to see what you saw, but I couldn't see a thing. I tried to wake you and the others up, but none of you would move. So I've been here alone."

I look to the opening above us.

From here I can see nothing but the empty night sky.

"What should we do?" I ask him.

"The water has become so thick that we can walk upon it. I went out there myself, but didn't go far, for fear of becoming lost," he tells me. "We have to go. We have to find our way across the sea, or else we'll be stuck here forever."

I rub my fingers into my eyes.

The pain within my vision moves back into my head, sending shockwaves through my mind. A headache forms that sits pulsing in the middle of my brain.

"We should go together," I tell him, attempting to ignore my pain, "and hopefully we will find something. Let's try to wake the others."

"They're too far gone." he says. "Far more than you were. If we can get away from here and perhaps find out why the water hinders us, then we can come back for them. But I fear you wont make it out there."

"Why is that?" I ask.

"You'll get caught, again, in the glowing world below us," he answers. "There is much more out there than you could see from your little window below."

"I guess I'll have to try and stay awake," I reply.

Les gives a small grunt from behind his mask, letting me know that he doesn't believe that I can make it. But I remember everything that's happened to us, and I can't let this journey end here. So I gather my thoughts together and I force myself into a place deep within my mind. A place that holds me tight, that keeps me where I am.

And we walk up the stairs
Into the strange, glowing world.
It stretches on forever.
A flowing light that shimmers white.
And green.
And gold.
A light that soothes my mind
Dissolving the walls that hold me in place.
I force them back up again.
But they keep melting into my thoughts.
How wonderful it would be to stay here forever.
How perfect it would be to live within this lie.
What is a lie anyway?

"Cyan," Les says in a stern tone, waking me up to what it is that I'm supposed to be doing.

So I build the walls higher within my mind.
And I keep my thoughts focused.
As we walk out to the edge of the ship.

"There's nothing," I tell Les, "in every direction."

"There's always nothing," he says back, "until there's something." He heads down the ladder on the side of the ship and walks onto the gleaming surface below. He waves his arms at me.

I climb over the ledge and head down the ladder.

As my foot touches the ground, the thick, shining liquid slightly sinks beneath my weight. It sticks to my shoes with each unsteady step that I take. I feel as if at any moment the surface will give way and I'll become drowned in the endless depths of light, the beautiful lie that rests beneath us.

But would it be so bad?
To live and die within a lie when it feels just like heaven?

Or is it hell?

I pull myself back to the present, away from the thoughts that get me nowhere but deeper into this attachment. Here and now, I move myself towards the place that I must go.

"Are you going to make it?" Les asks me.

"Yes," I reply. "Let's go."

We walk in the direction that the ship, which sits tilted and stuck into the sea, appeared to be heading. There is nothing ahead of us, but we must keep moving. Les strides across the glowing ground without a problem. He leads in front of me, mumbling words that I can't understand. Every so often he turns around to make sure that I'm still awake. That I'm still moving forward.

I feel as if I'm living in a converse world as the light shines upwards from below. Every so often I catch myself staring at my feet.

But it's not my feet that I see.

It's the light.

Shining brightly.

Soothing me.

Weakening my thoughts.

But I pull myself up.

And move myself forward.

Then fall back down.

"Cyan!" Les yells.

And again I pull myself up.

And again I fall back down.

And again.

And again.

The repetition wears me down.

Over and over I get caught and I escape.

I tell myself that I will keep my head up.

That I won't look back down.

But again I see the lights below.

Again I catch myself falling into nothing.

And again I tell myself a lie

That I won't look back down.

And every time that I do

I tell an even bigger lie.

Because more and more I want to lose myself

As the endless lies pile upon my mind.

I won't look down.
I won't look down.
I won't look down.
The weight becomes heavy.
And I can't stop.
But I have to.
So I tear myself apart
Every time I stare at the perfect world beneath my feet.
Until I'm nothing but scraps.
Torn apart thoughts that are weak and full of shame.
And if I don't stare at the lights
It hurts too much
To know who I am.
If I don't stare
I feel too much pain.å
If I don't stare
I die.
I don't stare.
And I disappear.

To the place that flows within me
And throughout everything.
I see the world.
The liquid light.
The endless night sky.
I fall deep into the glow.
I see every part of it.
Every.
Little.
Part.
And I see it for what it is.
So I move through it with ease.
Free from all the pain.
From all the desire.
And the light fades.
As I fly forward.
Far ahead.
Out of the glow.
And into a different place.

Where is it?
It's here.

I fall back into the world.
But the world is not the same.
I'm standing on a shore made of multicolored cloth. I bend down to touch the fabric and slide my fingers over its soft, billowy surface. Behind me lies the boundless, shimmering sea. It motionlessly collides with the fabric shore in long, glistening splashes of light.

I turn towards the coast made of countless colors. Listening to the empty air, I make out a faint noise coming from the distance. I move over the hill that sits alongside the beach. To my right lies the mouth of a river that joins with the sea. I stare down the length of it and decide to follow its course.

The farther I move down the river, the more its substance becomes fluid. Splotches of glistening light drift about the water as it flows more freely.

The light.
I remember the light and what it is.
It's the ghosts again.
Sparkling infinitely small, yet growing out across everything.
Colliding and multiplying.
Taking over this world and pushing us where they want us to go. But where do they come from? And why do they come here?
Do they follow us? Or do we follow them?

The river becomes a loud noise as I walk along its edges. The soft fabric beneath my feet has become damp from the water. Every step that I take becomes more difficult than the last, as my feet sink deep into the moist cloth.

Suddenly I see a bright light slide up into the horizon, as if the sun were rising. But this is no sun. It shines painfully bright with a light that cuts deep into my mind. It pushes dark thoughts into my head.

Thoughts that make me want to die.
I feel shame.
I feel depression.
I feel like doing nothing.
What's the point?
There is no reason to move.
And the walls in my mind crumble.

110

As my thoughts wreak havoc across my soul.

But my soul

Refuses to die.

And so I build the walls within my mind back up with every step that I take. And the pollution of the light that digs into my thoughts loses strength the closer that I get.

But one thought remains stuck inside my head.

Why?

And the only way to keep moving is to forget the question.

I reach the large glowing shape. From its mouth spews out the liquid that flows into the river, into the sea. A low gurgling sound radiates from within the glowing figure. Its body is large and round. It has no features other than its gaping, wide mouth. I move nearer to it and stare closely at its skin. It looks just as the glistening water, yet I feel no desire to lose myself within its embrace. Instead, I become repulsed by everything that it is.

By its lies and its oppression.

Its compulsion.

And deceitful charm.

I place my hand upon its surface.

And my left eyes burns more than ever before.

But only for an instant.

Though the instant was enough to send me to my knees.

I feel a vibration across the ground, and I look upwards to the glistening shape. The sound from within it has stopped, and its glowing skin begins to slowly drip down, revealing a dull gray surface below.

The river's flow has halted to a stop.

Silence.

And then it rushes inwards.

A powerful torrent

Crashing into the mouth of the round figure.

And the glowing liquid from the vast sea appears around the river bend, shining brightly as it surges into the gaping mouth.

Until the water no longer flows inward.

And the river again stops.

Silence.

That isn't broken.

I look to the mouth of the shape. Its insides glow with all the light of the sea. I can just catch the corner of something red upon its walls. I wade into the calm river and make my way into the radiating insides of the rounded shape. The thick glowing liquid swims against my waist as I stand staring at the words sprayed red upon the wall.

EVERYTHING EXISTS
WHEN NOTHING NEVER IS

The words shoot reason through my thoughts. Meaning collides with emptiness, and for a moment I see why it is that I must go forward. Why I must keep going on with this life. It's within the never-ending moment that I can truly find a purpose in the emptiness. It's the endless dance of life that gives meaning to nothing. I see it now, always moving, but always here.

I think about it too much.

And I lose myself to thoughts that make the moment disappear. I'm again within the self that feels so separate, yet so attached to this difficult existence. I know though, that what I felt is still there, hidden deep within everything, yet sitting in plain sight. And the knowledge of this truth gives energy to my mind.

I walk out of the glowing hollow and into the dark atmosphere of the river. I move back onto the land and remember the others stuck out at sea. What has happened to Les?

I left him there alone.

And the glowing thickness of the water has disappeared. Did he fall into the sea? Are the others free to move? Free from the grip of the lights appeal?

I run towards the coast in hopes of finding them.

The light, however, is gone.

The world is dark.

The ground often trips me, sending me falling to my face. The softness doesn't hurt though, so I quickly stand up after each fall.

My only guide is the sound of the river running beside me.

As I cross the fabric hill, I make out a faint glow rising over the horizon. There is, however, no sun that climbs into the sky. In its place I make out a moon that faintly sits round and gray in the pink atmosphere.

The wind begins to blow along with the light that comes into the world. Piece by piece, the cloth at my feet comes apart and drifts into the air. Countless vivid colors flutter about my vision, glowing bright in the pink light of the sky, until they all disappear with the wind. All that's left is drifts of sand.

The constant crashing of the waves reminds me of the others out at sea. Will they find me here? I stare down the coast, and in the distance I see a small figure sitting slumped on the ground. I move in its direction. As I get closer I can see that it is Les.

"Hello!" I yell out, but he makes no reply.

I walk up to him and kneel down beside him.

He's sitting with his knees pulled up to his chest.

His white mask reflects the pink light of the sky as he stares out at the sea. After a moment he turns towards me.

"You left me there," he says deeply from the strange place that his voice comes from. "You left me out there in nowhere. The ground began to melt away. I ran, but couldn't make it. I was pulled down into the water."

"Les," I stutter.

"I swam forward," he continues, stopping my words, "but I couldn't make it. With every push and pull through the water my arms grew weaker. I gave up and I sunk. But I didn't drown. I'm not even sure if I could. I was just sinking through an endless darkness worse than death. I was alone and alive. And I kept sinking deeper until below me I could see a light. It was the surface. It was the damn surface again!"

He firmly puts his hand on my shoulder and pushes down against me while standing up. I fall back by the force of his movement and catch myself with my hands upon the ground.

"I was sinking upwards," he says staring down at me. "And when I got to the top I could see the shore. I swam with what little bit of energy I had left. And I collapsed upon the ground. Alone. I was alone."

I see a few pieces of cloth sticking out from beneath his feet.

"I'm sorry," I say to him. "I had to escape. If I had stayed there I would have become stuck again. And when I came here I had to keep moving. I had to stop this from happening."

"I was with you," Les says walking away, letting loose the few pieces of cloth that were beneath him. "And then you were gone. I was alone there. I am alone here. I don't need you. I don't need the others. I only need myself."

"Les," I say to him, but he stops me before I can say more.

"You are nothing," he says angrily. "You are just like this place. An empty body. And an empty mind. I am different. I am not this. I am alive."

The shallow eyes of the mask stare deep into me, breaking my thoughts and making me believe the words that he says.

"So you're the one who is real?" I ask him.

He stands there silent.

The wind blows in from the sea.

The world flows with the colors of a sunrise without a sun.

Waves

Crashing on the shore.

My own heartbeat

Crashing in my chest.

"We are," he says moving closer to me.

I can hear a quiet vibration coming from behind the mask.

From within Les.

He stares deeper into my eyes.

The mask's horns seem to faintly grow longer.

Its fangs seem to cut a little sharper.

Its lips grin a little more evil.

"Who?" I ask without thinking.

Stillness.

Then movement.

And all I see is white.

V

Three moons.

And the Myriad flowing inward with the sea.

It's always moving.

Always following me.

I'm alone in this place.

As I've always been, and always will be.

The wind blows a humid breeze that moves serenely across my skin. The sky glows wide with a hazy pink light. My feet sit wet in damp sand, which is quickly becoming cluttered with bits of the Myriad.

The others are probably caught out there.

Tangled up in the chaos.

In themselves.

But here I am alone.

Where I am everything.

So I walk along my body.

Its form made from the world outside.

Looking for myself.

In everything I see.

Everything I hear.

I walk away from the water.

From the Myriad.

But over the gentle hill that rests along the shore, I find yet another coast with the same endless water and the same endless disorder. So I walk atop the ridge between the two seas.

And the farther along I move

The more the Myriad takes over.

To my left and to my right is the never-ending force of the Myriad. Tall poles of metal, sitting bent across the sky, jut out of its depths. Countless, vague shapes of every color slowly move amongst the clutter. The ceaseless groaning sounds of movement resonate in my ear

And as I walk along
Moving through myself
The shore becomes closer.
The ground becomes smaller.
And I become less.
For the Myriad is the only opposite.
The only thing that is not me.
And gradually it eats away at my body.
But it needs me and my mind.
Without me it couldn't exist.
But I don't need it.
I don't need a thing.
Other than this.
Myself.
I yell to the never-ending nothing that surrounds me.
But it says not a word.
It only grows closer.
And closer.
Until the ground is barely wide enough for me to travel.
My muscles begin to quiver.
And my stomach begins to turn.
I move faster, hoping to escape.
But my legs refuse to work.
And my heart races more with each step, as the Myriad grows
taller and taller until it towers above me on either side. I'm in a never-
ending hallway made of chaos.
Gray and red and green.
Blue and yellow.
White.
And orange.
Rusted pipes that dig into my narrow corridor.
Shredded plastic that clutters beneath my steps.
And the faint strip of light that shines high above.
My hands won't stop shaking.
Won't stop shaking.
Stop shaking.
Stop shaking.
Stop shaking.
And the walls are moving.

And everything is moving.
And I'm running.
I'm running.
I.
Am.
Running.
Away from all that is not myself.
Away from everything.
I shouldn't have done the things I've done.
But what else could I do?
No one really feels the truth that I feel.
That I am everyone.
That everyone is me.
My stomach churns inside my body.
And I'm filled with pain that flows into my eye.
It burns.
And it burns.
And still the walls grow inward.
The Myriad cuts against my skin.
Its touch feels like death.
Like the dead body lying out there in its depths.
Amongst the chaos.
Its shadowy skin being torn by the metal.
Bleeding cold black blood.
Its empty face staring vacantly at the clutter.
No eyes.
No mouth.
No life.
What else could I do?
I needed this.
This.
This is almost gone.
Almost crushed.
Metal scrapes against my skin.
I'm going to die.
It shakes throughout my mind.
My.
Mind.
I'm going to die.

I'm.
Going.
To.
Die.
I can't escape.
I can't disappear.
Why?
I'm stuck here.
Where the walls keep cutting
As I push myself through.
And I see the end.
I see myself.
Getting closer.
There is no more ground.
I'm walking on everything.

And the pain in my body grows so strong that my thoughts give up and die. They want nothing to do with this body, and my body wants nothing to do with them. They both just want to be free.

The light of myself grows closer.
And each movement is a war.
Cutting at my arms.
My legs.
My flesh.
Blood runs down my skin.
My blood.
My skin.
And then it ends
As the light takes over
And the Myriad collides with itself behind me.
I fall to the ground.

Turning over to lie on my back, I stare at the towering wall made of disorder. The pink sky instantly rinses away as a clear blue takes its place. Still, the three moons float statically above. The largest, or the closest, sits powerfully in the sky with a bright white glow. The two in the distance float faintly in the blue atmosphere, one shining dimly gray and the other a burnt and painful red.

A silhouette of movement over the edge of the wall.
Growing closer.
Closer.

And I try to disappear.

But I can't.

As it hits me in the stomach.

As it shoots more pain through my body.

I push the heavy piece of metal away.

Why couldn't I leave?

Why can't I escape?

Why?

Can't?

I?

I pull myself together and stand up.

In front of me a golden desert stretches on, colliding at the horizon with the blue sky. Large dunes sit scattered throughout the sand. Behind me the Myriad continues to resonate its ceaseless rumble, reminding me I should leave it behind.

I walk out into the sunless, sunburnt desert.

How long will I have to walk?

Why do I have to walk?

Because I have to.

I.

Have.

To.

Because no one else can.

With every gust of wind, the warm sand blows painfully into the scrapes along my skin. My eye burns stronger with every step that I take. The pain pulls thoughts from deep within my mind.

Is this pain me?

Is this me at all?

I have to be it.

I have to.

Yet this is not.

But this is.

Me?

This is me.

Me.

Me?

More sounds of the Myriad.

More proof that this is a lie.

Voices.

Voices?

Have they come to see me?

After all I am the one who saved them.

I turn to see the sounds.

And in the distance I see them climb down the wall.

Who can they be?

They are not me.

I am me.

And I am everything.

So they must be me too.

And they move.

And they see me.

And so I run.

From myself.

I shouldn't have done what I have done.

I.

Shouldn't.

Have.

Done.

What.

I.

Have.

Done.

He lands in front of me with a grin.

"So where are you going?" he asks me.

Wherever I want to.

"What did you do to him?" he asks.

Whatever I wanted to.

And he grins a little more.

I run at him.

But he swiftly moves past.

And I become surrounded by a wall of swirling sand. Each little grain soaring through the air sends a high-pitched sound into my ears. The spinning gets closer until it begins to rip at my skin.

I can hear her screaming, but I can't understand the words.

Then the sand begins to slow, letting me vaguely see their shapes through twisting movement surrounding me. I grind my feet into the ground and gather my strength.

Now.

I run through the wall as it cuts my skin.

And I'm moving through the golden landscape.

But again he lands in front of me.

"Well, this is interesting," he says with the same grin.

I turn to run, but instead collide into him.

Him.

The bastard.

I'll kill him.

I'll.

Kill.

Him.

I pull back and swing, hitting him in the jaw before he can react. He lets out a low grunt as he puts his hand upon his face.

I made him bleed.

"Why are you doing this?" she asks me.

I turn to her.

Because I have to.

Because.

I.

Have.

To.

I pull out the staff that rests upon my back.

And her eyes show confusion and fear.

As I jump in her direction.

But instantly I'm down.

And his hand is on my throat.

His silhouette covers my sight as I see his arm pull back.

With a movement he strikes.

Sending pain through my body as he hits me hard in the face.

Blood runs down across my neck.

Is it my own?

Or is it his?

I can't escape.

I can't move.

As he pulls back again.

And she yells at him to stop.

But he doesn't.

And again he hits me.

And again pain shoots through my mind.

More blood.
And something cracking across myself.
He pulls back again.
And she keeps yelling.
Down his fist flies.
And my left eye goes blind.
Half of me disappears.
Disappears as they stare.
Straight into my eye.
And he pulls at my face.
At my soul.
At me.
And he lifts me up.
But I can't stand.
I.
Can't.
Stand.
And she.
She touches me.
Past my skin.
Past my blood.
My bones.
My insides.
And into me.
The me that isn't even in this place.
And I see just her face.
Just her eyes.
Just her soul.
As she stares into my own.
And I'm gone.
Completely gone.
"Why?" she asks me.
Because I had to.
She steps back.
And I reach for her.
And she holds my hand.
For just a moment.
Then pulls away.
From me.

And the pain.
And the anger.
And everything pours out.
Because.
I.
Had
To.
Because I needed to be.
"Why did you do this?" she asks me shaking her head.
Because.
He lays me down upon the ground.
I.
He stands above my body.
Needed.
He pulls his fist back.
To.
His arm swings forward.
Die.

VI

Blood drips down his arm and across his knuckles, collecting at the bottom of his fist where it falls in thick drops to the ground beside my head. Indiana kneels down and puts her hand upon my chest. I close my eyes and try to remember.

Where I was.
What I did.
But emptiness is all that I can recall.
The shore.
And his face.
The mask.
A movement.
Then nothing.
Nothing at all.
No.
There was something.
A feeling.
Like I was surrounded by myself.
Crushed by the weight of my mind.
And then a collapse.
And the feeling cracked away.
As colors poured into my eyes.
And sound flew into my ears.
But I wasn't there.
Or anywhere.
I was nothing.
Becoming something.
Something fractured.
Broken.
Alone.
And I returned.
From nowhere.
To somewhere.

Indiana lifts her hands up to my face and stares into my eyes.

"Cyan?" she asks me. "Do you remember?"

"I do," I answer, "but not what happened here."

I try to sit up, but the pain that shoots across my body keeps me lying down.

"Don't move," Indiana says. "You need to rest."

"Sorry if I hit a little too hard," Vincent says while rubbing the blood from his hands.

"Sorry if I did anything that deserved it," I reply.

My left eye burns, but differently than before.

Its not a pain felt upon my eye.

My eye is the pain itself.

"It's completely red," says Indiana, as if knowing my thoughts. "The green of your eye is gone. In its place is pure red. Like blood. Like fire."

"What did I do?" I ask them. "What happened?"

"You didn't do a thing," Indiana says. "He did."

"Les?" I ask.

She nods.

"We awoke within the ship," Vincent says to me. "Everything was still and dark. The lights had faded away, and we we're alone with our confusion."

"The lights," Indiana adds, "they were perfect. I remember seeing them and nothing else. I could have stayed there forever. Not thinking. Not feeling. Not existing at all."

She turns her head to Vincent.

"But we we're released from wherever it was that we were," she says. "And that's probably for the best. What is life if there's no one there to live it?"

"We found that you and Les were gone," Vincent tells me, looking off into the desert. "And all around us was the sea beginning to shine with the light coming into the sky. Piece by piece the Myriad began to appear, floating up from the water's depths. Eventually the ship became stuck again. It was just another part of the chaos that surrounded it."

I gather the strength to sit up and ignore the pain that cuts inside my chest. Morgan floats by in the distance, staring out at the vast desert that surrounds us.

"Indiana led us through the sky, above the Myriad that groaned below," Vincent continues. "And we moved along with no direction, no idea of where to go."

"But then we saw you," Indiana says standing up, "or at least someone. In the distance we could make out the shore, and you were there sitting bent over the dark shape of a body. We were heading closer to you, but the Myriad began to growl louder from deep below. And with the noise came waves of metal crashing all around us. It grew higher and higher until you and the shore completely vanished. Again, we were lost."

"But as you know," Morgan says flying closer to us, "we can't stay apart for long."

"We climbed our way along until we again found the end of the Myriad," says Vincent. "And when we came to its edge we saw you running across the sand, leaving a trail of blood behind you."

"Honestly," Morgan says to me, "you were a lot more fun with the mask on."

"I was wearing that thing?" I ask them.

Indiana nods her head yes.

"We caught up to you," Vincent says. "But it wasn't you."

"But it wasn't Les either," Indiana adds.

I remember the darkness.

The emptiness.

"It was no one," I say to them as I stand up to my feet.

The hot air of the desert burns against my skin.

I look up to the three moons sitting in the sky.

"He's gone," I say. "Back to the dead."

"Why did he do it?" Indiana asks.

"Because," I answer, "he was alone."

But then I remember.

That I am too.

The blue above gives way to a bleak ashen sky. The desert sands begin to collide with fragmented patches of concrete. In the distance are lights shining sullenly white and yellow and green across the dismal landscape.

We walk along the concrete and sand, heading to the glow of a place that's unknown. My insides burn and my stomach wants to climb out of my throat and onto the ground below. My skin is sweating from the pain, and my head feels light or like its not even there at all. My lungs cut with every breath I take. My thoughts keep telling me that I'm dying. And then I think of death and it feels like the pain in my stomach and in my skin and in my lungs and in my head. My muscles begin to shake and I have to focus hard upon my steps just to keep from falling down.

"Are you okay?" Indiana asks me.

And I answer by spilling my guts out of my mouth.

The smell of the hot air and my vomit below burns my nose.

"Why?" I ask my body out loud through painful groans.

"We can't keep moving," Indiana says to Vincent. "He needs to rest."

"Night is falling," he replies. "If we stop moving, something is sure to find us."

"But if we keep moving," Indiana says back, "we're sure to find something."

"Lets go," I tell them in between heavy breaths. "I'm fine."

I continue to walk ahead, working through the pain.

I hear them follow behind.

The lights are getting closer.

The concrete becomes more as the sand become less.

"You're dying," Morgan says to me. "You're dying and we're dying and everything is dying. But especially you."

"Thanks," I answer while continuing to tread forward in sluggish steps. He hovers in front of me and floats backwards in the direction that I walk.

"Or maybe you'll never die," he tells me. "Maybe the pain will just go on forever." He flips in the air so that his body is upside down. He slows and moves his mouth close to my ear. "Which is worse?" he whispers. "The pain of death or the pain of life?"

He floats away and leaves me alone to his question.

But the agony in my body answers for me.

It tells me life is worse

Because death at least brings release.

And then something opens up inside my head, and I realize deeply that I really am going to die.

132

I.

Am.

Going.

To.

Die.

And my heart pounds so hard that my chest is going to rip open from the pressure. And the feeling I had before, when I was an emptiness behind the mask, builds itself up again throughout my mind. But it's different. It's not the feeling of being surrounded by myself, but instead it's being surrounded by everything else. I am nothing more than this bag of flesh. This living, dying thing.

And I begin to regret everything I've done, but I don't know why or what it is that I've actually done.

I just feel the regret of being alive.

Of having to die.

We reach the first light, an old rusted lamppost shining white across the flat, dusty concrete. Just a little ahead of us is the first building. Its walls are deteriorating away, revealing dark insides of rust and decay. We move down the street that forms beneath our feet, and slowly we become surrounded by more crumbling buildings and pale, grim lights. A low humming noise vibrates in and out of existence. It seems to come from nowhere in particular. The air is thick with moisture and the smell of something sickening.

"We should get out of this place," Indiana says while putting her hands upon a crumbling wall. "Nothing good can happen here."

"What makes you think something good can ever happen?" Morgan asks her. She doesn't answer his question. She just stares closely at the wall in front of her and rubs her hand across its brittle surface, sending bits of concrete tumbling to the ground below.

The quiet sound of footsteps moves into my ears. It comes from the shadows that line the street ahead. Each languid sounding step is louder than the last. And in between each footfall is the sound of something dragging heavy against the ground.

"It's coming this way," Vincent says looking into the darkness. The indistinct shape of a man begins to appear within the shadows. As it moves into the lights, its features start to take form.

His eyes are the first things that I see.

Large and white and staring directly at me.

Then his gaunt face, with its rotten yellow skin, shows itself in the light. His nose is torn away and his jaw is bent to the side. His body is naked and decaying. His bones push out against his foul skin.

He moves slowly down the side of the street, not moving towards me, but always keeping his gaze in my direction, always keeping his large white eyes, with their cloudy gray pupils, staring directly at me.

The broken mouth that sits below his face moves in little, violent motions, and a repulsive moan begins to grow out of his rotten throat.

Suddenly he stops.

His terrifying eyes staring deep into my own.

I move, but he keeps his sights on me.

"He likes you!" Morgan laughs as I back away, as the putrid man continues to stare into my being.

More footsteps.

And another walks out of the shadows.

His eyes, too, are fixed upon me.

"What are they?" Indiana asks. "And what do they want?"

"They seem to want Cyan," Vincent replies.

More of them appear behind us, wretchedly moving down the street and staring directly at me. I feel a terror run across my body as I pull the staff from my back.

"They fucking love you!" Morgan laughs louder than before.

"What do you want?" I vainly ask of the dead men as they stare hauntingly at me. They give no reply other than continuing their painful moaning sounds.

"We need to get out of here," Indiana says as more of the dead appear.

"Maybe you should stay close," Vincent tells me as he walks near and rests his hand upon my shoulder, "since they seem to be attracted to you."

"I'm fine," I tell him. "Let's just go."

We move cautiously down the street, amongst the crumbling buildings and the rotten men that haphazardly stand about and stare me down with haunting eyes. The more we move the more abundant the dead become.

No.

They must be alive.

They're here.

They exist.

And they stare at me with hidden thoughts behind their eyes.

But their bodies

Their flesh

Have long since lost the life that preserved them.

The shadows grow stronger as we pass the last streetlight.

"Here," Indiana says, holding her hands up high.

A small, barely visible point of light appears in the air above her hands. As she spreads her fingers wide and arches her arms apart, the speck of light grows into a brightly shining globe that sits radiantly in the air. Wisps of orange move about its yellow surface as it continues to grow in size.

"Morgan," she says as the sphere shines down upon her face, "would you mind holding the light?"

Closing her eyes, she brings her arms inward as the radiating sphere disappears back into the faint point it was before. Suddenly, upon quickly opening her eyes, the point of light explodes into a ball of flames, shooting a deep orange glow through the decaying streets and illuminating the multitude of dead surrounding us. They seem to take no notice, as their eyes remain fixed upon me.

"I see you've mastered fire," I tell her in amazement.

She smiles and nods as she stares at her creation.

Morgan floats above the ball of flames and moves it towards the air in front of him. The light shoots far down the city street, showing us more of the endless dead that crowd the road ahead of us.

"We've got to find another way," Vincent says.

I see a small grin grow across Morgan's face as he stares into the fire that floats in the air. His eyes show a glimpse of something wicked churning inside of him. He quickly shifts his view in my direction, staring at me deeper than the ghouls that line the street.

And as the fire reflects in violent movements upon his eyes, his penetrating gaze tells me something secret, something painful.

I'll kill them he tells me.

We'll kill them he says.

Everyone and everything.

I turn away from him to face the sound of someone screaming, someone running.

Towards us.

"What the hell is that?" Vincent asks.

I see it running in our direction with fear upon its face.

A ghost, shining bright white amongst the dead.

But he's terrified.

"No! No! No! No! No!" he screams over and over as he runs towards us.

Suddenly, one of the dead breaks his gaze upon me, and reaching out, grabs the running ghost by the face and pulls him inward. The screams grow louder as the dead man tightens his grip. Opening his rancid mouth wide, the dead man pulls back the ghost's head and bites down hard into his throat. The screams turn to painful groans as the dead ghoul eats away at the ghost, sending white blood shooting down across the street. Violently he rips the pale white head off of the ghost and holds it close to his face as he eats away.

And in the distance more screams begin to sound.

And the dead man, who chews gruesomely at the flesh of the ghost, stares back up and straight into my eyes. Bits of pale meat fall from his mouth as white blood drips down his rotting chin.

A fear churns in my stomach, and my head becomes dizzy upon feeling the nausea. More ghosts appear, running through the crowd of dead and screaming in horror. Each one of them gets seized by the rotting men and torn apart piece by piece.

Indiana grabs my arm and pulls herself close.

I want to protect her.

I want to end this.

But the fear in my stomach burns.

And it sends terror into my mind.

All around us is chaos and death.

At our feet lies pools of white blood that mix with the rotting slime that runs from the dead men's mouths and skin.

The fear in my body grows too strong.

The skin upon my face burns.

My muscles begin to shake.

And I vomit down into the white blood below.

"Fuck!" I gurgle out through the sickness that leaves my mouth.

136

Indiana lets go of me and moves to Vincent, who stands staring out at the hell that quickly surrounds us. Fear and shame take over my mind as I fall to the ground and painfully lie in the disgusting pool of fluids that coat the concrete.

And then I hear laughter above.

And as a turn over, I see Morgan flying by, spiraling the sphere of flames through the sky. Sending the fire down into the violence that covers the street, he catches ablaze the mass of bodies. Pure chaos overwhelms me as the ghosts and dead men tear at each other through the flames. Screams shoot out from every direction and I lose all sense of where I am. Indiana and Vincent disappear amongst raging mass of fire and death.

What am I going to do?

What the fuck am I going to do?

Disappear.

And it's too much.

The pain surrounding.

And the pain inside of me.

My mind feels weak before I have a chance to move.

And I fall.

No, I'm pushed.

Down into the darkness.

Beneath the street.

Beneath the chaos.

Beneath it all.

And I'm lying on cold, wet stone.

The fiery scene above has disappeared.

Now I lie alone in shadows.

I think of Indiana

Caught amongst the hell.

And I have to go back.

I have to go back.

I have to.

And so I go.

Into the darkness.

And upwards.

But it's gone.
They're gone.
Everything is gone.
I keep moving.
Up.
But endless nothing surrounds me.
Surrounds me.
Surrounds.
Me.

And again I'm alone in the cold, damp darkness.
The sound of water dripping is the only thing I hear.
Pure terror cuts throughout my body as I picture the unknown that lies so close to me. Anything at all could be there, and most likely of all is death as it flows amongst the omnipresent shadows.
I stand frozen in fear.
And I see Indiana in my mind.
Her hazel eyes staring at me as they did when I first met her.
For her I build myself up.
For her I gather the strength to move.
And I reach my hand outward into the nothingness.
Nothing.
Nothing.
Nothing.
Something.
Rough fur.
And it moves.
And it makes a deep sound.
And I'm not alone.
I'm.
Not.
Alone.
I'm fucking terrified because I'm not alone.
Indiana disappears from my thoughts as I hide myself inward.
I listen to the sound of heavy footsteps and of deep grunts coming from whatever it is that moves around me. I listen to my heart beating painfully in my chest and my lungs breathing in and out the cold and heavy air of the shadows.

Forever I sit stagnant inside my fear as the darkness wraps its cold grip around me. As I die alone inside myself.

"Go," he says to me.

And I awaken. I want to ask who's there, but the fear keeps me from making a sound. I sit confused, not knowing where I am. Not knowing who I am.

And then I remember.

Everything.

The darkness.

The flames.

The death.

Morgan.

Vincent.

Indiana.

Everywhere I've been.

Everything I've done.

It all floods into my mind.

How long have I been here?

Again, I move into the memory of my beginning as I stare into the silhouette of a child standing dark against a perfect blue sky.

And for a moment.

A single instant.

I hear the sound of paradise.

And I don't know where it is.

Or what it is.

Or if it is at all.

But I hear it.

And it sounds like everything I've ever done and ever will do.

And it's the voice of Indiana as she whispers in my ear.

"Love," she says in perfect sadness.

"Love," she says in endless joy.

And again I exist.

Not whole, but in pieces.

But I'm here nonetheless.

And so I put myself together.

And I stand up into the darkness.

Reaching my hand outward, I brush against the rough fur of something moving in the shadows. The large, coarse hairs glide across my skin as a deep groaning sound echoes through the blackness. My muscles tense as again I feel the fear inside my body, but instead of falling apart, I pull myself together and walk forward into the shadows. I slide my hands along the fur as I walk with no direction through the darkness.

Faster the sounds groan outward.
And faster the fur moves across my skin.
I fight hard against the terror that sits inside my head.
I have to keep moving.
I have to escape from wherever it is that I am.
Something snaps.
And something bites deep into my leg.
Ripping away at my body.
And all that I feel is pain
As I fall to the ground
And grab at my leg.
But my leg isn't there.
The fear tears at me, and I feel myself breaking apart again.

It takes every bit of strength that I have left in my mind to keep myself together. I pull my body along the ground. The wet, gritty stone beneath my hands digs at my skin. Behind me I can hear the sound of something chewing.

Something eating away at my severed leg.

I crawl along in pain until suddenly the ground gives way and I sink deep into a sea of dark water. Still, no light exists.

Just endless darkness surrounding.
I float down into the depths as water fills my lungs.
But I stay alive
Even though I should die.
And the limbs that I have left flail about in the shadowy liquid.
Something slick brushes against my skin.
But I don't feel fear.
I see it exist inside of me.
But it doesn't become me.
It just sits there in my mind yelling at me to be afraid.
I ignore it.
What else do I have to be afraid of?

Death?

I'm already dead.

And so I sink down deeper.

Deeper.

And deeper.

And as if the fear knows my thoughts, it gives me more reason to be afraid. In the distance a faint light grows. And against its glow I see a silhouette of something horrifying move about. Long, thin limbs that bend at strange angles sit dark against the light. The shadowy movements gain speed as they grow nearer. Suddenly, I'm surrounded by the grasps of countless, slender fingers that dig into my body.

I have no fear

As I leave it all behind.

And move into nowhere.

While everything becomes illuminated.

The endless beings that surround me.

Endless faces.

Wide-eyed.

With countless sharp teeth.

Staring into the place that I was.

The place that I am not.

Through them I move.

Towards the brilliant light ahead.

Until the radiance embraces me.

Until I'm there.

Until I'm here.

And I fall to the ground, landing upon my two legs.

I'm whole again.

Or was I never incomplete?

A new fear grows.

Not of the world outside myself.

But of the world within.

Of thoughts that I control, yet at the same time don't.

Everything that I am, yet everything that I'm not.

And the fear is equal to the fear of pain and death.

If not more so.

For it's a terror of myself.

It's a distrust of my senses.

Of my mind.

Of what I am.

I push the fear away in order to continue on. The water that surrounded me is gone. The nothing that was everything has been replaced by the bright light that glows from nowhere in particular. Around me are damp cave walls that shimmer blue in the mysterious light. I walk down the sapphire halls of the cave until it opens wide into a large hollow. Sprayed in fierce red letters upon the wall are words that arch over a small doorway.

ONLY THOSE WHO LIVE SHALL DIE
BUT NEVER WILL THOSE WHO LIVE BE DEAD

Who paints these words that pull at my thoughts? Who leaves red traces of wisdom upon this world of chaos? Whoever it is they know the answers to the questions I can't seem to ask. But they hide the answers well behind their words. And all that I get are new questions, new directions to head in.

Am I alive?

And will I die?

Or am I already dead?

I let the questions dissolve into my thoughts, where they become another part of me, another mystery within my mind.

Through the doorway that lies beneath the words, a crude stairway is chiseled out of stone. Moving upwards, I climb the steps in anticipation of what I will find. The higher I rise, the more the air becomes light within my lungs. With each step that I take, I breathe more easily.

I reach the end of the stairway, where I find myself standing within a dark forest. Moonlight cuts in through the canopy above, casting down a blue glow that swims amongst the shadows. Ahead of me lies a path that runs off into the woods. I follow it, breathing in the fresh air that smells of the pines that surround me. The darkness of the forest doesn't give me fear. Instead, I feel a sense of wonder towards what may lie in its depths.

But what of my mind?

What about the fear of what it is that I am?

Of whether or not my thoughts tell truths or lies?

The terror of myself gives way to the present moment, and I feel no dread sitting within me. Acceptance radiates through my soul, replacing the fear of self with a courage to face what I am and what I may become. The only fear that remains is for Indiana, whom I've lost somewhere out there in the hell of this place.

I can see her burning amongst the dead.

Being torn apart by rotten teeth.

And my legs move faster with every thought of her.

I have to find Indiana.

I have to find my way through this place.

I come upon a small spring that flows against smooth stone. Bright green moss grows upon the stone and glistens in the blue moonlight. To my right I hear a rustle in the thick brush of the woods. I turn in the direction of the sound and see two emerald eyes staring powerfully at me through the shadows.

"Do you know where you are?" a voice asks from some vague direction. "Or should I say, who you are?"

The green eyes move forward from the brush. Out into the moonlight walks a large gray wolf. Its fur sits smooth atop its great, muscular frame. Each step the wolf takes shows powerful grace. His emerald eyes gaze up into my own, digging deep into my being. They seem to ask me every question, yet they also know every answer.

"Both questions are really the same," the voice continues.

"Is that you speaking?" I ask the wolf.

But the wolf remains silent, staring at me with powerful eyes.

"We should ask you the same," the voice says from behind me. I turn to see a figure sitting upon the stones beside the spring. "For are you speaking?" he asks. "Or are your words giving life to themselves?"

"Who are you?" I ask him.

"I asked you first," he says. "But neither of us could ever really answer, so let's forget we ever asked it."

The figure jumps down from the stone, revealing himself to be small in size. His shape is vague, for he seems to be wearing some sort of hooded cloak. I faintly make out the whites of his eyes through the shadow of his hood. He walks near to me and stands beside the great wolf.

"I have no name," he says, pulling the hood of his cloak down behind his head, "so you may call me whatever you like." His face becomes revealed in the moonlight. His age is nonexistent; that is, he seems to be both young and old. I cannot tell if he is a child or an elder. His body appears to be a youth's, yet the way in which he carries himself, with his words and with his movements, radiates a wisdom gained from a long life of experience.

"Vidya," he says petting the wolf, "is what you may call him. What is your name?"

"Cyan," I reply. "Although I do not know what my name was before that."

"Before what?" he asks me.

"Before my name was Cyan," I reply. "I've appeared in this place and it's all that I've ever known, yet I somehow know much more than I've learned here. I feel as if I've come from somewhere else, but I have no reason to feel so. Do you know where we are? Have you always been here?"

"I do not know where we are," he says, "or whether or not I've always been here. But could I ever know these answers, no matter what life I lived? Do the answers even exist?"

"They have to," I tell him. "There must be an answer. How else could there be the question?"

"What question?" he asks.

"Any question," I reply. "Why? How? Where? The fact that the question can be asked means that the answer must exist."

"Maybe," he says walking to the water that lucidly reflects the moon above, "questions can only exist if there aren't any answers. If you have an answer then you no longer have a question."

His confusing reason, though seeming to be true, strains at my thoughts. His words, which flow with a familiar wisdom, open up new parts of my mind.

"So answers don't exist as long as there are questions?" I ask him. "But what then when an answer is born? Does the question die?"

"It seems so," he says, running his hands through the water. "But perhaps this means that neither the question nor the answer ever really existed at all. How can you have an answer without a question? Or a question without an answer? Perhaps all that exists is what lies between them."

"And what is that?" I ask.

He turns to stares at me through the bright moonlight.

"You won't find out asking a question," he says. "Or within what you think is an answer."

Vidya edges closer to me. I feel his soft gray fur brush against my skin. I rub my hand across his back, and as I do I feel a vague sense of virtue flow throughout my mind.

"Are you alone?" the ageless man, or boy, asks me.

"I was with others," I tell him, "but we became separated in a place much different than this. I fear that they're in danger."

I realize my hand is moving through the air, making the motion of petting Vidya, but the wolf has disappeared. Sounds begin to echo far off in the distance. Sounds of pain and torment. The memory of the burning dead returns to my mind. The nameless boy, or man, pulls his hood back over his head, casting a shadow across his face.

"Things fall apart," he tells me, "including yourself, and the ones you love and the ones you hate and everything else that ever was and is and will be. But when everything falls apart, everything collides together. In different ways. In different forms. In different times. It's always happening. Always dying. Always being born. And so we attach to the questions we ask ourselves and the answers we seek so hard to find, just to give a reason to our pain that never ends. But you know as well as I do that the truth cannot be found in answers. That it cannot be searched for in questions. It does exist. It's already here. Look for it, though, and it's gone. Find it, and it disappears."

He quickly walks backwards into the dark shapes of trees that surround us, dissolving into the shadows of the forest. I almost ask out for him, or for Vidya, but I know that they're already gone. The wind blowing through the trees is my only company.

The echoing sound of pain returns.

Where does it come from?

I turn to look down the path. In the distance I make out a faint glow across the sky. Is it the city where I was before?

I walk in the direction of the light.

I think of Indiana and how I must find her.

I can see Morgan's eyes as they gazed into the ball of flames.

What did he do?

And why did he do it?

And Vincent, is he alive?

Is he protecting Indiana?

Or is she protecting him?

The wind grows stronger, and the groan of creaking wood radiates from the tall trees. I can feel the life of the forest all around me, but I feel it mostly in its death as I walk closer to the lights ahead.

The sound of pain now flows strong through the wind.

Cries.

Moans.

Screams.

The trees become sparse.

The landscape becomes barren.

The moon still shines full, but no longer blue. Instead, an oppressive white light glows across the surface of the world, removing any sense of tranquility and replacing it with an overwhelming feeling of dread.

To my right I pass a pile of dead bodies.

No faces exist upon them.

Just featureless beings lying dead atop each other.

Were they ever alive?

Or were they empty from the start?

To my left I pass another pile.

And eventually the vast mounds of dead surround me, creating a hideous corridor for me to walk through. The smell of rotting flesh burns my nose, and the sounds of agony pound painful rhythms into my ears.

I remember the words that Sam spoke to me in the past.

Something bad is happening.

Something that shouldn't.

Yet it must.

Someone is dying.

Someone is being born.

I see him above an enormous mound of death.

Rotting corpses.

Shattered bones.

Rusting metal.

Fragmented pieces of concrete and stone.

He sits in the air, floating there as if seated upon a throne.

At the sight of me he sends a vile grin.

"Where have you been?" Morgan asks.

"What have you done?" I reply.

"Does it matter?" he tells me with an apathetic tone. "I've done what I've done and I'll do what I'll do."

"Where is Indiana?" I angrily ask him. "And Vincent?"

He snickers as his grin grows stronger.

"They're not here," he says, kicking at a skull beneath him.

Anger swells within me.

And I leave this place behind.

Past the dead.

The concrete.

The metal.

And bone.

"Where are they?" I ask him, grabbing at his shirt.

"I told you," he says mockingly, "not here. If they were they'd be dead."

"And why is that?" I ask.

He pulls my hand away.

"Because I would have killed them," he tells me, moving closer to my face. He stares at me with bloodshot eyes, and behind them lies emptiness.

He pushes me back and flies up into the sky.

"I want to end it all," he yells at me from above. "I want to end this ceaseless, endless, forever droning of life. What's the point of all this pain? This boredom? Just to feel a little less of it? Just to think there's somewhere better out there? I say fuck that. Let's make the worst of this pointless life. Let's start tearing apart this place here and now. Let's make it ours."

He floats back down to me.

His long hair blows in the wind.

His face shows no expression.

"I want it all," he tells me. "And you want it just as much as I do. You want to be everything you're not."

"I want nothing that you want," I tell him.

"Oh, but you do," he replies, moving closer.

His face sits near to mine.

His lips move close to my ear.

His hair brushes against my skin.

"And more than anything," he whispers into my ear, sliding his hand down my side, "you want her."

I try to step back from him, but his hand wraps tight against my body. I push against his chest as he lets go of his grip, sending me stumbling backwards. He steps forward, and in his eyes I see the look he had while staring into the fire. His right hand moves towards my body and I become locked into some elusive power that surrounds me.

Instantly, I'm shot through the air as I see the world fly past me. I collide with a solid wall of concrete, sending agonizing pain across my body. My vision blurs. My head and my mind and my limbs go limp. Fragments of concrete crumble around me as Morgan floats close by. He lifts me into the air with his mind.

"Surprised?" he asks.

But I don't have the power to speak.

I hang there

Lifelessly

As the pain moves through me.

"You see," he says while walking around my body, "I've found out that I do have the power to move what's alive. Or I suppose a more truthful way of putting it is that nothing is really alive. We're just lies in motion."

I try to collect myself from the pieces that remain.

But so few pieces are left.

Still, I gather the strength.

And I push myself away from here.

Away from this.

Into somewhere else.

And he floats statically in front of me.

His eyes.

His eyes burn through the nothingness.

And slowly I move forward.

Through him.

Through everything.

Faster.

And faster.

I move.

Away from the pain.

But I can't keep moving.
My thoughts begin to break apart.
And I find a place.
There.

In the darkness I sit.
In the shadows of a metal enclosure I hide.
From the small gap that sits in front of me, I can make out the place that I'm in. Countless metal pipes, with flaking bits of paint and rusted skin, project through the air. Scattered about are metal structures, one of which I am in. The sound of liquids moving through the pipes resonates throughout the area, along with the buzz of the bright white lights and the constant throbbing of painful cries and moans and screams.
Footsteps.
Moving closer.
And then I see someone limply walk past.
Fear sits in my stomach and it becomes amplified by the pain that cuts through my body. More shapes walk by and I realize that the dead are here.
I calm myself.
I have to.
I need to stop this.
This hell.
This pain.
This fear.
I watch my thoughts as they live and die.
I see my pain as what it is.
It is mine.
But it is not me.
And I pull myself together.
More and more.
And I hear Morgan.
Yelling out for me.
Flying high above.
But I ignore him.
No, I watch him in my thoughts, where the fear burns strong.
And it doesn't leave me.
So I must leave it.

The sound of footsteps stops in front of me.

A dead man stares into the shadows were I sit, his large white eyes gazing directly at me through the darkness, his putrid skin sliding down across his bone, his rotting jaw hanging severed from his face.

"There you are!" Morgan yells from above.

And the metal walls around me rip away. Countless dead surround me as I sit in the open bright lights. Every one of them gazes in my direction.

Then they all begin to float off of the ground.

Their limbs hanging lifeless from their torsos.

Thick black blood dripping from their bodies.

And Morgan sends them all flying.

I feel them collide against my body for just a moment.

But then I'm gone.

Within their insides.

Their decomposing skin.

Rotting flesh.

And rancid organs.

Moving past me.

Through me.

As I follow the metal pipes.

Swaying in the nothing of my mind.

As I move to where I am.

Landing upon the ground, I pull out the staff upon my back in a swift motion. I grip it firmly in my hands, and it gives me strength in my body and my mind.

I can't run from this.

From him.

I have to fight it.

I see him in the distance.

Flying fast through the maze of pipes.

Through the crowd of dead.

Even from a distance I can make out the wicked grin upon his face. Something follows close behind him, suspended just behind his back. He stops before me, hovering in front of a large, bright light and casting his silhouette into my eyes.

"Let's have some fun," he says lifting his hands up to the side. "What else is there to do?"

Spiraling out from behind him, five sharp blades, crudely hammered out from pieces of metal, drift around his body. Two swords float to his left and right. Diagonally, two smaller knives hover nearby. Above him flies the largest of his weapons, a vicious blade that cuts upward into the sky.

"I've had plenty of time to make this world my own," he says to me while floating divinely in the air, casting his shadow across the ground on which I stand. "And your life will be mine."

"My life will be my own," I say to him. "Even in death."

But my words slightly tremble from the distant fear that sits in my chest. That familiar fear of self-doubt cuts through, though it doesn't dig its way to the center of my being. I hold strong against its influence.

"Your life is nothing!" he yells.

The hovering blades begin to spin in circles around his body.

"As is mine," he adds dejectedly. "But in your death I find solace. To end your life is to mark my existence into this place. To be the only empty soul, the only living thing, is the only way to be what I am meant to be."

"And what is it that you're meant to be?" I ask him.

And the blades spin faster.

And he floats slightly closer.

Until I can makes out his dark red eyes.

"Everything," he says as if speaking to himself.

He throws himself forward and fiercely sends his blades shooting quick at my body. I spin my staff as it hits solidly with them, sending the sharp pieces of metal away.

One of them escapes and swiftly moves at me.

It cuts at my skin.

And rips at my flesh.

As I slip away.

And I watch my blood
Flow through the nothing.
My mind
Moves backwards.
Backwards.

To here.

And now the blades shoot throughout the air in savage movements. All around me they fly, as Morgan floats statically above with his hands raised high.

I reflect, with quick swings of my staff, each blade that shoots at me. Again and again they attack.

Faster and faster.
And I don't stop moving.
Don't stop swinging.
As each spin of the staff melds into the next.
Until my body is surrounded by a sphere of movement.
Until my muscles move without me telling them to.
One.
Fluid.
Motion.
And then I escape.

Upwards.
Above him.

I swing down fierce.
But he slips past and kicks me hard in my side.
He sends his large sword up at my body.
And I see it almost cut straight through me.

Then I'm gone.
Far in the distance.
I move.
And then I return.
Fast.
Towards him.
With all the power in my mind
I fly forward.
And the world blurs
Into a single flowing moment.
Until I'm there.

And with all the force of my body I swing.

And I strike hard against him.

And I feel his insides shatter.

I hear his bones break as his body goes flying.

And as I land upon the ground his lifeless blades fall beside me. I look up to see him spin about in the air, catching himself with his own mind. He hangs there like a dead body, his limbs swaying limp.

Slowly he starts to laugh from behind the long hair that drapes across his face. Lifting his head upwards, he raises his arms in my direction. I feel the air grasp my body.

No, not the air.

His thoughts.

His mind.

His everything.

He wraps himself around me and pushes hard against my skin.

But he can't move me.

I won't let him.

I can't let him.

I push my thoughts inward.

Yet I don't leave this behind.

I stay.

Here.

And fight his mind away.

As he pushes me in every direction

I stay firmly where I am.

And I feel anger in his thoughts.

In his motions.

And no longer am I being pushed and pulled.

But instead I'm being crushed.

As all around me I feel myself caving in.

Collapsing.

Until I have to escape.

I'm forced to escape.

And I implode

Into the place of nothing

As everything bursts through.

My thoughts burn up at the pressure

Of this and that

Being that and this.

And I let out a scream that no one hears
As I fall to the ground
That isn't there.

I'm lying on my back, staring at the blades flying high above my body. With my right hand I grab my staff and pull it in front of my face, barely blocking the two quick, sharp knives sent flying at me.

Again, I escape.

Again
I move
Through there
To here.

And I swing at him.
And he swings at me.
And we collide in pain.
Over and over.
Falling to the ground.
Until his blood covers my staff.
And my blood covers his fists.
And we slam into the concrete.
Collapsing apart.
I stand up to my feet.
And I pull the staff high above my head
As I walk to his body lying upon the ground.
But then my shoulder screams in pain
As his blade cuts deep into my body.
From behind, it slices through
Sticking out the front of me.
And my blood drips down the jagged metal.
And I push myself away.

As I feel the pain
Sitting in my thoughts.
Of death
Becoming part of me.
Of myself
Becoming death.

And I move.

Landing on my feet, my muscles go weak.
And I drop my staff to the ground.
Its weight is too much to bear.
"This is it," Morgan says to me while slowly floating upwards.
"Is it?" I ask him behind heavy breaths.
His arms violently swing downward as all five of his blades
shoot into the ground. They stick deep into the concrete around my
body. I feel his grip upon me as his arms lift upwards, but I'm too
weak to stop him, and I'm forced into the air.
"You understand it, don't you?" he asks me through a
painful voice.
"There's nothing to understand," I answer him.
He pulls me closer.
Until I sit fixed in the air near his body.
He forces my face upwards and pulls the largest of his blades
out of the ground, levitating it in front of my neck. His hand rises up
to my face and caresses my bloody skin.
"Exactly," he quietly says to me as tears move down from his
bloodshot eyes. I take what strength I have left and force my arms
forward, grabbing him where he stands.
He looks at me with his empty eyes.
With his empty soul.
And I take him with me.

Into the place where I am all there is.
Where I'm alone.
As I hold his lifeless body
His endless sadness becomes my own.
His dead eyes staring at everything that I am.
Telling me things I already know.
That I'm not what I think I am.
That I'm dead.
That I'm empty.
That I am evil.
I.
Am.
Evil.

I'm everything.

And I'm nothing.

But he also tells me things that he didn't know.

That I am everything that I am not.

I'm alive.

I'm full.

I'm good.

I.

Am.

Good.

And his sadness becomes me.

And his dead eyes seem to move.

As his lips seem to say.

Nothing.

I let go.

And he fades away.

Into somewhere.

Deep inside myself.

Into nowhere.

And I'm alone.

In the place where I am all there is.

His body is gone.

I stand alone amongst the wreckage of this place.

But something strange moves through the air. I feel it on the skin of my neck. I feel it in the quiet buzzing in my ears.

Someone is here.

Watching me.

The dead still scatter the area, though they neither move nor stare at me. They just stand motionless, looking down at the ground. It's not them that I sense, though. It's someone else. Someone who is everyone and everything and everywhere.

I try to move, but the pain in my shoulder from the cut of Morgan's blade rips at my nerves and stops my body. My eye burns hard in echo of the anguish. I fall down upon a ledge of concrete that sits amongst the rusted metal pipes.

Still, I feel that someone is here.

No.

More than that.

Someone isn't here.
Here is who they are.
None of it makes sense.
But all of it does.
I become dazed from the pain in my body.
And the confusion in my mind
As I sit alone.
But not alone.
Letting my body heal itself and my mind cut loose the confusion that tangles up my thoughts.

I know it to be true now.
Someone is here.
I know it.
As I walk along a narrow bridge of metal that connects where I was to where I'm going, I feel a thousand hidden eyes caressing my every movement and an endless sea of thoughts touching my own mind. From the eternal depths that lie beneath me, from which the thin grates of metal are my only protection, I can sense the one who watches.

Suddenly, I see something rising to my right. I jump back in surprise, catching myself before I stumble too far in the wrong direction. A small red ball hovers up to where I am. It sits still in the air, staring at me through its muted skin.

Nausea builds in my stomach from the fear of where the shape has come from and how it got here. I stand motionless, staring at it floating dauntingly in the air. After moments of stillness I gather myself together and move towards the hovering shape. I reach my hand outward and press my finger onto its surface. Its skin wavers across its form, and as I pull back, the red liquidness of its body sticks to my hand. As I try to shake it from my skin, I see another shape rising up from below. It too is round, and its color is the same blood red.

The shape still sticks to me.

And as it sits against my skin, I see it begin to grow.

Slowly, it moves across my hand.

I try in vain to pull it off and only succeed in getting it to stick to my other hand as well. While the shape grows across my body, more

157

of the crimson spheres come rising up from the shadows until all around me are the liquid globes of red. They hover in the air, staring at my every movement, at my every thought.

The fluid red skin of the sphere now crawls up my arms.

And I move my mind inwards in fear as I try to escape.

But the pain is too much.
The feeling of my arms
Being ripped away.
Ripped.
Away.

And I'm shot back to where I was.
Stuck where I am.
These things keep me here.
Where they can see me.
Where they can become me.

Moving across my body, they enclose every part of me besides my head. I'm caught within the mass of red liquid that surrounds me.

Is this it?

Is this where it ends?

And answering my thoughts, the spheres begin to violently shake. The metal bridge beneath me crumbles away, and now the only thing protecting me from the endless depths below is the enemy that controls me.

I begin to scream out as the spheres sing a painful noise.

A constant vibration of agony.

The red begins to grow along my neck.

And into my mouth.

Into my body.

Across my eyes.

And all around me.

Inside me.

Where pain is everywhere.

But it's not my own.

It's theirs.

Whose?

Everyone's.

So it is mine.

But it feels so distant as it sits inside my chest.

Cutting at my heart.

Ripping at my lungs.

And the shaking goes on.

Until everything falls apart.

And I'm lying on the ground in a pool of red.

While blue lights shine bright above me.

The pain collects itself into a place deep inside my eye. I stand up and find myself again in a city street, yet it ends not far from where I am. It drops in jagged fractures down into the endless darkness. This place is a single point within a boundless nothing.

In front of me stands a tall building shinning vibrantly a blue light. Countless glass windows cover its sides. Two large doors stare out at me from where the building meets the crumbling concrete sidewalk. I walk to the edge of the small floating island I'm upon and stare out into the endlessness surrounding. Faintly I hear a humming coming from within the tall building beside me. I have no choice but to go inside.

I walk up to the doors of the building.

As my hand touches their cold metal handles I feel something terrifying move behind them.

Without even opening the doors, I instantly find myself inside the structure. My vision begins to blur, yet at the same time things become more lucid. It's as if by seeing less of what is here, I'm really seeing more. I realize that my sight is not blurred. I can see the shapes as they sharply cut into reality. It's what sees these shapes that is blurred. It's what's inside my mind the blurs the lines of existence. I feel as if I've been here before. And then I remember the feeling.

It's the feeling of being asleep.

Of dreaming.

But this is no dream.

Its more real than I can even call myself.

Bright lights wash out the room that I am in. Dirty white walls surround me in every direction. In front of me is a sharply angled desk that sits heavily on the rust colored carpet below. Other than a stairway that sits in the far right corner, the room has no other features. I walk past the solitary desk, and turning to look behind it I see a vile pool of thick black liquid bubbling up from the ground. Its consistency

159

matches that of the red spheres that surrounded me just moments before, yet somehow I can sense a difference within the liquid.

It's something evil.

And suddenly I feel them again.

The ones who watch me.

The shadowy liquid begins to rise upwards as the vague shape of a hand forms against its edges. I step back in horror as the shape grows in equilibrium to my fear. The more it becomes terrifying, the more I fear it and the more it grows. Now standing complete is the shape of a man dripping heavy drops of black to the carpet below. Three hollows form in his face. From the cavities opens wide an evil mouth with teeth that drip dark blood and two large bloodshot eyes that stare hauntingly at my soul. Their gaze makes me realize that it is him who watches me. He is the one who is everywhere. He is the one inside my thoughts. Inside every part of this world. And he is the one who wants me to die.

My fear grows uncontrollably as I move away from him.

He steps heavily forward, and as his foot touches the ground one of the lights above swiftly shuts off. With each step he takes the room becomes darker.

I try to disappear, but somehow my fear keeps me here.

Is it a weakness in my mind?

Is it the grasp this creature has upon me?

I turn to move up the stairway that sits in the corner. Running up the steps, I sense the man watching every movement I make. As I turn upon the landing and head up the second stairway, I catch a glimpse of him as he stands at the bottom of the steps.

Quickly I move upwards.

And before I reach the top, the lights of the stairs shut off.

I can feel him there behind me.

So close

To my body and my mind.

And I can feel the death of myself

As his hands reach out for me.

I rush forward, tripping to the floor, in total horror of what's behind me. I quickly stand up and see in front of me a long hallway with the same bright white lights as before. Along the sides of the corridor are countless wooden doors with metal numbers attached to them.

160

As I run down the hallway I hear agonizing sounds resonating from behind the doors at my sides. Blurring together into one terrifying noise is the sound of people screaming in pain and fear, the growl of creatures as they tear each other apart, and the groan of wicked things that want to chew upon my flesh and bones.

The lights begin to snap off behind me, and I know that he still follows close behind. I hear the sound of creaking wood, and just in front of me I see a door open slightly. I stop in fear. But still the lights go dark behind me, so I force myself to run forward past the door that hides the unknown. I move quickly and continue to run, not looking back to see what lies inside the room. I run until my lungs burn from the strain. As I reach the end of the long hallway, I find myself before another staircase. I turn back, however, and the darkness has disappeared along with the man who followed me.

Terror shakes my mind and I almost wish he were still there just so that I would know the source of what haunts my thoughts. I turn to the stairway and cautiously step upwards. At the top of the stairway I find yet another long hallway of doors. I move slower now, in caution of what may come at any moment.

In front of me I see a doorframe with no door in its place.

I know that within the room lies something horrible. I know that within lies the evil that watches my every movement.

I push my fear aside in order to move.

As I come closer to the opening I hear the sound of someone's throat as it painfully grasps for air. I move to the side of the wall opposite the empty doorframe and slide slowly past.

As I reach the hollow doorway I see nothing.

Just a dimly lit room with emptiness inside.

But I stare at the edge of the entrance.

And I know that the room is not empty.

In my mind I see everything imaginable, every terrifying thing that could exist, as it appears around the edge of the wall. I stare in complete fear of what may lie behind the corner.

But nothing ever comes.

The sound of an agonizing grasping for air continues from the room. But from whose throat does it escape? My fear faintly turns to curiosity, sending me closer to the empty room. I slowly move inward until I'm standing in the middle of the empty room.

The sound echoes from the inside of my head.

From the inside of my thoughts.

Then suddenly it moves behind me, and I turn to the open doorway. Standing there is gaunt man with skin pale white. His limbs are long and narrow. Thin hands, with drawn-out fingers, frantically move about the ends of his feeble arms. He grasps for air from the small narrow mouth upon his large pale head.

His eyes, which sit sunken deep within his skull, stare bright and wide in anguish at me. The noise from his throat grows louder as he awkwardly steps in my direction. His footsteps leave behind viscous black imprints.

Closer he moves.

And I pull the staff from behind my back.

Still he moves nearer while my feet dig into the ground.

Closer.

And I pull back.

Closer.

And his thin hands reach out to me.

Closer.

And his mouth opens wide.

Closer.

And I swing

Ripping his body apart

Sending black liquid spraying across the room.

Still, his legs keep moving towards me. I step out of the way, but they keep moving in my direction. And out of the black liquid slowly rises the man from before. I move quickly out of doorway. Within steps of leaving the room, the lights surrounding me shut off. All that is lit is the small bit of hallway I stand in. The closed door that sat against the opposite wall of the hall is my only exit. I try again to leave this place behind and move into the nowhere within my mind, but still I'm unable to escape. In the open doorway stands the oozing man, his eyes open wide and his mouth chewing at the air as blood drips from his gums.

I reach behind me and feel the handle of the door I lean upon. The horrifying creature stretches forward. His arms wrap around me as I quickly turn the handle. Just as his fluid limbs close inward, I open the door and fall back into the cool night air. The doorway that leads inside becomes engulfed in his shadowy form as his body seeps across the air.

I stand to my feet and look about the area.

I realize that I'm on the roof of the building I was just in. Moving to the ledge, I look over at the vast length of building that sits below. Somehow I've climbed its entirety.

Looking upwards I see the night sky glowing bright blue in the light of a full moon. Countless stars burn bright enough to cut through the moon's light, giving the sky a shimmering glow. A breeze blows across my skin, and with a deep breath I fill my lungs with a cool air that seems to heal my body and mind.

I feel happiness faintly move through me.

I feel hope build up within my bones.

I can escape this.

No.

Not escape.

I can end this.

An eruption of light and noise bursts out of the shadows hanging across the doorway behind me. I turn to see the black film stretching out across the rooftop, cracking away as vivid light burst through growing fissures within the liquid black skin.

With a sharp snap, the black membrane rips apart as an enormous creatures flies out from the bursting light. Landing upon the ledge of the building, the beast flutters its long translucent wings in the night air.

It turns to me, and every single fear I've felt until now collects itself within this terrifying moment, sending me to my knees as the pain inside my mind becomes a physical agony within my body. My chest burns heavy as my heart pounds a fierce pulsation across my body. At the sight of its eyes, its gruesome face, my stomach churns a sickness through my soul.

Stretched across the head of the creature is familiar skin.

Familiar flesh.

Sam's pale white face is thinly drawn over the hideous bones that jut about the creature's head. The soft skin stretches from the tension of the creature's shape. Darkness sits behind the holes where eyes should be.

Below the horrid face lies the beast's chest, a ribcage ripped open revealing within a glowing, pounding heart.

Beneath the monster stands four legs made of black bones that glisten in the moonlight. Stretching out at its sides are its massive ghostly wings and two large arms that pulse with the glowing blood of the creature's heart.

The bones within its chest begin to fiercely bite at the air as the creature bats its wings and rises into the sky.

Still my fear overcomes me.

And I'm left weak upon the ground.

The beast soars above me and swoops down, grabbing me by my arms. I drop my staff to the ground and hang limp within its grip. It stares at me with the black holes of Sam's dead face. Its rib cage violently gnaws at the air as I hang helplessly in its clenched hands. My skin tears within its grasp, sending blood dripping out from beneath its jagged fingers.

A terrifying roar comes out from within the pounding heart.

And as I hang within the creature's hands, waiting for death, waiting for the fear to end, the few thoughts that remain within my mind collapse together into a single awareness.

This.

This is all there is.

This pain and this death.

But there is no me.

So what is there to fear?

And with these thoughts I gather strength within this body and this mind. The fear remains, but no longer holds me in place.

I see it for what it is.

Nothing.

And the muscles in my arms pull hard, sending more blood flowing out from within the creature's grip. Still, I'm held in place.

Still, I'm caught within its hands.

And I focus.

On the pain.

On the death.

And Sam's lifeless face staring into my eyes.

I leave this hell behind.

Moving.

Back into the nothing.

The place where I am everywhere

And nowhere

And all that is.

The creature's heart glows tranquil in the vacuum.
A golden beacon of the world I was in.
The world I escaped.
And the world that I shall always return to.
Moving forward through the radiant heart.
I collect myself within this place of nothing.
And I stay.
Here.
Forever.
But forever is only a moment
That never ends
And never begins.
And so I collapse.
Back into my thoughts.
Thoughts that scream at me from every direction.
Pull at me from everywhere.
I can't stay here.
I can't.
Stay.
Here.

And I fall to the ground, grabbing my staff and jumping back to my feet as the creature spins around high above. Looking forward through the night air, I see her standing in the distance, her bow held high and her eyes shooting fiercely in my direction.

She stands upon the roof of a building that wasn't there before. It sits in the distance and looks just as the building that I stand upon does. Her white arrow flies as she lets the string of her bow go. Cutting through the air, the arrow lands deep into the back of the flying creature. It lets out a roar as it turns in her direction. Already she moves out into the sky, creating ground beneath her feet.

I pull myself inward.

And move myself up.
Beside the beast's body.
Beside its ghostly wings.

And crashing down upon it, I swing my staff wildly at its body. Its bones crack upon the impact and it lets out another roar. Spinning in the air, it hits me with its skeletal legs before I have a chance to move. I'm sent flying down into the rooftop.

But before I land.

I escape.

And swim against the pressure of my mind.

Against the flow of my thoughts.

Until I'm above it.

And falling downward, I again crash into the flying creature.

And as we collide, an arrow shoots past my vision. It sticks deep into the pale skin that stretches across the monster's face. I land upon rooftop, far from the beast, as Indiana runs close.

"Glad to see you're still alive," she says to me between heavy breaths. "I was worried."

"The same goes to you," I tell her.

A faint smile moves across her lips.

"So let's try and stay alive," she replies, turning to the creature that now hovers in the air above us.

Shooting quickly downward, it cuts through the air with its large translucent wings, sending a strong gust of wind that pushes us backwards. I swing my staff, but just miss the beast's body as it flies past and grabs Indiana. She drops her bow to the ground, but quickly forms a sharp blade within her hand that she shoves deep into the creature's back.

The beast remains ahold of her as it flies out into the emptiness that surrounds the rooftop. More and more she digs into its body as they soar throughout the abyss. The monster cuts back around through the air, and as it moves past above me I pull myself away.

Until I'm there.

Until I'm here.

In front of it.

And I swing hard at its chest as it strikes against my body.

I feel my staff cut deep into the beating, glowing heart that lies within its open ribcage. And as its radiant blood shoots through the night sky, I catch Indiana by the wrist and fall along side her. All around us is the shimmering blood of the creature that plummets lifeless to the rooftop.

But the rooftop isn't there.

Nothing is.

And the creature begins to slow to a stop within the air.

Yet we continue to fall.

And there's nothing left but Indiana and myself.

The endless starry sky.

And glistening blood.

Alone

We fall

Together.

Shimmering from the blood that paints our bodies.

Falling through nothing

Towards nothing.

I hold her close.

And feel her body against my own

As she stares into my eyes

And her lips

Touch mine.

VII

We fell through the stars.

Our bodies.

Our minds.

Embracing one another.

Yet, even though we were falling, there was no up and there was no down. Just a path that we moved in through endless space, through endless darkness glazed with the countless blazing stars that glimmered all around us. Planets in the far distance would move in vivid colors, dancing amongst softly spinning galaxies that drifted through this vast expanse.

Closer we grew into each other

As our life together became our home.

Our own falling world.

From her hands, from her mind, she created it.

A large, soft bed for us to lie in, with green blankets so smooth that the only thing softer was her perfect skin. Beautiful paintings of worlds that didn't exist, hanging upon walls that weren't there. A bookcase full of books with no words upon their pages. And a long, dark wooden table with matching chairs for us to sit at and talk.

Talk of things that were and things that would be.

Of ourselves.

And of each other.

Of the day that we were separated.

And the day that we were found together again.

"I lost him," she told me, as the stars drifted past, "not long after the fires began. He held me close within the flames, but the flames grew too strong. And as his grip slid away from me, I looked into his eyes. They showed something I couldn't understand. Was it guilt? Or anger? Either way, they burned as hot as the fires that danced around us. The last thing that he said was for me to go. And the ground disappeared below me as I fell into somewhere dark and cold."

Her face showed sadness. And deep within her eyes I could see her thoughts trying to push themselves away.

"I walked through the damp, dark world, for how long I don't know," she continued as we sat at our softly falling table, "until I came back up to the city, where it was burning in ruin. High above it all I could see him, Morgan, causing all the destruction. And so I ran from him and the flames and the streets full of death until I reached the end. Until I reached the cliffs that fell into nothing. But the street wrapped around the ledge, along with the buildings and the sidewalks and the scattered streetlights. So I put my hand down upon the ground and moved it over the side. As it slid over the edge, I felt it fall inward towards the ground. I stood up, closed my eyes, and walked outward, ready to catch myself within the air. But instead of falling, I moved through some strange push of gravity that felt as if my entire existence was being turned around. And again I found myself upon the street. But the ground didn't stretch on long. Ahead was another ledge, and there I did the same. Around the next bend I saw the building you found me upon. Inside of it was just one thing. You."

"Me?" I asked confused.

"Yes," she replied. "You. But not you. It was your body, but there was no one inside. You just stood there, motionless in the middle of the large white room, with a certain look upon your face. Mostly empty, but not completely. Swimming somewhere inside of you was a hidden sadness. A hidden sorrow. I could feel it. And so I put my hand upon your face. And as I did a tear fell from your eye. A tear that held that hidden bit of sadness, that single piece of emotion within you. And then it was gone. You were empty. Completely. And I was alone. I walked back to the doors that I came in, but as I left the room I found myself upon the rooftop of a building. That's where I saw you. The real you. And I was never alone again."

She put her hand upon mine and pulled it in close.

I gave her a smile to let her know.

She wasn't alone.

She never would be.

I was hers.

Forever.

And so we lived within our falling home.

And there, in our peaceful existence, where no others came to break our lives apart, I came to know the depths of my mind.

As we fell through the endless nothing
I pushed my thoughts inward.
And I watched
As the boundless space around me
Became a part of myself.
And into that fused emptiness
I moved.

And I stayed.
Against the force of my thoughts.
Against the currents of my mind.
Until I would collapse.

Back into my home.
With her.
And each time I left it behind
I grew stronger against the movements within my mind
Pushing me away, yet pulling me inward
So that the hardest thing to do was to stay completely still.
And stronger I grew against the destructive force of time.
I would stay within the nothing.
Longer.
And longer.
I would watch the countless stars burning bright within the liquid emptiness, swaying amongst the seas of my thought.
Until it would break me apart.
And bring me back home.
"Where do you go?" she asked me.
"Somewhere within myself," I answered. "Though where that is I'm not sure. All I know is that I collect every part of my thoughts, my mind, my soul, my body, and push them into wherever it is that I go. And there I can see how I'm connected to the world around me, yet also completely separate. I'm nothing, as is everything else. There is no here or there. There's just one single place within. And in that singular place, I control everything. That is, I control nothing."
She told me that I never really left.
That I would sit there falling through the air, as everything else did, and for just a moment my body would blink away.
But what I felt was forever.

Where I went was somewhere else.

"I love you," she told me as we fell past a golden pink nebula of dust and light. And everything was perfect.

"I love you," I told her, looking into her eyes as they reflected the surrounding stars.

And upon the soft green blankets
Our bodies intertwined.
Our skin pressed against each other's
As I moved inside.
As she pulled me close.
As the stars disappeared.
In glorious explosions.
We were all that was left.
As one.
And we were love.

"Take me there," she asked while lying by my side.

"Where?" I asked back.

"Wherever it is you go," she told me.

And I stared out into the endless black that surrounded us.

Were we even falling anymore?

There was no way to tell.

"No," I told her. "I can't."

"Why?" she asked back.

"Because," I replied.

"I want to go in there," she said to me while putting her finger upon my forehead.

"It's too dangerous," I told her.

She moved her finger down my face and along my neck until her hand rested upon my chest.

"I want to go in there," she added. "Inside that beautiful heart of yours."

"That heart," I said, "is yours. You are inside of it. You're every part of it."

She climbed on top of me
And pressed herself against me.
Her lips ran along my neck and down my chest.
Her perfect touch melted my senses.
Her perfect movements softened my mind.
Sliding back up, she pressed her lips against my own.

Then she moved her mouth beside my ear
As her hand slid down.
"Take me there," she whispered.
I pressed my hands against her slender back.
And slid my fingers down her skin.
As we loved what was
And what would be
I pulled her inward.

Where everything collided
And became less than one.
And I watched
As her skin flaked away
Like old paint.
And her body crumbled
Until her eyes were all that was left.
They stared with no thoughts
No life
No love
Into my own.
And they spoke to me
Without words.
Bleeding beauty from within.
Her emotions.
Empty.
But something hidden.
Something painful.
Dripping away.
Until there was nothing.
As her eyes closed.
And I was alone.
Would I lose her?
If I returned?
Would she be gone?
I didn't want go back.
And so I remained.
Within my mind.
Watching myself.
Alone.

Inside.
Until time
Broke through.
And now I know.
That I can't.
Stay.
Here.

And she's still in my arms.
Her skin is still pressed against mine.
But she's crying
And shaking
As I hold her tight.

"You're back," I whisper into her ear. "You're back and everything's fine. You're here. And I'm here too."

But she won't stop shaking
As she pushes me away
And falls over the edge of the bed.
Over the end of our soft green blankets.
Over our home.

And down onto the floor that isn't there, where she shakes and she screams and she pulls her body inward.

"Indiana?" I ask her, moving to the edge of the bed.

"No!" she yells to me. "Go away! Go away!"

Her hands push at me.
Tears run down her face.

"No. No. No. No. No," she repeats as she violently rocks back and forth.

"What's wrong?" I ask her with fear of what I may have done.

But she ignores my words
And looks around at the nothing that's all around us.
Her entire body shakes in terror.

"Where the fuck am I?" she yells out, standing up to her feet.

"You're here, Indiana," I say to her softly.

"There is no here!" she screams. "It's empty! Everything is empty! I'm empty! I'm fucking nothing!"

And she nervously steps away from me while staring into my eyes. I stand and reach my hand out to her, but she quickly moves away.

"You," she stutters, "What the hell are you?"
"It's me, Cyan," I tell her calmly.
"No. No. No," she says to me, "You are. You are."
"I'm what?" I ask her.
But she ignores me with violent screams
As her body shakes with each step she takes backwards.
Until she falls over the edge of the floor that isn't there.
And I see her body tumble through nothing.
I jump after her.
But the floor that isn't there stops me.
I pound my fists in anger against the hidden something.
And I move inward.

Where I see her.
Falling with fear in her eyes.
And I move to her.
Close.
Yet far.

But she's gone when I return.
And I'm nowhere.
"Indiana!" I yell out in desperation.
But she doesn't answer.
So I go back inside myself.

Where I saw her last.
But see her no more.
Where I stay.
Until.
I.
Fall.
Apart.

And I land upon nothing.
Falling through space
As the fear that I defeated returns.
It's a fear for her.
And what she felt.
And where she's gone.

What did she see there?

Inside the place I know so well.

Inside myself.

I fall faster.

And faster.

My limbs pull upwards against the speed of my movement.

In the distance, far below, I see faint objects beginning to appear. And as I fall closer, a sun that slowly drifts into existence high above me illuminates the empty sky. The darkness that surrounded me has given way to a vast blue atmosphere.

And I collide with the world that forms beneath me.

Endless sticks and twigs and leaves and thorns scrape against my skin as my world becomes enveloped by vibrant green plant life. Plummeting downwards I collide with thick branches that shove my body about. Something hits me solid in my chest, shooting all the air within my lungs out in a violent rush. I go limp, tumbling in pain through the brush, until I break through the thickness of plants, whereupon my fall becomes a graceful drifting as I enter into a tunnel made of grass. I wearily drop through the green shaft as it slowly rotates around my body.

And then I realize.

I'm not falling down.

I'm falling up.

I'm rising through this green passage. I can feel it in my body that what is in front of me is not below, but above.

Small glowing specks of lime colored light float about the air. The higher I rise, the more they become. And as they float past my body I faintly hear them singing soft melodies into my ears. They vibrate unknown sounds of unknown words with unknown meaning. And as the grass becomes greener and the music grows louder and the light becomes brighter, my body regains the strength that it lost from the fall. My mind collects itself and I remember Indiana. Again I feel the fear of what she experienced inside my existence.

Above I see the bright blue sky growing outward from a small spot of light at the end of the grass tunnel. As I come closer, it grows larger. As I reach the end of the passage I fall upwards out of the shaft and softly onto the green grass that sits beside it.

178

I now stand within a wide valley of abundant flowers limitless in color and shape. They gently sway in the cool breeze that blows through the canyon of flora.

Standing tall in front of me is a mighty tree, which glows from the sunlight that shines inward from behind its many leaves. Its branches twist about in massive spirals, growing outward from its wide trunk. I feel drawn towards the huge tree. Its aura pulls me closer, sending the sensation of peace throughout my body.

As I walk through the vibrant field of flowers, moving forward through the influential forces of the great tree, I think of Indiana and where it is she may be. Where did she go? And why?

And as sadness swallows my heart whole, I reach the base of the large tree. I gaze up at its countless leaves dancing in the wind, each of them outlined by the golden radiance of sunlight. A bright object falls with a thud to the ground at my side. It appears to be the fruit of the tree. And as I pick up the heavy purple fruit in my hands, I feel a desire grow within my thoughts. Though I feel no hunger, nor ever have, I feel a craving to devour the plump fruit.

I hesitate.

For just a moment.

And then dig my fingers deep into its soft, violet skin, ripping it open to see its vibrant red insides. With one hand I grab a large handful of the glistening red fruit and shove it into my mouth.

I become overwhelmed as its sweetness glides throughout my mind and opens up a world never known to me. I taste its perfection and it envelops my senses until all that's left is this feeling of sacredness. More and more I grab for the ripe fruit, shoving its sweet red insides into my mouth until a hollow shape is left sitting in my hands. As I stand beneath the magnificent fruit-bearing tree I feel its pureness rest inside my body.

The gentle breeze that blows across the valley suddenly disappears. The sun that sits behind the tree grows faint, sending rusted colors through the sky. The sensation of the fruit within my body collects itself within my head, where it sits above my eyes and pulses throughout my thoughts.

At first the feeling brings perception.

I can see myself as I am.

As the world around me is.

Perfectly, I know this place.

Yet with each pulse within my mind a sickness grows.

And the throbbing becomes painful.

And the world echoes my pain as the abundant flowers begin to wither and die. Their colors drain away with every pulse inside my head. And as the last bit of color dies from the world, all the pain within my body moves into my left eye.

Falling to my knees, I curse myself for eating the fruit.

But no matter how much I regret what I've done, the death that surrounds me remains. The pain within me stays. And so I sit in misery within the field of colorless flowers that wither against the rust colored light.

This place is sorrow.

This place is suffering.

I think of all that I've felt.

All that I've done

Up to this point in time.

And how it's all passed away.

With every bit of good comes every bit of sorrow.

The taste of fruit is sweet.

But the death that lingers within its essence

Is always waiting for its time to come into ripeness.

No more will I taste the sweetness of life.

And no more will I taste its death.

And with these thoughts another plump fruit falls beside me.

As I ignore all of the convictions freshly born within my mind

I think of eating the fallen fruit beside me.

Of devouring it here.

Amongst the lifeless landscape that I've created.

For in its taste I can find escape.

And within escape I will find death.

Within death I find myself.

But as I reach for the fruit the sound of footsteps begins, stopping me before I enter into my own vicious cycle. Brushing past my skin is the soft fur of Vidya. The warm air of his breath flows across my senses as he turns and moves in closer. His green eyes look deep into my suffering as I sit, burdened by my thoughts, upon the ground.

He speaks to me through the depth of his eyes.

Without words he tells me things that I don't understand.

But that I must understand.
And so I stand to my feet
As he walks past where I am
And leads me to the sacred tree.
The tree that gave me the sweet fruit of sorrow.

And as the great wolf reaches its wide trunk, the thick bark of the tree falls in burning embers through the air, sending ash throughout the sky. Carved into the bare wood of the tree is a doorway that glows from far within.

Vidya turns to me, speaking again with his jade eyes, before he walks into the tree's passage. As he disappears behind the mysterious entrance, I watch the pain within my eye. With each step I take towards the tree the pain dwindles away. As I cross the wooden threshold I am again given a sense of tranquility.

Not a shallow calm as before.
Not a false sense of perfection.
But an acceptance of the pain that I feel.
The lingering sorrow within my body, my mind, and my soul.
It falls into place.
And I move forward.

The walls warmly glow with an auburn light that radiates from deep within the wood of the tree. Each step I take eases my thoughts, yet each step also wears at my body. My muscles grow heavy. My lungs become full of the warm air that flows through the narrow wooden corridor. Sweat drips in heavy drops from my skin.

After some time I reach a small window carved into the tree. Looking out of it, I see that I'm far above the valley of colorless flowers. The sun has now disappeared, and a blue darkness lies beyond the reach of the golden light pouring out of the tree. Over the edge of the tall mountains that surround the valley, I vaguely make out a glow far in the distance, and with it the faint sound of life.

But the life that I hear brings me no joy.
Instead I feel dread move into my thoughts.
Of what is out there.
Of where I will go.
Of where I have been.

And so I continue up the spiraling wooden staircase.
Keeping my thoughts on my weary muscles.
On my heavy lungs.
As the hot air pulls sweat out of my skin
I lose myself in the movements.

Still, I keep climbing.
Does time pass?
I can't say.
The only sense of it comes from the steps that I take.
And the exhaustion in my body.
I pass more holes in the wall.
Windows that stare out into the landscape.
At the valleys and mountains.
And the daunting city in the distance
Glowing in tempting, yet painful colors.
At first I stopped and gazed out each window, taking in the vast landscape that lay in the distance.
But gradually I began to pass them by.
And now I no longer notice them, aside from the cool air that blows in from the outside. It chills the sweat upon my skin and breaks my comfort, my adaptation, to the warm air of the tree. And with each pass, the strain of my climbing becomes renewed.
Yet I continue.
Upwards.
As I climb.
Towards somewhere?
I rise.
Towards myself?
I move.
Nowhere.

The glow of the wood begins to fade, along with the warmth upon my skin, as I continuously climb each draining step, until eventually I move through the crisp air of complete darkness.

I find myself standing within a large dome of leaves that rustle in the wind. Behind them lies a night sky full of brightly shining stars. A large, radiant moon cuts through the dark shapes dancing above me, illuminating the place that I stand.

"This is not the end of your climb," a vaguely familiar voice says from the darkness.

"There is more?" I ask out.

"There is always more," the voice replies.

Out of the shadows walks the nameless child, the nameless sage that I spoke to in the woods. Beside him treads Vidya.

"I expected to find you here," I tell him.

He pulls away the hood that covers his face, revealing his changed features. His skin has aged, with creases forming at the sides of his mouth and eyes, though still seems to be young. Growing out from the edges of his clothes are delicate green leaves that slide against his skin. They wrap around his hands and rise upon his neck.

Though they don't seem separate from him.

They don't grow on him.

He is them.

"Did you enjoy the taste?" he asks me.

"I did," I reply, "before I felt the death that it caused within and without me. Until the taste left my senses and I was left within the sorrow that remained."

"But do you not remember that sweet flavor of life?" he laughs out at me. "That wonderful feeling of being alive! Of quenching your desires! Of tasting existence!"

"I do very well," I tell him. "But the pain that followed is not worth bearing for such a small amount of pleasure."

"Ah," he says walking closer to me. "So what then would be enough pleasure to merit the pain?"

"No amount of pleasure," I tell him, "for pain is always equal to the joy that is felt."

He looks away to the many leaves blowing in the wind.

He stands there in silence for some time.

"Why have I climbed this tree?" I ask him. "And why does it exist? What is it that flows through its sacred fruit?"

"Emptiness," he says darkly. "It grows the taste of emptiness. The taste that you desire, though you say otherwise."

Following his words, countless moans resonate from far off in the distance. The sounds move through my senses and caress my body. For a moment I taste the memory of the sacred fruit that sat within my hands and the death that followed.

I do want it.

I want to die.

So that I can feel alive.

I want the taste of existence to move across my tongue.

And into my thoughts.

My mind.

My soul.

"The seed, however," he tells me, bringing my thoughts back together, "of the sacred fruit that you devoured, can grow into many different things. And it grows not within the ground, but deep within yourself."

Vidya walks up to me and again rubs his soft fur against the palm of my hand. I turn to the large wolf, who stares not at me, but up at the bright moon that hangs behind the leaves. What does he see there? What does he know?

"It can grow to be a source of knowledge. Of wisdom. Of truth," the nameless, ageless being tells me. "Or it can grow into yet another tree that bears its emptiness for others to taste, spreading its seeds further on. Or it can even grow into sharp vines that yield no fruit at all, yet cut away the life within just to grow more vicious, more cruel."

"And what if it doesn't grow at all?" I ask him.

"Then the seed will sit forever inside you," he says, walking back into the shadows. "And you will always be a part of it, as it is a part of you. And you will be the emptiness that stirs within it, as the emptiness will also be you."

The moans grow louder in the distance, pulling my thoughts away from our conversation. In my mind I picture the places from which they come.

"You shall rest," the child tells me. "Sleep here tonight."

"Sleep?" I say confusedly. "I cannot sleep, nor have I ever slept before."

"You're sleeping now," he says from the darkness. "Your thoughts are not clear. Your mind is not your own. While you do move closer, closer than many ever have, you still dream far away within yourself, unaware and unable to realize it. So stay here tonight. And in the morning you will awaken to yet another dream."

And with these words he's gone.

I'm left alone with Vidya, who remains at my side as I sit upon the wooden floor, dreaming wide-awake of my life and all that has become of me.

And as the great wolf sits close by
As the night slowly passes
I sleep.

The morning arrives
Waking me from my slumber.
Though I did not sleep separate from here.
I was instead within the dream of my mind.
The dream that was this place.
Quickly I look about, seeing that Vidya has gone.

I sit alone within the dome of vibrant leaves. They move about in the wind, swimming green against the bright blue behind them. I stand to my feet and stretch my body wide. I feel renewed. I feel as if my mind and body have become reborn. I think of what I thought throughout the night, of what I felt flowing through my mind.

Yet all that I can remember is the emptiness
My endless grasping at nothing
As I sat aware of the chaos of my thoughts.
Until, with the morning light, I broke through.
Shedding away the disorder in my mind
I awoke.
Yet am I really awake?
Or am I, as the ageless, nameless being said, waking up to yet another dream?

With no direction to go, I push my way through the side of the vibrant leaves and walk out upon a long branch of the tree. As I pass out of the sphere of green I find myself not within the clear blue sky I perceived from within, but instead I'm surrounded by an endless gray atmosphere. I cannot see the ground below, as thick fog sits beneath me. The branch that I stand upon seems to stretch off into the distance, though the melancholy haze masks what lies ahead.

I walk forward, carefully, upon the branch that hangs within the gray sky. As I move onward, the wood beneath my feet becomes slick from the fog. Its bark turns nearly black from the dampness. There's silence as I balance upon the wet and narrow walkway that juts through the mist. The silence, however, becomes broken by distant moans, the same of which I heard last night. And as they grow louder, I sense a slight glow up ahead through the fog.

Appearing in front of me is a pulsing red light.

It cuts in red rhythms through the mist. As I approach it I see its shape. It blinks in steady rhythms the form of a large, penetrating eye. I stand upon the wet branch and stare at the neon light vibrating red through the gray fog.

Ceaselessly, it lives and dies.

I push myself forward and find myself passing more objects. Wet brick buildings vaguely sit in the distance, just barely visible enough to see. Tall iron structures, rusting from the mist that surrounds them, stab through the thick gray from below and rise upwards back into the haze. More neon lights, in extravagant shapes and colors, buzz their lights and sounds through the atmosphere.

As the objects become more abundant and the brick buildings begin to move closer inward, cramping the area that I move along, the fog begins to dissipate and reveal to me the place that I am in.

I walk amongst tall buildings that glow from the countless neon lights attached to them. The radiance of the city surrounding me flows with the many colors of the lights, mainly that of the lustrous red that burns the brightest.

Yet with all the lights throughout this city, the world is still dark. Shadows sit dauntingly in every corner.

And from behind them come the many moans.

The branch that led me through the mist now lands upon the ground. Thick patches of plant life grow outward where it collides with the concrete. Small flowers, which glow like the neon lights all around me, rest gracefully in the mound of green grass. The city, however, envelops the small growth of flora, suffocating the patch of life into a small knoll upon the ground that scarcely makes its way into the damp city streets.

I move onto the concrete.

The night sky hangs dark above the tall buildings that surround me. Neither stars nor moons exist within the vast shadow that covers the city. Walking along the wet concrete, listening to the moans that reverberate amongst the buildings, I come upon the shape of a woman standing below a tall red light. She leans against the wet brick behind her while casually holding a lit cigarette in her hand. As I approach her she turns her eyes towards me. They glow red from the light above.

She takes a long drag from her cigarette and blows the smoke sharply into the night air. I walk up beside her, where, from the door that sits next to her, I can hear the low pounding of music from within. She casts a grin in my direction after exhaling another cloud of smoke. Her hair hangs long and dark against her neck. Her skin glows pale in the red light. Upon her wrist, below the hand that holds the cigarette, is a tattoo in the shape of dark circle with six hollow lines moving out from the inside.

"Do you want something?" she asks me.

"Perhaps," I answer. "I wouldn't be here if I didn't."

She gives me another grin from behind a cloud of smoke.

"You have no idea how much fun you're gonna have," she quietly laughs as she snubs out her cigarette on the wet brick building. She turns to the door to her left and opens it wide. The music grows loud and shoots out through the streets.

I hesitate.

For in my mind I know that what lies ahead will only pull me deeper into this place. And for a moment I think of Indiana.

As she held me close.

As we fell together through the stars.

The stars which are now gone.

Yet I know that I have to move forward.

And the pounding of the music pulls me closer.

I have to.

Just to know.

"Go ahead," she says to me, tilting her head towards the entrance with the same grin that she's given me twice before.

And so I move through the door and into the wall of sound and light. A thick sea of people moving to the music flows through the room. Their bodies are empty forms, dark shadows with no features other than their shape, their bright white eyes, and their softly glowing lips. Yet I can feel them against my body. Their skin glides against my own, as the lights flash blindingly from above. And as I move farther into the crowd, I become more and more a part of the swaying mass of bodies.

Someone's hand touches the side of my face, spinning me around. It's her, the girl from outside. She holds her hand out to me, revealing a brightly glowing pill sitting upon her palm. I recognize the radiance. It's the same as the flowers that grew beneath the branch that led me here. She puts the glowing pill in her mouth and pulls her body close to mine. She kisses me, spreading my lips apart with her tongue and pushing the pill into my mouth. She glides her hands across my body as she pulls herself away, softly biting the edge of my lip as she disappears back into the shadowy crowd of people.

And as I feel a strange sensation begin to burn across my body, I fall into the music, into the lights, into the touch of skin against skin.

I don't exist.
Just this.
The push.
And the pull.
And I turn to shadows.
My skin darker than the night sky.
As I become just a body
Just a craving
For more.
As people touch me
And I touch them.
And everyone is touching everyone.
While the music sends vibrations
Deep into my senses.
Until I find myself separate.
Not knowing where I am.
I can feel my blood rushing.
Through my body.
I can feel the glowing light.
It flows throughout my senses
As I stand alone
Beside a massive wall of white.
No.
Not alone.
Together.

With the shadows that touch me.
We slide as silhouettes against the bright wall.
Her tongue in my mouth.
His hands upon my skin.
Our bodies intertwined.
The sound of music pulses through the concrete.
And with my hands
I tell her.
With my tongue
I move my words.
Give.
Me.
More.
And she does.
As I swallow the glowing pills.
And they burn through my veins.
Through my mind.
The music cuts away.
And all that I am turns to touch.
Nothing else.
Just her body.
And mine.
And everyone's.
As I enter the warmth.
As she digs her fingers deep into my skin.
And I push.
Into her.
My body burns perfect
As I collapse into a single point.
Inside.
And out.
Inside.
And out.
The movement shoves me deep into the moment
As the universe explodes in eternal light
And my mind orgasms
Across the world
And back into this single place and time.
Beneath the sea of people.

My heart races.
And I fall in love.
With nothing.
With no one.
And I fall into somewhere else.
Wet brick and red lights.
Moaning shadows that slide along the buildings.
Their white eyes watching me move.
Someone pulls me to the side.
Holds me close.
"So do you like the taste?" she asks me.
And I answer with my touch
As she pulls me into the darkness.
"Do you like the emptiness?" she whispers into my ear.
And I recognize the voice.
But my thoughts have no control
As she licks the skin upon my neck.
Her hands move into my body
And we become liquid.
Our touch moves in waves of shadows.
Gliding into each other.
Mixing our skin.
Someone gives me handfuls
Of brightly glowing pills.
I swallow them all
Through my skin
As her tongue moves
Across my body.
As the lights swim around us.
And the red turns to violet.
And violet into blue.
"We can give you anything," she tells me.
"As long as you want it," she tells me.
"But you have to give us something," she tells me.
"If you give us yourself," she tells me.
"We'll give you everything," she tells me.
And the five of them lie naked against my skin.
Their words.
Their hands.

Caressing more than my body.
Caressing my mind.
My soul.
My soul?
There is no soul to get in the way.
There is no stopping this bliss.
And I want nothing else.
I'd die for this.
I'd kill for this.
As I touch what's not my own.
As I take what isn't mine
Make it a part of me
And feel it swallow me whole.
Then I see it.
The tattoo.
The circle with six lines.
Upon her wrist.
Her back.
Her ankle.
Her hips.
Her neck.
They glide across my body.
As I move above them
And below.
More shadows enter the room.
Touching.
Everyone.
Becoming.
The taste of skin.
And the movement.
The endless movement.
And I recognize him
As his eyes look into mine.
He puts his hands upon my back.
And pulls me close.
"Vincent?" I ask.
But he ignores the question.
And my thoughts begin to collect themselves
As our shadows collide.

Where am I?
And what am I?
This body?
This endless touching?
And again I yell out to him.
But he ignores me as he turns away into another part of this.
And I remember it all.
Where I am.
What I'm doing.
As they surround me
And merge
Into one
Perfect
Body.
She moves.
Close.
And I smell her fragrant skin
As it clouds my mind.
And I stare at her body.
Her perfection.
As she stands there.
Naked.
Her long black hair gliding against her skin.
Her slender waist.
Her curving hips.
Her full, round breasts.
"What do you want, Cyan?" she asks.
All I want is to be inside of her.
I want to touch the curves of her body.
I want to taste every inch of her skin.
Nothing else matters.
Nothing.
And she floats through the room
Wrapping her soft hair around my body.
As I touch her
As I melt in her grip
She spreads herself apart
And pulls me in.
Where I collide.

I dissolve.
I disappear.

And I'm surrounded by their insides.
Her insides.
Rotting organs.
Glowing in vibrant colors.
Shoving against each other.
Fluids gushing in and out
As their eyes burn with emptiness.
And I remember.
Again.
Where I am.
What I am.
And think of Indiana.
And the way she made me feel.
As I held her close.
In the emptiness inside of me.
And as I stare out at the liquid nothing.
At their entrails glowing bright.
I become repulsed at everything I've become.
Which is nothing.
And everything that I've lost.
Which is love.
And I move through their bodies.
But don't feel them against my own.
And I stare deep into her eyes.
The one who held me close.
And I push.
Myself.
In.

And the bodies that surround me explode
As they dissolve into the air.
Their shadowy skin ripping apart.
Their insides bursting away.
And I stand firm upon the ground
As the dead fall beside me.
She sends me a grin that I recognize.

"No more fun?" she asks. "Or is the fun just beginning?"

And instantly her long black hair rushes at my body and sharply cuts across my skin. I spin myself about and escape her grip. As I land upon the ground, I reach for the staff upon my back, but find that it's gone.

Everything is gone
As I stand naked
My shadowy skin slowly turning back to normal.
And again I'm surrounded by her flowing hair.
As I push myself inward.

And move myself forward.

Where I land in the air beside her and spin my body around, kicking her to the ground. She catches herself with her long hair as it solidifies into sharp pillars behind her body.

"I could have given you anything you wanted," she scornfully says to me as her body rises high into the air, "but now I'll have to force you to take it all. Every touch. Every taste. Every smell. Every sight. Every sound. You can't resist it. You could have just accepted it, could have relished in the pleasure, but now you'll live in misery at your endless lust. Your endless desire for what you hate."

Her hair grows even longer
As it whips about violently in the air.
She sends a painful smile into my eyes.
"You can't," she whispers.
"Say," she hisses from behind her hair.
"No!" she screams out, lashing forward.
And as her dark skin surrounds me
Enveloping my body
I collapse.

Into the void.
Where everything
Is nothing.
Where her attraction disappears.
As her vile insides float about the air.
And I push.
My thoughts.

My mind.
Forward.

And I cut into her body
Forming into her insides as she rips apart.
But she gathers her skin.
Her flesh.
And her insides.
And puts them back together as she whips her body around
and slices me with her long, sharp nails.

Her face shows its true nature as she turns in my direction.
Her mouth opens wide, revealing countless, thin, sharp teeth. Her eyes
burn red with thin black slits within the middle. Upon her forehead is
the symbol of the circle with its six hollow lines shooting outward.

She growls at me from behind her many sharp fangs.

"You're fucking mine!" she roars out as she quickly moves
towards me in jagged blurs through the air.

Suddenly she's upon me, and I'm sent forcefully to the ground
as her hands grip deep into my throat. And as she chokes me with her
slender fingers, I feel again a craving for her touch. As she digs deep
into my skin, I lust for her body. And in her eyes I can see that she
knows my desire. Her hair goes soft, falling gracefully down her arms
and to my skin, as she returns to her beautiful form.

"It's so much easier," she whispers into my ear, her body lying
on top of mine, "if you just let go."

And so I do
As I let my desire loose
As I take what I want
And I watch myself die.
My body becomes hers.
And my skin turns
Not into the shadows as before
But into a glowing, bright white.
I become nothing
But the touch
Of our bodies.
And I watch
As this moment
Melts away.

She burns against my skin.
"What are you doing!" she screams as I move inside of her.
As I dig my hands deep into her back.
In.
And out.
I rip at her liquid skin.
In.
And out.
I pull my staff from deep within her body.
In.
And out.
I watch the emptiness behind everything I see.
Hear.
Smell.
Taste.
And touch.
In.
And out.
Everything dies.
In.
And out.

I'm nowhere.
I'm somewhere.

Above her.
I pull back.
Above her.
I swing down.
Her body rips apart.
And doesn't come back together.

VIII

Naked and alone, I walk amongst the shadows of the dead. Their bodies, melted into liquid pools of black, glaze the rooms that I walk through and alleys that I roam.

My mind feels awakened

But also in pieces

As stumble through the places where I was.

The sky burns blue above the urban landscape. The sun's light reflects off the thick black puddles of the dead, which collect in fluid heaps against the brick buildings at my sides. I search for Vincent in the hope that he didn't die along with the rest of shadowed bodies.

I find myself where it began, the room where I swallowed the colors of life and joined into the waves of sight and sound and touch.

My clothes lie upon the ground where I must have left them before becoming just another naked body. I grab them together and put them on. As I dress, the sound of someone screaming enters the room from far outside the front door.

I move out into the brightly lit streets. The melted shadows don't cover this side of the city, yet I still feel the sensation of death rising from the concrete below.

I travel towards the cries of a man in pain.

Is it Vincent?

I run past the tall brick buildings until I find myself in a new part of this city, where the air turns cold and high buildings made of concrete, with no windows or doors or any features at all, sit alongside the streets that I move through.

I see someone standing in the distance upon a large slab of concrete. The plateau sits within the center of a hollow filled deep with gleaming water. Before reaching him, I can tell that it is Vincent, for in a violent thrust of anger he tears apart the building beside him and sends it vanishing into nowhere. He follows his destruction with a painful scream as he falls to his knees. I yell out to him, but he doesn't reply, either from not hearing me or ignoring my call. I reach the edge beside the water-filled hollow.

I gather the pieces of my mind.

And I pull myself inward.

Pushing myself forward.
Through the emptiness.
Faintly I see to my left
The slight shimmer of a building
As its form fades away
Into nothing.
And I land.
Beside him.

"Vincent," I say as I touch the ground.

And with my words he stands and spins swiftly around, ripping a sharp valley in the ground towards where I am. I quickly jump out of its path and land beside the gash dug deep into the concrete. He stares at me in confusion, breathing heavily as blood drips down his naked body and lands in thick drops below.

"Cyan?" he asks me in between his painful breaths.

I nod yes and slowly move forward, but as I do he steps back. Falling to his knees, he shakes his head and mumbles words beneath his breath.

"I'm surprised to see you alive," I tell him.

But he doesn't respond.

"I thought you died in the fire," I continue, "from what Indiana told me."

"Indiana?" he asks violently as his eyes turn up to me.

"Yes," I tell him. "I found her. She told me what happened. Of the fire that overtook you both."

"She's alive?" he anxiously asks, standing to his feet.

I hesitate to give an answer.

Is she alive?

"Where is she?" he asks moving closer.

"I don't know," I tell him.

"You don't know?" he questions me angrily.

"She left," I say, "and I don't know where she's gone."

With my answer he gives out another painful scream.

200

"We will find her," I tell him. "We always find each other."

"No," he says. "We don't."

And so we stand in silence upon the concrete plateau.

The only sound is the dripping of Vincent's blood.

"We should fix you up," I say to him.

"I'm fine," he replies.

"What happened?" I ask.

"What do you mean?" he asks back.

"What happened to you?" I ask, "What happened after the fire? And how did you get here? And why are you bleeding?"

"Nothing happened," he replies. "And that's why I'm here. I did nothing during the fire. I tried to stop him. But I couldn't. I didn't. And I ended up here, where they gave me an escape. And I did nothing. I let myself die. Until you tore my death apart. Until you woke me up. And I made myself bleed for what I didn't do."

"Why?" I ask him. "Why would you do that to yourself?"

"Anger," he says to me slowly. "Regret. Shame. Hate."

"For yourself?" I ask.

"I let her go," he tells me while walking to the edge of the concrete and staring down at the water below. "I lost her in the flames. I couldn't hold on. And when I came here I forgot about her completely. I forgot about everything."

"You did all you could," I tell him.

"I did nothing," he replies.

"And so did I," I say back. "I left you there to burn."

Silently he stares at the water.

His body slowly swaying

As he lifts one arm up

And gazes at his bloody palm.

"Nothing," he whispers before falling forward into the depths below. I run to the side of the massive concrete slab and watch as his body splashes heavily into the water. I see his shape sink deep beneath the surface until he's no longer visible.

I wait for him to rise back up.

But he never does.

And so I disappear.

Moving through myself.

Past the shimmering surface of the water.

Through its dark depths.
And its blue glow.
And I see him there.
Swimming down.
Towards something burning bright.
And I move past him.
Watching his face as he swims motionlessly.
And below
Through the bright light
I see a separate world.
A separate life.
And there I move.
And there I am.

I land upon the dry ground.
Beside me is a small pool of water.
I look around and see nothing but an arid landscape.
Crumbling roads move through the sky, sitting upon decaying pillars of concrete that lie in the cracked, dry ground. The sky shines deep blue amongst the many large, dark clouds that float slowly by. I stand shadowed by thick white cloth hung loose across rusting poles stuck into the ground. The ragged canvas blows in the dry wind.
I hear the sound of Vincent rising through the water.
And he reaches the surface
The blood cleaned from his body
His wounds no longer there.
I reach my hand out to him, which he accepts, and I pull him out of the depths. He stands breathing heavily beside the small circle of water.
"And where are we now?" I ask.
"Does it matter?" he says after filling his lungs with air.
"We will find her," I tell him. "I know that we will."
"Why did she leave you?" he asks me with spite in his words.
"I don't know," I say back. "Or at least not exactly why. I took her to the place that I go. To the place that moves me through this world. And she saw something there. Or from the things that she said, perhaps she saw nothing. Completely nothing."
"And she let you take her there?" he asks me moving closer.

"She asked me to," I tell him. "I didn't want to. I knew it would be dangerous. But she insisted. And so I did."

His fists clench as I speak.

And his eyes try to hide emotions

Though they escape enough for me to notice.

"So what can we do?" he asks me. "Where did you see her last? Where should we go? And what happened to Morgan?"

"He's dead," I say. "I killed him myself. And the last I saw of Indiana was someplace far from here. Someplace we could never go. You know there's nowhere permanent here. Everything is always changing. There is nowhere to look for her besides wherever it is that we end up."

"So we keep moving," he says to me while looking out at the crumbling landscape. "We keep living in this ever dying world."

I move to his side and stare at where we must go.

"How did you kill him?" he asks me.

And I hesitate.

For I killed him in the place that I dared to take Indiana.

"He fought me," I tell him, "and I almost died by his hand. But I took him away from here. I took him into nowhere and let him go."

"You don't make much sense," he tells me. "But what here does?" He turns to me and gives me a strange look. "So Morgan is gone," he says. "As is Les, or whoever he was. And Sam."

He stops quickly after speaking and stands quiet and still.

I can tell that he's lost in some memory.

Of what was.

Or maybe what could have been.

"So it's just me and you," he continues. "And Indiana, somewhere out there."

"You know," I say to him, dampening the seriousness of our conversation, "you are completely naked. Would you like to find some clothes?"

"There's no need for them," he tells me. "Unless, of course, you're the one embarrassed?"

"No," I stutter back. "No. I just thought that maybe you wouldn't mind getting dressed. I mean, all that sand ahead, it could end up somewhere painful."

He gives a deep and loud laugh at my remark, which is the first time I've heard him laugh at all. I laugh in return, not from the pathetic joke that I had made, but from the sound of his laughter alone.

"Maybe you're right," he says to me. "But we don't have Indiana here to make us what we need. So I guess I'll have to do it myself."

With this he turns his vision up to the white cloth above us. He holds one of his palms flat outward and begins to curl his fingers in. As his hand closes, a line shreds into the canvas, cutting away a long square of fabric that falls to the ground. He picks up the cloth and twists it about his waist until he is partially covered by the white fabric.

"This will have to do," he tells me as he stands there in pride of his work.

"Let's hope the sand doesn't blow too hard," I say with a grin.

The large clouds above sit motionless.

Yet every so often, from what cause I don't know, they quickly drift towards one direction, their bodies billowing about and changing shape until they again come to a halt within the deep blue sky.

We've been walking through this arid land for some time.

For how long I can't say.

But this is something I've come to accept.

That time doesn't really exist.

There's just an always-flowing present.

The constant death and birth of now.

We move amongst the crumbling overpasses that slither through this vast desert. There are no signs of life here, neither past nor present, aside from the colorful graffiti sprayed across the tall columns of concrete that hold the roads high above us.

No words are painted upon their surfaces.

Just intricate shapes of red and yellow and blue and green.

"Where do you think we are?" Vincent asks me as we move into the shadow of a large cloud above. "What do you think this place is? Not just here, but everywhere we've been and will go. Every part of this strange life we live."

"I think a better way of finding the answer," I tell him, "is asking who we are. And how it is that we know the things we know.

We're a part of this place. And what can we understand more than ourselves?"

We stop walking forward as Vincent turns around to face me. We stand surrounded by the massive shadow cast down on us from above.

"How did these feelings of strangeness become born in our thoughts?" I ask. "How do we know that we live in some sort of anomaly? Some glitch? That people shouldn't fly and shouldn't make things out of thin air? And how do we know what telephone poles are? And cars? And anything at all? How de we even speak the words that we do? Or think the thoughts within our heads?"

"Because we lived a life before this," he says. "Because the only way of knowing anything at all is by experience. So we must have come from somewhere else."

"But how do we know that we really lived some other life?" I ask him. "We have no memories of a time before this. We just feel these peculiar thoughts that tell us that this isn't normal. We have this deep seated notion of what things really are."

"So how do you explain knowing anything at all?" he asks me as he turns around and continues to walk forward. "How can we know without having known? How can you explain the fact that we woke up here with all this knowledge of life already within our heads?"

"When did you wake up?" I ask him, which again stops his movements.

"What?" he asks turning around.

"When were you born here?" I reply. "What did you experience?"

His fingers slowly curl inward to his palms.

His large brow digs down over his eyes.

"I," he stutters, "I don't remember."

"You don't remember!" I yell in amazement.

"No," he quickly says back. "I don't recall when I awoke here."

"So then what do you remember?" I ask him as I walk closer to where he stands. "What's the first thing that you can recollect?"

He looks down at the dry ground below.

And stands quiet for a moment.

"Indiana," he says awakening from his mind. "I remember her standing there, upon the edge of a dark lake. Beside us were tall beams of metal with soft green plants twisting all about them. I remember seeing her there, her feet sitting in the edge of the water and her hands held out in front of her. White flower petals formed within the air beneath her palms and flew about her body as they fell into the water below. She turned to me. And I remember thinking how beautiful she was. How perfect. And I remember the scent of something divine. And it was her. She looked me in the eyes and asked me who I was. Not knowing what to say, since I didn't know who I was, I asked her the same. She told me she had no name, but that she'd been there for some time, alone. And suddenly a strange sound began to resonate from above us as the lake began to slowly seep upwards. We were swallowed by the water. She swam to me as I swam to her. And we held each other as we floated up to the rising surface, where we came into this world we know."

In my mind I see her.

Standing beside the lake.

Perfectly.

Her body.

Exists.

Her eyes turn to me.

And I remember holding her close.

As we fell through the stars.

As I loved who she was.

And our home.

My.

Home.

"I suppose that's my first memory," Vincent says, breaking me from my thoughts of her and us and everything that I had and lost.

"So you can't even remember the beginning of this life," I tell him, "yet you believe in a life before it?"

"I do," he answers. "What other reason could there be for the knowledge within us?"

"Perhaps our own thoughts are painted upon us," I say to him.

"By someone else?" he asks.

"Or by ourselves," I tell him. "Or by no one at all. Perhaps chaos is the only creator of existence. What we know has no real substance. All that our knowledge is, all that it can be, is a concept within our minds, an idea of obscure existence that we project onto our lives. So are the memories, our knowledge, within our minds true? That is, were they born from actual experience? Or were they just placed there, born there, in our thoughts, where they seem so genuine, so real, that we could swear we've lived the life within our heads? Could it be that what we think to be true is merely what we think and nothing else?"

"The truth is impossible," Vincent says looking up at the large cloud above us and then looking back down at me. "All that we can understand is our own life. Our own experiences, whether they are real or not, are the only things that we can truly know. The closest thing to truth is our own beliefs. And so we have to believe in ourselves. Our faith must become our reality."

"You used to be a man of reason," I say, "yet now you preach faith?"

"I found no answers," he says in a dark tone. "No reason behind anything. Not even within myself."

"So you gave up?" I ask him

"So I gave up," he replies. "And I lost Indiana in the flames. And I lost myself in the escape of lust. And now that I'm alive again, all that I have left is my faith in this life, in this experience without reason. Nothing else."

"But you can't deny that even your own life could be a lie?" I ask him.

"Even if it is a lie," he answers, "it is all that I know."

"So where are we then?" I ask him, returning to the point of the discussion. "What is this place? And who are we?"

"We are here," he says waving his arms about at the landscape. "And this place is nothing more than the life we live. And who we are is the same."

"It's too simple," I say. "Too easy to think that way."

"And why does it have to be difficult?" he asks me.

"Because," I reply, "I am here. I accept that. I know that. Yet even though I see the truths that you claim, I see no everlasting beauty, no meaning in this life."

"And why must there be beauty?" he asks. "Why must there be meaning?"

"What reason is there to live without meaning or beauty?" I ask back. And as I speak, the shadow that covers us quickly shoots away as the clouds glide fast through the sky, releasing us into the bright sunlight.

"Neither can exist," he tells me. "You know this. Meaning and beauty, they're just ideas in our minds."

"Are our thoughts not what you said we must trust more than anything?" I reply. "We create this life. So meaning can exist, just as much as reality, within our minds. Somewhere deep inside myself lies beauty. Lies truth. And it's as real as the place that we are in. Yet it's hidden beneath the questions. Beneath the answers. And so we must always dig deeper."

"You speak of beauty and meaning as the same thing?" he asks.

"I speak of them as opposites," I reply. "Thus, yes, they are the same. For opposites are merely compliments of the one. Beauty is the chaos. Chaos is the reason. Reason is the meaning."

"You live too much in words, Cyan," Vincent says to me, waving his arm in my direction. "You take too much meaning from the sounds that float about your head and out of your mouth. This existence is indescribable. It's beyond what you call beauty, meaning, reason, and truth. What word, what idea, could possible describe the absolute? The notions that you have are merely a part of it all, a part of this life, and how could a part of the whole describe its entirety?"

"Perhaps it never can," I tell him. "But how can one become whole unless they build together every part?"

And before we can continue talking, a loud crash of thunder rings throughout the air. We look about us, but see no storm. Abruptly, however, the clouds move again. Stopping in the blue sky above, a large dark cloud sits within the air and casts its vast shadow upon the ground beside us.

Another loud ring of thunder breaks through the sky.

And suddenly a vivid yellow body of a man lands with a thud upon the shadow beside us. He lies there limp. We move to him, but find that he has no features. He's just a body, with no face or life, but with vibrantly colored skin.

And looking up, I see another falling in the distance.

A green body shooting down through the sky.

Crashing upon a concrete overpass.

"Well, this is strange, isn't it?" Vincent asks.

"No," I tell him. "It's not. I know the trap that you're planting. I know what you plan to say. That you think this is strange because we know from another life that this shouldn't happen. But if what you say is true, that all we can really know comes from experience, then from all the experiences that I have here, this is not so strange."

And again a body falls beside us.

A red figure lying lifeless upon the ground.

And again.

But blue.

Then orange.

Then purple.

Then white.

And black.

And every color there is.

As we run out of the cloud's shadow.

And watch as mounds of color grow beside us.

As bodies pile upon themselves.

And the heavy sound of the vibrant figures falling upon each other resonates all around us like thick rain.

We move through the sunlight.

The space amongst the shadows.

The only place safe from the shower of bodies.

And with every abrupt shift of the clouds we must quickly move to the displaced safety of the sun.

We travel this way for some time.

Until the ground becomes buried beneath the mountains of bodies that grow across everything. And the colorful figures, with no life within them, become the land that we walk upon.

"This seems so familiar," Vincent says to me, stopping and looking around at the vast chaos of colors all around us.

And I feel it too.

I know this place.

And as we continue on, I begin to notice objects forming from beneath the bodies. Rusted poles of metal grow from the depths below. Decaying wooden walls, which look torn from some home, float across the colorful surface. More and more things appear.

An old, worn down refrigerator.

A child's broken bicycle.

Bits of paper blowing in the wind.

Two halves of a huge boat

Drifting apart

And colliding into countless other objects.

The chaos becomes too much.

And I can't distinguish one thing from another.

And looking around at the lifeless bodies lying within the endless disorder of things that slowly move about, I recognize where we have gone. Or more so, what has come here.

"It's the Myriad," I tell Vincent. "It's found us once again."

The sound of everything.

All around me.

And the wind blows harsh against the skin of my face

As we climb our way across the Myriad

Yet never find an end to it.

Every step we take could send us sinking into its depths.

Every object that we climb could collapse into the chaos.

"How long does it go on?" I ask Vincent even though I know he has no answer.

"As long as it wants to," he replies, climbing over a dome of pale blue metal. He stops atop the round object and scans the horizon.

The gray clouds have swallowed the blue of the sky.

The bodies, however, no longer fall.

The wind blows a loneliness that moves through my mind.

And I think of Indiana and how I was wrong.

There is beauty in this world.

And it's her.

Only her.

And I long to hold her again.

As my body aches.

As my thoughts scream out against this place.

"Why don't you go up above?" Vincent asks me, pointing to the pale gray sky. "See if you can't find something."

I nod in agreement.

Calming my thoughts of Indiana.

And pushing them deep inside.

I collapse into nothing.

The chaos falls beneath me

As I'm rising to the clouds above.

Until I stop.
Where I am.

And appearing beneath the clouds, I rise just slightly upwards. As my body slows to a halt, I float for a moment in the sky, staring at the Myriad that stretches on all around me.

But my body begins to drop.
And I fall fast.
And as I do, I glimpse something in the chaos.
A shadow?
A hollow.
Where the disorder sinks into itself.
And down.
I fall.
Into my mind.

Where I push against the movement.
Against my thoughts.
And falling down through the nothing.
While swimming upwards through the heavy emptiness.
I find myself.
Where I was.
Where I am.

"Did you see anything?" Vincent asks as I land upon a sheet of bright green plastic.

"Over there," I say, pointing in the direction of what I saw. "It sinks down. Into where, I don't know. But at least it's something."

"Then that's where we'll go," he replies.

And we move, climbing over the countless objects that grind against each other below. After some time of traveling across the harsh landscape, we make out the contour of the hollow that I saw from above, where the Myriad begins to sink downwards. And as we move along with it, we make out the clearing that it descends into.

A massive round area sits surrounded by the Myriad.

The chaos encircles the clearing, stopping suddenly at its edge, creating walls of disorder around the hollow. The concrete overpasses from before dig their way out of the walls and shoot through the open area.

"Are there people there?" Vincent asks, stepping closer.

And looking harder, I make out vague white shapes that move across the ground and over the concrete roads that cut through the air.

"Ghosts," I tell him.

"Damn," he says under his breath.

And I see a strange shape in the center of the clearing, sitting upon the peak of where all the concrete highways collide into each other.

"And what is that?" Vincent asks, staring at the same shape that I see.

"What else is there to do besides go down there and find out?" I reply.

And so we climb our way down the hill made of everything, as bits of the Myriad tumble down from our steps. We reach the edge and see below us one of the concrete highways that protrude out from the wall. Vincent jumps down and lands heavily on the dilapidated concrete. I move myself inward.

And down.

Appearing next to him, I see the clearing lying out in front of us. The road that we are on stretches out for just a short distance before it breaks apart and crumbles to the ground. We walk forward and down the piles of concrete at the end of the road, which leads us to a field of yellow, dead grass.

To our left sits a group of the pale ghosts. They slowly move about, walking with no apparent direction, sometimes running into each other but making no notice of it.

"Why do you think they're here?" Vincent asks me. "What is this place?"

"I'm sure we'll find out soon enough," I answer. "They're always drawn to something. And that something seems to always be drawn to us."

"Or are we the ones drawn to it?" Vincent replies.

And as we walk through the dead grass that crunches beneath our feet, we find more and more of the slow moving ghosts. Their small black eyes stare blankly forward. Their wide mouths sit shut with no expression. And we make our way to the center of the hollow, towards the strange shape we saw from above.

212

Another road crumbles to the ground in front of us. We climb our way up its collapsing heaps of concrete and steel, and find that the overpass stretches on towards our destination. The languid ghosts move about the street's surface, paying no attention to the world around them.

We come upon the point where all the roads collide, where they form a sort of ruined intersection that rests high above everything within the clearing. Sitting in the center, upon a slab of concrete formed into a derelict throne, is a giant in the shape of a man, yet with the head of a fearsome lion.

He stares emptily, as the ghosts do, down at the ground that cracks away beneath his massive feet.

"He's huge," Vincent whispers to me as we sit beside the edge of the intersection. "He's at least four, maybe five of us in height."

"Let's hope he doesn't want to put up a fight then," I reply.

And I slowly walk to the colossal figure.

Vincent follows close behind.

When we approach him, time seems to stop, and we watch as he sits magnificently upon his decaying throne. He appears not to notice us, as if he was frozen within his mind.

But ending the timeless moment of stillness, the huge beast slowly turns his vision upwards and stares at us with his fearsome, yet vacant, eyes. The heavy clouds above crash with loud thunder.

And the stillness painfully returns

As Vincent and I stare into the massive beast's eyes.

"Hello," I say to the giant, bringing life back into motion.

The sky flashes bright above us, bathing the world in its bright light. The colossal mouth upon the beast's terrifying face casts me an unexpected smile.

"Hello!" he roars out across the entire expanse of the clearing.

And the sun's light shifts to gold, as from all about us we hear shouts in reply. I feel a sensation flow across my skin. Is it happiness? I turn to Vincent, and he's smiling while staring at the golden light that shines upon everything.

The huge beast laughs at all the joy around him.

"Yes!" he shouts out between heavy sighs of delight.

"Who are you?" Vincent asks him, stepping forward.

But the giant only replies with more cries of joy.

More bouts of laughter.

"Who are you?" Vincent yells again.

"He's the life that he lives," I tell him.

"No," he quickly says back. "He's more than that."

"No," I reply. "He is nothing more than this place."

And all around us is the laughter of a million ghosts.

They run through the clearing together, embracing each other as friends. As family. Family?

And flashing by in my mind is a vague image of a house.

And the people that live in it.

But before I can see it clearly, it disappears from my thoughts.

And leaves me alone within this place.

Vincent falls to his knees.

Upon his face is despair.

And his hands dig into the pavement as bits of it vanish away into nothing, turning the area around him into thin webs of concrete.

"It's more than this," he says with sadness. "I'm more than this."

And ghosts stop running.

And the giant loses his smile.

The clouds above return with spite.

And all around me, but not within, I feel sadness.

"Why?" I ask Vincent, staring not at him, but at the giant's miserable face.

"No," the beast sighs as he falls back down into his throne.

"Because," Vincent says as his head hangs down, "I'm nothing without her. And she is this world. She's everything. And I am not."

But before I can reply to his curious words, rain floods down from the heavy gray sky above. We become drenched by the downpour, as both Vincent and the giant cry together with the rain.

The ghosts move faster now, though they no longer hold on to one another as friends, as family.

But instead they move alone.

Weeping with sorrow.

With pain.

And my left eye begins to burn.

Echoing the misery within the world around me.

Vincent slowly stands to his feet.

Not saying a word, he weightily walks forward through the violent rain.

"What are you doing?" I ask him, though the pain in my eye keeps me where I am.

He ignores my words.

And he moves beside the enormous beast.

"Vincent!" I yell out.

"You're more than this," he says, lifting his hands forward, dissolving the concrete throne of the giant.

The huge beast falls heavily backwards to the concrete, shattering it with his weight and sending parts of it crashing to the ground far below.

"What are you doing!?" I scream out to Vincent, forcing the pain in my eye away and running forward to where he stands.

And as I reach his side, the massive creature stands to his feet.

His terrifying face of rough fur shows rage.

His eyes cast down in our direction.

The sky above burns red as blood.

He growls out with fury as the many ghosts around us begin to scream in anger. I watch as they grab at those who stand nearest them and rip each other apart limb by limb. In the distance I hear loud rumbles of some power unknown, as the ghosts fight in rage across the clearing.

And I'm surrounded by war.

By hate.

Again I see an image within my mind.

But it's an image with no shape.

No form.

Just a single color.

Red.

And my eye explodes with pain much stronger than before.

To my right I'm struck with the great power of the giant's massive hand. I fly fast to the left and tumble painfully to the concrete. Gathering myself back together, I see Vincent being crushed within the giant's grip. He roars out at Vincent with his immense voice, throwing him from his grasp forcefully into the side of the overpass. Vincent tumbles over the edge and falls to the ground far below, where the war of angry ghosts rages on.

And the beast turns his eyes to me.

His great lion's mane blows in the strong wind.

I step back and pull the staff from upon my back.

While he runs at me with full vigor.
And I pull myself away.

Feeling the waves of anger flowing through this space.
I struggle to stay within.
And my mind fails to move.
As I fall apart.

And I appear where I was before.

The giant jumps forward and lands upon me with his fists, shattering the roads apart and sending everything crashing down below. I lie crushed within the piles of concrete, yet my body is somehow still alive. I see through the cracks amongst the rubble the silhouette of Vincent standing against the intensely burning flames behind him. And as the ground shakes, I see the giant come to his feet beside me. He moves toward Vincent, as Vincent turns to him, yet doesn't step away.

The giant reaches down and grabs him where he stands.
And I try to push myself inside.

But the anger.
The overwhelming rage.
Keeps.
Me.
Where.
I.
Am.

And appearing back beneath the rubble, I yell out in vain as the beast rips at Vincent's body with his immense teeth. His fangs tear Vincent's head away in gruesome silhouettes.

I watch as the giant devours him.
Piece by piece.
And I feel the anger around me
As it seeps in through my burning left eye
And devours my mind, becoming all of me.
And I move.

In through the fury.

With the passion of my rage.
I push.
Through the emotion that is everywhere.
Within myself.
And I dig.
Through.
My.
Mind.

And I stand amongst the flames, staring into the beast's
fearsome gaze as he laughs in loud roars.
But not the same laughter as before.
Instead its rings out with vile agony.
With pure wrath.
And I run to him.
And I feel it.
The rumble.
Coming at me from my right.
And I turn before it hits me.
And jumping upwards, I move myself inside.

Where I fly through the rage.
Past the body of a massive elephant.
Moving beside him.

And appearing back within this war, I stare at the flames that
burn upon the huge saddle wrapped around the thick, round body of
the creature. Standing within the flames, upon the back of the fierce
elephant, is Vincent. His face shows no emotion. His eyes, which are
now two empty holes within his head, burn with fire from deep within
his body.

I stare as he pulls the raging elephant around and heads in my
direction. In the distance, I see another charging beast. Upon his back
as well is Vincent with his burning, hollow eyes.
The two of them charge towards me.
And as I feel the heat of their fire
I pull away.

And watch.

As the two sit motionless
Within their imminent collision.
And I flow
Far from their paths.
And I stop.
Here.

They collide in explosive force, sending waves of heat outward
in all directions. The massive giant growls in anger through the flames,
running towards where I stand.

I spin about and catch my mind.
Just as the huge beast reaches me.
And I instantly fade away.

Through nothingness full of rage.
To the space beside the beast's head.
And his eyes I know
As Vincent stares into my mind.
Not with the hollows that glow from the others.
But with his real eyes.
The ones I know.
And the anger within me.
Crumbles.
Away.
And I feel the pressure.
Of all the rage.
Push.
Me.
Back.

And I swing forward through the hot air, smashing my staff
into the beast's skull, in between Vincent's eyes. The blow sends us
both back as we fall in unison upon the hot grass below. I feel heavy
vibrations beneath my body, and I turn to see another massive
elephant rushing towards me. I watch as it moves closer. Vincent stares
down at me from upon it with the fire of his emptiness. And before I
become trampled under its enormous hooves, I shift into the void.

Where I spin my body about.

Flipping myself upwards.
So that I float there upside down.
And I rise
To see his hollow, burning eyes
Staring down at where I was.
His insides fiery with hate
As the frozen flames wrap around his body.
And surprising me
He moves his gaze
With obscure motions
Through the liquid emptiness
Until he looks deep into my thoughts.
His lips begin to slowly move
As I hear
Not with sound
But with sensations upon my mind
The words he speaks.
You are everything.
He tells me.
And everything must die.
And with his words.
I fall away.

Landing in the air in front of the charging beast, I collide with his thick skin, with his heavy muscles, with his forceful movements. I fly through the air and land high upon the concrete of an overpass held above.

I lie there in pain.
My body beaten into weakness.
My mind collapsing alongside it.
And I see his shadow fly through the air.
Then land hard upon the concrete beside me.
Sending cracks through the pavement.

The flames burn bright from below, yet the sky has turned a deep, dark, almost-black blue. The giant stands illuminated, his top half glowing red from the fire, while his legs shine blue from the night sky. His heavy steps shake my body as my vision blurs everything into a haze. I feel his large fingers wrap around me and squeeze my body tight as he lifts me up to his face.

The blur of his eyes, which reflect the brightly burning war that engulfs us, digs deep through the distortion of my mind and awakens me to the painful place that I am in.

"I am more than this," the beast growls at me.

"I am more than nothing," Vincent snarls.

His grip tightens as I feel my bones grind together.

My muscles crush inward from the pressure.

"Vincent," I cough as blood pours out of my mouth.

"He is no one," he roars back at me. "He is nothing."

And he drops me down.

Where I fall limp to the concrete.

And he stares at me with his wrathful eyes.

"You, however, are not," he growls.

And I try to reply.

To say anything at all.

But my body is too weak.

"And for nothing to become something," Vincent says in the beast's rough voice, "the something must die."

And he lifts his leg high, moving his giant foot above my body.

And my body can't move at all

As I watch myself

Lie helpless.

And feel myself prepare to die.

Embracing death

As I become nothing.

And I move.

But I don't.

From here to there.

And there to here.

I see his insides glow black with hate.

As the anger of the emptiness

Flows throughout his body.

I awaken myself.

To him.

And in a vicious burst, his body rips apart and shoots across the pavement. I lie within his insides, his body missing from the space that I occupy. I fall out of his torso, and he tumbles to the ground.

I catch myself upon the concrete, pulling my strength together enough to stand to my feet. I move to his side.

The giant lies upon the crumbling road.

Vincent stares out from deep within the dying creature.

With tears gathering along the sides of his eyes, he turns to me and stares, saying nothing as the flames surrounding us die away.

And I'm left alone in the silence.

In the darkness.

Standing high upon the overpass.

The wind blowing warm against my skin.

I feel something fade away.

And then.

I feel nothing at all.

IX

The world around me collapses away in chaos.

The Myriad dissolves, its countless objects disappearing in wild flashes as I walk along the tunnels that form from its dissolution. The passageways lead through thick darkness, as the moon's light barely cuts in from above. The disjointed walls reverberate the endless grinding noise of the Myriad as it collides against itself.

I move deeper down into the darkness, swallowed by the shadows of the Myriad. Swallowed by its loud noise.

I sometimes come across small sources of light.

A buried lamppost that radiates its golden glow throughout the tunnels. A flickering light bulb hanging down from the roof of a passageway, dying and living and dying again. Faintly lit strings of lights lying behind thin sheets of cloth lining the sides of a narrow corridor.

In blinks of an eye, parts of the world vanish into nothing.

Yet this cessation is what leads me forward through the sparsely lit tunnels that dig through the Myriad.

I begin to rise as the hollowed out paths digs their way up into the night, where the moon shines bright across the vast landscape of disarray. Scattered throughout the distance is the shimmering of the many lights that occupy the Myriad.

The pieces of metal and plastic and wood, the endless amounts things that crowd the chaos, become slick from the cool dampness of the night air. I often trip upon the unstable ground, catching myself before I fall hard onto the disorder that I move across.

I go in no direction.

I have no reason to be here.

Or there.

Other than to find Indiana.

Who could be anywhere.

Or nowhere.

Bits of grass begin to grow across the wet objects below. Green vines wrap themselves along the moist wooden poles that protrude upward from deep within the Myriad. Moss develops on the sides of the countless plastic pieces of junk that scatter the vast wasteland. And as I climb across the abundant plants, the deep green substances that spread across eternity, I find myself moving towards some strange sensation ahead of me. I feel drawn towards a peculiar emptiness, as if being sucked into a void.

The Myriad gives way to solid ground as the masses of flora drift against an endless expanse of flat, cold metal. Nothing lies ahead of me, yet still I'm drawn forward.

And so I walk onward
Into the desolation.
The stars begin to disappear
Until all that's left is a flat landscape
And the brightly shining moon above.

Even the smooth ground begins to vanish just behind my steps, crumbling into nothing with each stride I take.

Where am I going?
And why?
I find no reason.
Other than her.
And so I continue on.
If not for her, for the fact that I can't turn back.

There is nothing behind me besides the abyss, the infinite wall of blackness that eats away at the space that I travel.

So I walk.
And.
I.
Walk.
With thoughts of Indiana in my mind.
And how I long for her and our home and our love.

Suddenly, as I take another step forward, the ground in front of me vanishes, just as it does behind me. The vastness that lies ahead falls into emptiness, and I'm left standing upon a strip of cold metal. In confusion I step forward, and as I do the ground again evaporates both behind and in front of me. In agitation I move, over and over, until I'm left upon a narrow sliver of metal that cuts through this vacant space.

So I stop.
And I stare.
At what's left.

And I turn to my side.
And I move across the thin strip of ground.
As I do, the metal again fades away behind me.
And eventually ahead as well.
Until I'm left upon a single point of space.
A single small bit of metal that hovers in the void.
I sit down in hopelessness.
With nowhere to go.
And I stare up at the moon
My only company
As I fade this life away.

Where I watch myself.
And nothing else.
As I push my thoughts into place.
As they try to shove me far from here.
Yet at the same time pull me inward.
And I'm caught in the violent pushing and pulling.
As my mind dissolves.
And I become nothing.
But the awareness of the forces.
Of these thoughts.
Of these motions.
And I collapse.
Into.
This.

Back upon the suspended piece of ground.
I stay for just a moment.
For again I fall away.

And flow into this.
Into what?
Into that.
And everything.
Which is nothing.
Which is what I am.

And appearing.

I disappear.

Into.
Myself.
Into.
Something.

Again.

Nothing.

Again.

Something.

Again.

Am I here?

Or there?

Inside?

Or out?

And a sudden thought
Moves through this
That
And me.
As I find myself staring
Through the vast emptiness
At a liquid sphere of light.
And I plunge into the vacuum.
Which tears at my mind.
But I only push harder.
I only pull stronger.
Swimming through the water of my thoughts.
The deep, dark water of myself.
As the light grows brighter.

And brighter.
Until the light is this.
Until.
The.
Light.
Is.
That.

And I'm standing upon the glowing surface of the moon.
Its bright white shining upwards from beneath me.
Yet it illuminates nothing.
For there's nothing to shine its light upon besides myself.
I feel a faint vibration colliding against my feet and echoing through my body. It grows stronger as I stand staring at the barren, glowing landscape. The vibrations begin to shake my body so intensely that I'm forced to fall to my hands and steady myself against the ground. Yet the ground is what causes the vibrations.
And the ground is what crumbles away
As I fall into the center of the moon.
I land heavily upon a soft bed of green grass, where I lie within the hollow sphere that was the moon. It radiates a brilliant white light throughout its interior, so brightly that I'm forced to shut my eyes.
I stand, slowly opening my eyes until they adjust, and I find myself upon a floating island of grass levitating within the center of the white, empty globe.
"So has the seed you swallowed grown into anything yet?" a voice gently asks me from behind. I turn to see a figure half buried within the plane of green grass. His body seems to be a part of it, as it grows up his sides and becomes most of his shape. Only his small arms, like that of a child's, and his face are separate from the green grass.
"It's grown into nothing," I answer him, "which to me seems better than growing into anything at all."
He very slowly blinks his eyelids and sits staring at me as I walk closer to him.
"Do you know?" he asks before taking a long breath.
And then again sits silently still.
"What becomes of nothing?" he finishes after some time.
"What do you mean?" I ask back.

And I wait for the answer.

"It becomes something," he slowly replies.

And the grass grows gradually up his torso.

"What's happening to you?" I ask him, and as I do a piece of the white moon around us vanishes away.

"The same thing happens to something," he answers before taking another long breath. The grass moves slowly down his arms, which sit lifeless at his sides.

"It becomes its opposite," he says. "It becomes nothing."

His limbs now hang fully covered in the green grass. His childlike face sits above the mound of plant life. He stares at me with his large eyes as they again blink in slow motion.

"Nothing makes sense," I tell him. "No matter what happens. No matter what I think or do. And why must it make any sense? Why do I always look for something that isn't there? That isn't here?"

"Because," he replies with a frail voice, "there is something within you that's becoming something without."

"What do you mean?" I ask him, stepping closer.

"And what's outside of you," he weakly adds, "is becoming what's within."

And his head falls low as he finishes his strained words.

"What do you mean?!" I shout.

But he remains motionless.

Silent.

I move to him and lift his head.

And watch as the grass grows up his neck.

And along his face.

Until only his eyes, large and white and round, are visible.

And they stare at me with complete understanding.

Complete empathy.

And I feel his answer in the way that he looks into my being.

But I don't understand what it is that he's trying to say.

Still I know nothing.

Still I am ignorant to the reasons of my existence.

To the answers of my endless questions.

And he slowly shuts his eyes

As the grass consumes him entirely.

I'm left alone.

Within my thoughts.

And all around me
Bits of the bright sphere vanish
Piece by piece
As my world becomes black
And the void becomes everything.
I fall to my knees in the darkness.
And feel the grass against my hands.
Endless nothing.
Endless.
Nothing.
Until I hear faint steps.
Until I hear the sound of breathing.
And brushing against me is a heavy body of soft fur.
I know the sensation.
It's a familiar feeling.
And I reach my hand out to embrace Vidya.
But I feel him walk past, so I stand quickly to my feet.

I hear his soft paws moving through the grass, and I follow his sounds as we travel through the darkness. The grass seems to go on much farther than it did before, as we continually move forward, as I follow the sound of his steps.

And the sound is all there is.
His paws against the soft grass.
The air that moves in and out of his lungs.
Then silence.
And I'm lost.
With no direction.
With nothing at all.
But then I hear the sound of his heavy breathing.
And again I follow
As he turns about the darkness
In winding paths.
And I struggle to stay close.
Until I collide with something solid.

I listen for Vidya, but hear nothing. I slide my hands against the wall that now sits in front of me. It feels warm to the touch, as if there was a world burning with life behind it. I move across its surface until my hand strikes against something protruding from the wall. I grasp the shape and realize that it's a doorknob. I turn it slowly, listening to the sounds of its rotation cutting through the vast emptiness that I am in.

I take a deep breath before opening the door.

And as I push forward I become bathed in sunlight.

Lying beyond the doorway is a narrow city street, yet it's not like the kind I've experienced before.

It's alive.

As the trees sway with the breeze.

And lights plays amongst the windows.

Echoes of everything flow all around and into my ears.

The aroma of life enters my senses and awakens me to something I've never experienced before.

Something that feels so real, so familiar, and so alive.

Yet I see no one.

I am alone within this presence of life.

I walk out onto the sidewalk and stare down at the cracks in the pavement, where small bits of grass burst through. I turn my eyes down the road and see the many buildings that line it. They sit in various colors, in dark reds and light blues, in yellows and soft whites. Along the street are parked cars, yet they don't rust and decay like the ones I've seen before. They exist as if someone uses them, as if someone cares for them.

In the windows of the shops that I walk past are different sorts of things. Within one brick building is a collection of musical instruments. In another are countless books. The window of a small yellow building is lined with blue and green bottles full of liquids that blur what exists behind them.

I find myself standing upon a street corner where there is only one direction to go. In front of me and to my left the road crumbles away into empty space. To my right it continues on as it gradually goes downhill. The buildings give way to small houses with chain-link fences surrounding their well-kept lawns. As I move along, the grass becomes more unkempt and the fences begin to rust. I walk upon an open gate that leads into a yard of dead grass and a house with dirty white siding. The front door of the house is held open by a heavy clay pot with a tall dead plant sitting inside of it. I walk across the lawn and up the few steps that lead to the door. The smell of smoke enters my senses as I approach the open door and stare into the dark insides of the house.

Walking inward, I find myself within a cluttered room of bookshelves and boxes and clothes that scatter the floor. In the corner is an old chair of green fabric. Beside it is a tall yellow lamp sitting upon a round wooden table. A small blue ashtray full of burnt cigarettes sits beside the lamp on the table. The smell of smoke grows stronger as I move deeper into the house. To my left is a narrow hallway that leads to closed doors. To my right is a kitchen brightly lit from the sunlight that comes in through the windows. I walk into the kitchen and stand upon its brown linoleum floor. The shelves and counters are bare. Hanging from the ceiling, in front of the two large windows, is a red and blue glass shape of a hummingbird. It turns slowly as the thin string it suspends from twists about.

I look to the back of the kitchen, through the sunlit air, where a small metal table sits beside two more large windows. Thin white curtains hang in front of wide windows. Through the white cloth I can make out the shape of someone sitting behind the house. I walk across the linoleum floor to the screen door in the corner of the room. Upon its glass are words painted in red.

ALWAYS AND FOREVER
THE NEVER EVER NO
THE EVER NEVER YES
AND THE EVERYTHING THAT FLOWS

I place my hand upon the glass and feel the peeling paint against the palm of my hand. I push the door open and walk out onto the concrete patio that sits behind the house. I turn to see her sitting there, a cigarette burning in her hand as she stares emptily out at the backyard.

"Indiana?" I ask her.

She slowly takes a drag from her cigarette and blows the smoke into the air. Turning to me, she says nothing. Her eyes look somehow different than before. They're still hers. They're still the eyes that I've known, that I've loved. Yet something lies heavy within them, crushing and burning away her connection to this world, to this life. Though she sits close beside me, her mind is too distant to see.

"Would you like a cigarette?" she asks me as she flicks her hand forward and creates one that rests between her fingers. "I know that you do."

"Yes," I answer without thinking. I grab the cigarette from her hand, and as I rest it within my lips, Indiana waves towards me and lights it with a flame that sparks in and out of existence. I fill my lungs with smoke, and as I exhale, my body sort of melts into place. I become more existent. I become more real. And I have to sit down upon the metal chair beside me, for the sensation almost becomes too much.

Indiana stares out at the small backyard where the sunlight shines upon the green and yellow grass. The patio that we sit on is shadowed blue by the metal awning above us. We sit in silence even though endless questions, endless things to say to her, clutter my mind. Over and over I fill my lungs with smoke, and over and over I exhale gray clouds into the crisp air.

Suddenly, a jagged hole appears upon the lawn as the grass dissolves and the dirt that lies beneath it fades away. From where I sit, I can make out that nothing lies below the ground.

We exist upon a thin layer, which hovers within a void.

"You made this place, didn't you?" I ask her.

"I did," she replies while turning to me and staring deep into my eyes. An emotion escapes the hot something that burns away at her relationship with this world. A splinter of contempt shoots from her to me, and I feel it collide against my mind. I take a long drag from my cigarette and stare out at the hole in the lawn.

"He's dead," she says. "Isn't he?"

"Vincent?" I ask.

But she says nothing as she continues to stare straight at me.

"Yes," I say. "He's dead."

"It doesn't matter," she tells me.

"It doesn't matter?" I say back quickly. "That he's dead? That we're the only ones left?"

"No," she replies.

"What happened to you?" I ask her as I stand from my seat. "What did you see inside of me?"

"I saw nothing," she answers, exhaling the last of her cigarette, then tossing it to the ground.

"That doesn't mean a thing," I tell her. "What did you see? What happened to you?"

She quickly stands and grabs me by the wrist, pulling me close to her body. I rest my hands upon her back, holding her as I've longed to do for some time. She moves her lips to mine, gently kissing me. Closing my eyes as we embrace, I feel something strange happening to the world around me.

She lets go.

And as our lips separate, I open my eyes.

To someplace new.

Yet someplace known.

I stand again in front of the small white house; however, it looks less ragged, less aged, less oppressive. Its white sides are no longer coated in thin layers of grime. Its lawn is cleanly cut and its fence is free from rust.

"We're home," she says, pulling me towards the house.

We walk up the steps that lead to the front door, which is now closed. She opens the door and we walk inside. The front room, which was cluttered before, is now cleanly organized. The green chair still remains, along with the table and the lamp and the bookshelves that line the walls. In the corner of the room is a small television set. Sitting on top of it is a picture frame without a photo inside. Indiana moves to the green chair and sits softly upon it.

"This is where I lived," she tells me. "This was my life before now."

"How do you know?" I ask, sitting down upon a small wooden chair opposite her. As I do, I see a small photograph lying on the floor beneath her chair.

I quickly move away.

And slide through the room.
To her.
Still there.
Within the nothing.
And drifting down
Below the chair
I see the photograph.
And I know her.
The girl with the tattoo.
A small circle upon her wrist.
With six lines cutting through.
She sits not alone.
But with a man.

Just outside the picture.
And I move.
Back to there.
Where I was.
And where I am.

"My father and I," she says, ignoring my question, "we lived here together. This was always home. We never moved. We didn't have the money to. My father could never leave his job, could never risk going without money."

I think of asking her again how she knows these things, but I let the question go and listen to what she has to say.

"And would you please not drift away into that empty, little place you know so well," she cuts across the room at me.

I say nothing back and just stare into her disconnected eyes.

"I never called him dad," she says, gazing into the vacant air between us. "Or father. I called him by his name. Or at least by his nickname."

"And what was that?" I ask her after she ends her statement with silence. A painful grin grows across her lips as she moves her stare to me.

"I called him Vin," she says. "But his name was Vincent."

"So you're saying Vincent was your father?" I confusedly ask, leaning forward in my chair.

"I'm saying Vincent was my father," she answers, "though not the Vincent you're thinking of."

She stands from her green chair and turns to walk down the narrow hallway. I rise and follow her.

"I never really knew my mother," she tells me as she opens one of the doors within the hallway and walks into the room. "She left us when I was young, maybe two or three."

We now stand in a bedroom with walls painted dark gray. A large green bed sits against the wall, and beside it is a small nightstand. Indiana sits on the edge of the bed. She opens the drawer of the nightstand and pulls out a small cardboard box.

"She got pregnant a second time," Indiana says holding the box, "not long after they had me. But she didn't want it. And so she got rid of it without telling my father. He came home one day and found her lying drunk on the kitchen floor. She was screaming out loud, over and over again, what she had done to the life inside of her. I know this because he told me so. He told me everything. He never hid things from me. He wanted me to know the truth. He would tell me that the truth is what matters most. And that the truth would lead to what is good in this world. The truth would lead to love."

She opens the small cardboard box that lies on her lap and stares at what's inside.

"They had already named the baby," she says looking up at me. "A name that would fit both a boy and a girl. They named it Sam."

"So we're all a part of you?" I ask her skeptically as I walk to where she sits. "Why do you think this is true? How do you remember?"

She stares at me with eyes that know me well.

And I'm forced to sit beside her.

And to forget my questions.

She pulls a photograph from the box.

"Vincent used to show me this when I was young," she says, staring at the photograph. "It's a picture of my grandfather, Les, standing on the shores of somewhere. My father had tons of them. Pictures of Les all around the world. He traveled everywhere, my grandfather. And he wrote letters to no one. To himself."

She pulls a stack of papers out of the box and unfolds a single sheet.

"The night is different here," she reads aloud. "The stars burn bright across the blanket of darkness, unpolluted by our city lights. You can see every one of them shining through eternity, dancing with each other, being nothing more than what they are. It's incredible. And it makes you feel so small that you barely exist at all. And that's when you become everything. But again the sun rises. And again I feel much too large for this place. So I must move on. I'll write again soon. Love, Les."

She folds the letter and puts the stack of paper back into the box. She holds the photograph again, staring at it with eyes that wish they felt more, that wish they didn't bear the weight that crushes their connection to this life.

I almost say something, though I don't know what. Before I do, she hands the black and white photograph to me. It's a picture of her grandfather standing on the shore and staring out at the ocean.

"It's Vincent," I say, remarking on her grandfather's appearance, for in the picture I see Vincent standing in the sand. He's staring at the water with heavy thoughts behind his eyes.

She hands me another.

And leaning upon a long stretch of metal railing, high above the skyline of a city, is Vincent dressed in a pinstriped suit. He's looking at the camera with eyes that hide every question we could ever ask.

And another.

Of Vincent, or rather, Les, smiling across a table scattered with bottles and cards. He wears a torn white shirt. He's young, though his beard is grown long.

She turns over another photograph, but doesn't hand it to me.

She instead puts them all back into the box.

Pieces of the room quickly vanish as she shuts the cardboard box.

"That wasn't me," she comments.

And the rest of the room quickly follows. Piece by piece it disappears until Indiana and I are left standing upon bare concrete. Behind us, where a wall had vanished, is the house next door. Indiana walks out into the daylight, which radiates through the bright white sky. I follow her out into the street.

"I lived here," she says. "Even when I went to college."

The street bleeds out into a vast concrete surface.

Indiana moves along, lifting her arms to her side and effortlessly creating a world around us. Large buildings appear to our left and right. Trees grow out of nothing. She even forms people, which scatter the area, their faces blurred and their movements frozen still.

"I was alone," she tells me while staring into one of the blurred faces, "amongst all these people. I had a few friends, but no one I ever really became close with. No one who could ever make me feel less alone, less surrounded by something separate."

She suddenly turns to me, and as her eyes meet mine we become swallowed by walls that grow into this world from far within her mind. For a moment there is nothing but the pitch-black interior of the room she has made.

Fluorescent lights flicker into being above us, and I see Indiana standing on the opposite side of a classroom. All but one of the seats is taken up by students, yet the student have no heads. They're just hollow bodies with necks that lead up to nothing.

Indiana slowly walks across the room, gliding her finger along each desk she passes until she reaches the single vacant seat. She sits at the desk and stares forward at the empty blackboard.

"I studied religion," she says gazing forward, creating streaks of chalk upon the board with no apparent purpose, "and philosophy. I didn't really want to go to school. I did it for Vincent. I wanted to make him happy. I wanted to let him know that his life spent raising me wasn't a waste. That I could become something."

The white lines dancing upon the chalkboard become violent in their movements as Indiana's hands begin to tremble upon the desk. Suddenly, the lights cut out, and again we're in darkness.

The walls fall away as a miserable sky engulfs us from outside the room. Along with it comes a heavy downpour of rain. A meadow of dark green grass sits around the fallen walls, and scattered about are trees with damp, black bark. Indiana remains at her desk, staring forward at the blackboard that is no longer there. I walk beside her and lay my hand upon her back.

"No," she says. "You can't."

"I can't what?" I ask.

"Make me feel happiness," she answers. "Or your compassion. Or anything at all."

She stands from her seat and walks forward across the fallen blackboard. Out into the wet grass she moves, where she stops beneath a tall dark tree and rubs her hands against its moist bark. She turns and slides her back down the tree until she sits upon the ground.

Tears form in her eyes, collapsing down her face and mixing with the raindrops that slide along her skin.

"They're not real," she says. "They carry with them as much life and sorrow as the rain."

"What are you hiding from me?" I ask her. "Why is it that you deny everything about yourself?"

"My father died not far from here," she tells me pointing at a distant white building. "It was his heart. It stopped, and along with it his life."

She stares at the building. I can see, hidden far within her eyes, behind the weight that burdens her mind, a memory forming within her.

"They called me," she says. "I was alone, surrounded by people I didn't know and never would. I came here, but by the time I arrived he was gone."

She pauses.

And the rain begins to die down.

Until a faint mist collides against my skin.

"I remember," she whispers, hesitating for a moment between her words. "The smell. What was it?"

She shakes her head and silently mouths her question again.

"Someone was cleaning," she suddenly says, "the floors and walls. Making them white as snow. And the smell of it burned the inside of my nose and swam around in my lungs. I couldn't get away from it. It was everywhere, like poisoned lemons crowding the air. They told me that he had passed, and the entire time tears built in my eyes, but not from the sadness. From the painful smell. And after that moment I felt nothing. My emotions we're murdered by my senses. And I was empty."

"So this is why you feel nothing?" I ask her.

"I dropped out of school," she tells me, disregarding my question. "I had no need or desire to be there. It was my last year, but I couldn't stay any longer. And so I left and lived alone in what was my father's house. It was entirely my own."

She closes her eyes.

And as she does, the house from before begins to emerge around us. Yet the damp trees still remain, digging their way out of the floor and cutting up into the ceiling. Indiana stands and walks to the disordered bookshelf. Her hands run along the spines of the many books as she tilts her head to the side and stares deeply into them.

"I wrote," she says, "everything that I could. I wrote about what I thought and what I felt, or really what I didn't feel. Of how this place was empty. And even though I was no longer in school, I studied and read all I could about religion, philosophy, and even psychology."

She pulls a small paperback book from the top shelf. Its cover, which is dark blue and green with vague yellow words written upon it, is worn and bent upon the edges. She opens it and appears to read its contents.

"This was my first and only book," she says while turning the pages. "It was awful, but it was true. I put everything I knew about life in its pages, which was nothing at all."

240

She turns to me with a dry smile while handing over the book.

"I wrote it in my penname," she says as I look down at the cover.

EYES OF RED
A Novel
-Les-

"You wrote in your grandfather's name?" I ask her.

"I learned to write from his letters," she says. "The way he described what was within him and outside of him as if both were the same thing. It's what I wanted to accomplish. In my writing and in my life. It's how I wanted to explain what I thought I knew. I didn't want to be separate, but I was. It wasn't my name that was writing, it was this bodiless person made of me and him and the world around us."

I look back down and open the book to its first page.

Everyday I feel this strange nothing as it swims against the even stranger something within me. I become their collision, their endless romance. I become a hollow moment that instantly gives way to more. More love. More hate. More this, that, and everything. Yet the feelings are empty. They crumble away in fragments of consciousness to reveal the desolation within. And that is where I live.

My hair has grown long. Its color has vanished. And my skin is just as white. My eyes have become darker. Their brown has turned, in equal to my loathsome mind, almost red, like blood. My social life has all but disappeared. My only friend is the man I talk to every morning at the bus stop. What is his name? I cannot remember. Yet every cold morning, as we stand in the dirty, gray piles of snow that line the street, he greets me with a smile that only makes me feel more awful. More alone.

My chaotic words, which spill out of my mouth without my mind giving birth to them, often lead me into painful situations.

And I watch from far within as I wreak havoc on my life.

As I dissolve away at every connection I have with this world.

Why do I live this way?

Because I have to.

It is what I am.

I stop reading and glance up to see that Indiana is gone. I look around the room, with its mess of books and clothes and trees that grow up into the ceiling where the plaster crumbles away against the damp, dark wood.

I smell the smoke of her cigarette, and I follow it down the narrow hallway to the final door on the left. The room inside is painted every shade of blue.

Dark cerulean spirals collide against bright waves of teal.

Teal fades in drifts to deep indigo.

Indigo glides across splashes of pale azure.

And above, where the blue is painted darkest, almost black, are specks of gold that shimmer across the ceiling.

Indiana sits, listlessly smoking her cigarette in long, drawn out drags, upon the edge of a large bed with golden blankets and soft white sheets. The only other objects in the room are a dresser covered in piles of clothing, more books that scatter the floor, and a stained glass lamp that sits in the corner and glows its blue, yet somehow golden light across the room.

"I wanted to be sad," she says, exhaling a cloud of smoke. "Maybe I really was. Maybe all the emptiness I felt was just sorrow disguised as pathetic apathy. But nonetheless, the apathy is what I thought I felt. And so I tore myself down for feeling so empty, for not mourning Vincent. I was everything to him. He worked his life away to give me my own. And when he died, my life died too."

I try to say something, anything, but nothing is able to escape my mind and make the words that I need to say.

"The book gets less depressing," she says, looking up at me. "I tried to write something beautiful. But the only beautiful parts were the sad ones. Everything else was just a forced attempt at happiness. At seeming like I knew the silver lining of life's pain."

"All this," I finally spit out, "how do you know it's true? How do you know that this life you seem to remember is the real life you lived. Have we all just been pieces of your mind? Am I just a fragment of your memories, turned into some dream life?"

"No," she says bitterly, yet almost with a small laugh. "You're much more than that."

"What am I then?" I ask her. "And what the hell did you see inside of me?"

"My father," she says while standing up, "used to tell me that I would become who I was and nothing more, so I had to make myself what I wanted to be."

She walks past me, softly brushing against my shoulder and heading towards the hallway. I grab her before she leaves and spin her around. She stands close, staring at me with her hazel eyes. They burn even stronger with disconnect.

"Indiana," I whisper softly, but she pulls herself away before I can say more.

She walks out into the hallway and opens another door.

She moves into the room, and I slowly follow.

Walking into the room, I become amazed at the massive landscape I find myself in. Indiana and I stand beside towering objects that at first seem strange, yet slowly become evident as to what they are. To our right is a sink that stretches far too high for us to see the top. In the distance ahead of us is a bathtub, with someone sitting statically inside of it, the size of a mountain range. Each tile that we walk across, each massive square of black, of white, of black, of white, stretches on for a distance long enough to exhaust us by the time we reach the next. My lungs become full of humid air as we walk along the gigantic bathroom floor, towards the ominous bathtub and its inhabitant.

"What is this place?" I ask her. "Why did you make this?"

"It's the oldest memory I have," she tells me while crossing the shallow valley in between two tiles. "It's to me where I began."

"Your life began beside the lake," I tell her, "where Vincent found you alone."

"He told you that?" she asks, turning around.

"He told me that you'd been there for some time," I say walking closer to her. "So tell me, what happened in between this life you seem to remember and the beginning of the one you live now?"

"Nothing happened," she says quickly. "There was no space between then and now."

And again she walks forward across the vast ceramic tiles.

"You don't have any answers, do you?" I ask, following her.

"No, I don't," she replies. "Do you?"

Do I?

"No," I stutter quietly. "I don't."

And we continue to walk onward, passing beneath the shadows of the towering objects around us. When we come within a shorter distance to the bathtub, Indiana begins to create steps of gray stone beneath her feet that lead us up into the air. We move in intricate paths of ascent as Indiana walks upwards in random movements.

We rise to the porcelain bathtub, reaching its high edge. Sitting to the right in the water is an enormous man. His naked body glistens from the droplets of water upon his skin. His face, however, lacks any detail. There's just a flat plane of blurred skin in place of a mouth, a nose, and eyes. Far below us is motionless water. It sits in static waves, splashing still against the sides of the tub and the colossal man. To our left is a hollow form within the water. It's shape is vague, yet just barely I can make out the contour of a small child.

Indiana turns to me and says nothing, staring at me with her distant eyes before walking down to the solid water below. I follow her steps until we reach the clear ground. We walk into the hollow form of the child, past static splashes of water that scatter the air and motionless waves that push the ground beneath us up and down.

I run my hands along the curves of the empty space, along the edges of the still water. I move into tunnels that lead into projected spaces of a child's hand, of a child's fingers. I feel, as I touch the outline in the water, the small wrinkles of a child's skin.

Indiana stands in the center of the hollow form, staring out into the vast space between the shape that we are in and the faceless man that sits far across the water.

I walk to her side and turn to stare at him.

"Your father?" I ask.

And she turns to me, lifting her hand and caressing the skin of my face. She closes her eyes as her fingers trace the outline of my features.

I stand captured in her touch.

And I remember our home.

Our love.

Her gentle skin against mine.

And what I feel now is different.

It's not the same loving embrace as when we fell through the stars, making a life that was to be lost forever. I know now that she is gone. That what we had can never be again.

"Morgan," she says opening her eyes, "he used to tell me, was the most beautiful name there was. And that's why he named me that. But then he would look away and rub his rough chin and whisper, just loud enough for me to hear, that I was in fact so beautiful that the name must have been made just for me."

She turns to her left to stare at her faceless father sitting in the water. But as I turn to see him, I see that he no longer wears a featureless mask.

"His face," I say aloud as my thoughts pour out of my mouth, "looks so familiar. His eyes. Are they?"

"Yours?" she says, finishing my words.

And I sink deep into the moment.

As I stare at myself.

Yet I don't.

No.

I don't.

It's not me.

It's not anyone.

It's just a hollow face.

An empty shape.

"This isn't real," I say to her. "That isn't me."

"No, it isn't," she replies in agreement.

"Then why does he look like me?" I ask. "Why did you make him this way?"

"This has to end," she says staring vacantly at the space between her eyes and mine.

"What has to end?" I ask.

And she stands there with a lost look on her face, her body swaying, just slightly, as something stirs within her thoughts. Her arms begin to tremble. Her hands begin to shake. And she falls to the solid water below.

"No," she murmurs between heavy breaths of air.

"Indiana?" I ask her from a distance both physical and emotional. She continues to shake, her hands skidding along the clear ground. Suddenly, large chunks of the world begin to vanish in quick cracks. The walls around us vanish.

The man.

Her father.

Me?

He crumbles away into nothing.

And the destruction continues until all that's left is the thin outline of water in the shape of a child upon which Indiana and I remain.

"The rain is going to fall now," she says in a quivering voice.

And the rain begins to fall from the nothingness above us.

"The lights will shine," she continues.

And across the void, lights of red and blue and yellow and white blink into existence.

"The wind," she whispers.

And the wind blows cold against my skin.

"Where are we?" I ask her.

And she stands to her feet.

And she walks off the platform of water and out into the emptiness, creating thin sheets of metal beneath her feet. The heavy rain above collides with the steel, making loud noises as each drop drums against the metal. In the distance she stands, slowly spinning her arms about as a metallic world becomes created around her body.

Large beams of steel jut upwards from the darkness below, appearing to hold up the platforms of metal that glisten from the rainwater. Strings of white lights dance into existence across the sides of the metal platform, along with thin sheets of yellow plastic that flap in the wind. Piles of pipes and panes of glass scatter the surface that Indiana stands upon.

I follow her path out to where she is.

And as I stand beside her

I feel a vague sensation arise inside myself.

A familiarity?

The rain.

The lights.

The wind.

The cold wet metal surrounding.

It all feels unique.

Both known.

And unknown.

"This is the place," Indiana says, staring at me as rain drips across her lips. Her dark hair blows in the wind, sticking in smooth curls against the wet skin of her face.

"Where you killed yourself," I answer from the depths of my mind, pulling the words from somewhere hidden.

And sliding amongst the raindrops upon her cheeks, I see tears glide heavy against her skin. They reveal themselves, separate from the rain, with their weighty movements, their tragic forms.

"You're not empty," I tell her.

"I'm not anything at all," she says back.

"Why are you here then?" I ask her. "Why did you end your life? And why did you come to this place?"

The rain grows stronger.

And the wind blows harder.

"Because it never ends," she says forcefully through the loud sound of the downpour. "Because I saw the truth. That I was empty. And that I was everything. I was nothing. Alone. So why not kill myself? What did I have to lose?"

"I don't believe you," I tell her. "This life is more than just some echo of your past. Who am I then? What memory of yours do I belong to?"

"Now you're just lying to yourself," she says, walking backwards to the edge of the metal platform.

I watch her every movement.

"I have to end this!" she yells out, her hands trembling at her sides. "I can't do this anymore. I can't exist anymore. No. I can't not exist anymore. I can't be this empty something. This part of you."

"What did you say?" I ask, stepping closer to her, to the edge.

"Do you want to know what I saw inside of you?" she yells through the rain. "I saw myself. I saw what I really was and am. Which is nothing but an empty part of you. I have no mind. No soul. I'm just a cause and an effect. A projection. A machine. An empty reflection of your past. But when I was inside of you, a part of you, I was your mind, your soul, and for that single moment I was alive. I saw the life that I lived, that you lived. That I came from."

She steps back again. The heels of her feet hang over the edge of the wet, steel platform.

"I fell," she says as the rain dies down into scattered, heavy drops of water, as the wind slows to complete stillness. "I bled myself dry and slipped away with the falling rain. And that life ended. And a new one began. I woke up here, in this place of fragments, of pieces of my mind. And I saw the bright blue sky. And the sun shining bright behind the silhouette of a child."

"No," I say to her, to myself.

"I came into this world," she continues, "where I met myself. And killed myself, again. And I became who I was, who I am, and nothing more."

And I can't think.

I can't do anything.

Besides watch.

Myself.

And listen.

To her.

And the rain.

And the truth.

"Do you remember it now, Morgan?" she asks me, I ask myself. "Or are you Cyan? Or Indiana? Or Les? Or Vincent? Or Sam?"

And I remember it all.

The life.

The death.

Of who I was.

Who I am.

"I think," she says through the still air, "that you are no one. That you're alive and that is all. And what I am is what you're not. I'm dead, but I'm something. And as long as you're alive, I'll exist as this dead something inside of you, this hollow, lifeless other. But I want to be alive, Morgan. I want to be you, Cyan. And so you have to die. You have to become me. And I have to become you."

Her feet dig into the metal.

Her heels lift upwards as she puts all of her weight forward.

"Indiana," I whisper beneath my breath, as if reaching out for what's already gone, for what never really was.

She moves.

Lunging towards me, her body becomes surrounded by flames that burn in and out of existence.

Before she reaches me.

I drift away.

And through her liquid fire
As it glows across her skin
I move.
Forward.
Through this familiar place.

Within myself.
Within.
Nothing.

Landing upon the ground, I quickly turn to see her stumble forward to a stop. She stands with her head hanging down to the metal beneath her feet. The flames still spark around her body.

"You know that you can never touch me," I tell her. "You know that I'll always separate from here, from you."

She says nothing.

And the rain heavily returns, crashing loudly down upon the metal and extinguishing the fire around Indiana's body.

The body that used to be mine.

"I know," she says, lifting her head up, yet still staring in the opposite direction of me.

The faint sound of movement, of something cutting through the air, enters my ears. I can't tell where it comes from, since it seems to come from everywhere. As it grows louder, clearer, I sense that the movement is above. I look up to see countless white dots sitting in the black sky. They at first seem static, yet soon I make out their movements. And then their shape.

Endless, sharp, white arrows fall down to where we stand.

And as quickly as I realize their existence, they shoot into the ground around me. One of them sticks deep into my left shoulder just before I rip myself away.

From the downpour of arrows.

From this painful world.

And into the emptiness.
Swimming amongst the lines of white.
Until I'm beside her.
Where the arrows don't fall.
Where she stands alone.
Inside the dead something.

I pull the sharp arrow out of my flesh. Bright red blood pours from the wound and drips down my arm and torso. I grab Indiana and pull her around to me. Her face is partially covered in a black mask that swims around her eyes.

"You can stop this, Indiana," I say to her.

"The only thing that I can stop is you," she replies, pulling herself away.

"The life that we lived is gone," I tell her. "This life is the only thing that really is. The only truth is that we are here."

"We're dead," she says back. "There is no us. There's only you and me, completely separate. If I could kill myself to escape this place I would. But it wouldn't work. I'd still be the same empty other inside of you. And so you must be the one to leave this place, me, behind. You must be the one to die, so that I can become the life within you."

"You can't kill me, Indiana," I say moving closer to her. "And I won't kill you."

"I already have," she replies. "And so did you."

She takes a step back before turning to run out towards the nothingness surrounding the metal platform. As she moves into the darkness, she forms clear glass beneath her feet. I quickly run towards her, though her path is hard to follow. The transparent ground seems to vanish into the dark void. The only signs of its existence are the drops of rain colliding against it and the faint glare of distant lights upon its surface.

The space between us begins to grow, as I move in measured steps across the nearly invisible path.

I lose her to the darkness.

And so I pull myself in.

And glide.

Through nowhere.

Appearing beside her on the glass platform, I reach out for her body. She spins and swiftly kicks at me, sending the both of us falling from the sides of her path. I grab the ledge and hold myself up, where I watch her tumble down through nothing. She falls without making a sound, without making a movement.

I pull myself up and stand upon the clear surface.

I'm not sure what to think.

All of my thoughts try to live at once.

Yet they only succeed in killing off each other.

Until nothing is left inside my mind.

Besides one lonely thought.

One sole survivor.

It's the memory of my father.

Lying dead in the hospital bed.

And the smell of something burning in my nose.

As tears collect along the bottoms of my eyes.

Where they collapse in thick drops over the edge.

Down to my dead father's skin.

I feel so alone, feeling nothing at all.

And I'm brought back to where I am by a sudden flash of light through the darkness. Beneath me lies an ocean of turbulent water. Violent waves quickly move below, as the downpour of rain seems to fuel the water's rage.

No sun exists within the gray sky that now surrounds me.

Instead, high above me hangs a massive, glowing light bulb.

It burns bright across the violent sea.

Illuminating every fierce wave that rises.

I see Indiana's small black mask floating across the surface of the water in whichever direction the waves wish to push it. I collect myself and jump down from the glass.

Yet I collide with the water almost instantly.

And the massive, violent sea is nothing more than a puddle at my feet. I walk against its waves, sending small splashes into the air and across my legs. I look to the gigantic light bulb hanging above me. As I reach up to it, my hand grasps completely around it.

"I may not be able to kill you," I hear Indiana say from somewhere, "but I do control the world in which you live. You're nothing without me. Just as I'm nothing with you."

"Where are you?" I ask out to her.

"Does it matter?" she asks back. "I'm everywhere you are."

Suddenly a wooden door appears in front of me.

"I won't open it," I say.

"Yes you will," she replies. "I control this place."

"But not me," I say back.

"You are what's around you, Cyan," she answers from her hidden existence. "You're nothing living within something. And I am that something."

I stand staring at the door in front of me.

And at the strange, shallow, violent sea that stretches on in all directions. I reluctantly step forward for some unknown reason inside of me, or perhaps just curiosity, and grasp the door handle.

Opening the door, I see a long hallway with countless doors, much like the one I experienced long ago, where I was chased by fear. Water from the ocean at my feet pours into the hallway and soaks the rust colored carpet, turning it dark. I move through the doorway, and as I do the damp carpet makes wet sounds beneath each of my steps.

I walk along the hallway, passing the numbered doors.

All of them, however, are marked with the number seven.

Behind them I hear familiar sounds.

I stop and reach for a handle.

But the door is locked.

I listen closely.

And hear a known voice.

Is it my own?

I push hard on the door, but it wont open.

And so I dissolve.

Into my mind.

Where I swim through the door.

And find nothingness.

Complete darkness.

In all directions.

Besides where I was.

And where I return to.

"Does it go on forever?" I ask out to Indiana.

But I get no reply.

So I continue to walk forward.

Past the numbered wooden doors.

Seven.

Seven.

Seven.

Past the familiar sounds.

Seven.

Seven.

Seven.

Past my own thoughts.

Seven.
Seven.
Seven.

All of them open at once.

With a loud scream of wind.

A violent torrent of air blows inward through the doors, pushing me both forwards and backwards. I collide against the wall and grab ahold to the side of an open door. Outside of the hallway I see the endless void, the eternal darkness.

And suddenly I feel myself not just gripping to the doorframe, but hanging by it, as gravity pulls me downward through the hallway I've been walking. The strong wind dies down as I hang from the doorway, and I'm left within the stillness of the corridor.

"Just let go," she says from somewhere.

"And fall?" I ask.

"What reason do you have to live?" her voice asks through the still air. "You're forever mine. And the only escape is to just let go. To die."

"I have no reason," I answer.

And so I let go.

But I don't die.

I just.

Disappear.

Into myself.

Where she is nothing.

And I watch the empty doorways floating past.

I watch my body.

I watch my thoughts.

And I relax.

Into the falling movement.

Until the doors no longer exist.

And I'm drifting.

Above the ground.

Where five vicious blades cut upwards.

Blades that I know from before.

And beside them is Indiana
Looking up through a mask of pure black
Into the tall column of brightly lit doorways.
And to her.
I move.

Spinning myself around in one swift movement, I grab the staff from my back and swing. I feel her body collide with the heavy weapon, the weapon that she had made entirely for me, and the collision sends vibrations of sorrow through my hands and into my mind. I feel her soft skin, her thin bones, her slender muscles, her entire body colliding in pain with the staff as she goes flying to the ground.

The grief within my mind turns to regret.

This shouldn't happen.

I stare at Indiana, the woman I loved, the woman I built a home with, the woman that was everything to me. She lies in pain upon the ground from my own doing.

But I know that she's no longer the one that I loved.

I know that she is empty.

That she is nothing but myself.

Yet.

Still, she holds a place inside my mind.

Inside my soul.

And I want nothing more than to be no longer separate.

To end this opposite existence within one self.

Her hands grasp at the hard stone ground. Standing to her feet, she turns and stares at me through the mask that now covers her entire face. Only her eyes, disengaged with everything but her nonexistent thoughts, are visible.

"Kill me again," she says mockingly in muted tones from behind the mask. "It doesn't matter. You'll eventually die. And when you do, you're mine."

"I'm already yours," I tell her. "I always have been."

And in her eyes I can see that she smiles.

Though it isn't in happiness.

"So you think you've got it all figured out?" she asks.

But I don't answer

As I walk in her direction.

"You can't end this," she says stepping back. And as she throws her arm in my direction, I shift into nowhere.

Drifting to my right.
I glide.
Against nothing.

And appearing beside where I was, I see a massive block of violet colored stone occupying the space that I was in. Indiana stands with her arm lifted towards the solid cube. She quickly turns to me as I begin to run in her direction. Again she aims her arm at me and again I move away.

Where her creation doesn't exist.
Where I move
Through the liquid
Static
Emptiness.

I land behind her.
Spinning around, I see the bright green cube of stone she forced into the space that I was in. Jumping towards her, I quickly swing my staff, but before I strike her body she turns and blocks my swing with a sturdy wall of white. The collision shakes my senses, stunning me within the moment.
I see her movement.
And I can't escape.
I only fall to my right in reflex.
And the solid stone block of dark red exists in the same place as I do. My left arm shatters away as blood drips down the stone. The pain sends me to my knees, where I kneel with one arm gripping my staff.
The other.
Gone within the stone.
"I envy your pain," Indiana says, walking to where I am. "I thought I felt it before, but no, I never have. You're the one who's felt everything."
She rests her hand upon the top of my head.

"And now," she whispers from behind her mask, "I can take your pain away. I can make it mine. And you can watch from this empty place. You can be the dead. And I can be the living."

I fall back and swing the staff towards her body with my one arm. It collides against her legs as she forms a small chunk of yellow stone where my head was before. She stumbles to her left and catches herself. I collapse inward as she turns in my direction.

> And I push myself.
> Far past where she is.
> As my mind pushes back.
> With thoughts of pain.
> From my severed arm.
> Until it becomes.
> Too much.
> And I.
> Stop.

Where I can see her standing in the distance beside another colored stone. I squeeze the staff within my hand and feel pain within my arm. I have to end this.

> And she screams.
> I dig my feet into the ground.
> The sound of creation.
> And waves of color shooting towards me.
> Countless blocks of every hue form in the air.
> And all around me are the scattered stone cubes.
> As I run in her direction.
> Silently amongst the blocks of color.
> Hidden from her vision.
> Until I see her.
> And she sees me.
> As I jump, throwing my heavy staff at her body.
> She spins just out of its path.

And it digs its way deep into the pale, almost blue, wall behind her. She steadies herself and swings her arms towards where I am.

> Just as I slip away.

And I drift within the pain.

Forcing myself to stay within my mind
As I see my only arm
Disconnect
Within her creation.
And I hold onto the nothing
As long as I can.
Until my soul.
The hidden source.
Of who I am.
Makes.
Me.
Collapse.

Back into her world.
Where I lie on the ground beneath her feet.
She stares at me from behind her mask with eyes that show no emotion from the pain that she brings to me.

"Just let go," she says, shaking her head. "You won't feel a thing anymore."

I move to my knees and shove my head forward against the ground, difficultly pushing myself up and standing to my feet.

I step close to her.

Close enough to touch her, if I had arms.

"Show me your face again," I say to her.

"Why?" she quickly asks back.

"Because I want to say goodbye," I tell her.

And as the words leave my mouth, I wonder whether or not I really do. No answer ever comes.

"I wish I knew what that meant, to love," she says, pulling the mask from her face, revealing an empty smile across her once perfect lips. "I suppose I will soon enough. That is, if the life that you give me is better than the life that I've lived before."

Silently, I move my lips close to hers.

And her smile dies away.

For a single instant.

I see her.

The one I loved.

The one.

Who I was.

As her soft skin touches mine.
And I kiss her.
"Goodbye, Cyan" she whispers.
As our lips separate.
And she lifts her arms forward behind my body.
"Goodbye, Indiana," I quietly reply.
Moving in for one more kiss.
One more touch.
And as her lips meet mine.
I know.
That I love her.
And always will.
As I pull us both away.

Into a place she's been before.
Where she was my life.
And she is my life.
Now.
Our mind flows across this single moment.
Our lips embraced.
And my love keeps us together.
As we drift.
Forward.
Through the timeless nothing.
I can't let her go.
Into the emptiness.
Where she longs to be.
And I belong.
We stop.
Our bodies so close.
Yet forever separate.
I slide my lips away.
And caress my face against her skin.
Her perfect skin.
And I drift.
Down her long neck.
Her shoulders.
And her arms.
Until I reach her hand.

Where my lips return.
Kissing her palm.
Goodbye.
And our life.
Together.
Ends.

She appears upon the staff stuck deep into the pale blue wall.
My body stands just outside the weapon's reach. With a violent cough
of pain, she reaches for the object that cuts through her chest.
Red blood pours from the hole in her body.
Dripping down the dark gray staff.
I stare at her pain.
And I know that it is empty.
Just as my love for her.
Left to die within that separate something.
She looks to me.
And I look away.

X

The rain pours down from above as I sit upon a small white block at the edge of her world. She is gone from here, as are my arms, yet I bleed neither sadness nor blood, for what was lost was never really anything at all.

So here I exist.

Here.

I am alone.

And I become what's inside myself.

In front of me lies the vast space of nowhere.

As it always has.

And always will.

What is left?

Besides my thoughts.

My hollow body.

And the constant push of time.

A time that never ends.

And never begins.

There is no other, now.

There is only me.

And here I am.

In the same spot I was before.

Where I'll stay for the rest of time.

The rain slows down to a stop.

Static droplets in the air.

And into my mind.

I go.

Where I live.

Forever.

And then.

Forever ends.

And I appear amongst the motionless rain, where time begins to move again. It returns not with its forward push, but instead it pulls me back to the beginning that never happened.

The rain flies upwards.

And my thoughts swim against the reversal, watching as everything dissolves into what is was before. My past burns into existence, eating away at the present as I see before me the ones I've known. Yet, their faces are my own.

I see myself.

Only myself.

In everything.

I'm impaled upon a dark gray staff, bleeding my own blood.

I'm eyeless and burning atop a raging beast.

I'm staring face to face with myself, within myself.

I'm alone, shattered upon the sand.

I'm dead, against a wall of ghosts.

I'm alive.

And it all falls backwards.

Into my only life.

My only mind.

I drift.

Separate from time's movement.

Yet always attached to its existence.

And I flow.

Along with my seclusion.

Seclusion from who?

And my thoughts go violent.

Refusing to be alone.

And.

My.

Self.

Falls.

Apart.

I emerge into substance, where I still remain on the lonely white block, staring at what happens. All that I've experienced here flows past my existence in a single quick motion until I'm where this all began.

There is no clear blue sky above.

No shallow pool of water below.

Instead, I'm standing on cold, wet metal.

Staring out at cold, distant lights.

My arms, which aren't there, bleed from wrists that aren't there. They drip colors, from nowhere, down to the ground far below.

And the colors echo back as the Myriad begins to form, digging its way up and out of the ground. In the dark sky surrounding me, objects of every shape and size and color blink in and out of existence, sending loud snaps into my ears.

The Myriad flows against the metal I stand upon, splashing its chaos against the edge of the platform.

I watch as everything is.

As everything moves.

Around me.

Within me.

I remember what I felt when I ended my life.

Was it mine?

Or hers?

Or no one's?

I saw what I thought to be the truth.

That this world was meaningless.

Forever fleeting.

And I was a part of it all.

No.

More than that.

I was all of it.

I was the pointless existence of existence.

And so I moved on.

I let go.

Of what I was and wasn't.

I let go of nothing.

Onto another something.

So that I could forget myself and what I knew.

But deep down I wondered.

Was there nothing more than this?

Would I never exist again?

Or would I be dragged onward?
Into a heaven?
A hell?
Or both?

A violent shaking sends me falling to the ground. Unable to catch myself because I have no arms, my face falls hard onto the metal. I move to my knees and watch as the platform I'm on rises upwards, the Myriad remaining down below. Climbing alongside my movement are tall buildings that ascend out of the disarray.

I stand to my feet and walk to the edge of the metal.

My left eye burns, pulling me deeper into my existence, deeper into feeling who I am, as I stare out at the buildings that scatter the area around me. Their long glass windows glisten in the upwards-falling rain, while chaos flashes in and out amongst them.

Random objects.
Forming.
For only an instant.
Then vanishing.
Into the void.
Where I follow them.

And I glide forward.
Through my mind.
And see the world.
That is nothing more than me.
And I become.
What I already was.

I'm upon the rooftop that sat nearest me.
Its surface is made of smooth concrete.
As I look outward, more buildings rise ahead.
I run forward.
Jumping off the ledge.
And dissolving.
Into the air.

Where I become the movement.
The forward push.
And I soar.

Through the thoughts within me.
Onto the next rooftop.

And I land running.
Never stopping.
I move.
Until I again jump out into the empty air.
Into myself.

I fly.
There.
Which is here.
As I return.

Into the world that's lost itself.
Crumbling away in chaos.
I run.
I jump.
I disappear.

Leaving it behind.

Appearing again.

Fading away.

And moving into place.

Running.

Collapsing.

Jumping.

I let go.

Landing upon another rooftop, I stop before leaving its edge. The nearest building doesn't rise upwards like the rest. It grows from some distant point to my side, sitting horizontal in the air.

I run.

And I jump.

But I don't disappear.

I let my body flow against the world as I fall towards the building ahead. The rain stops within the air at the same time that I land hard upon the glass surface. Yet for only an instant it is still, for it quickly begins to pour down against the long glass building I stand upon.

I look about me and see that nothing else exists anymore, besides myself and the rain and the building and the Myriad far below. A pain grows faint in my chest as I think of my endless future here, a ceaseless flow within my mind of chaos and emptiness.

And the pain grows strong.

And I reach for my chest with arms that aren't there as I fall to my knees. I slide against the wet surface of the building. The agony within me moves. It flows through my veins and collects itself within my mind. I follow it.

And I see the pain.

Swimming amongst my thoughts.

Asking me.

Without words.

Questions I can't answer.

Yet I try.

And the answers that I find.

Break.

Me.

Apart.

The pain grows viciously outward, looking for an escape.

And it finds one in my left eye.

Complete agony envelops my senses.

Burning away at my vision.

As a pressure grows within my eye.

So strong that I feel myself ripping apart.

And I scream out into the rain.

As the pain escapes.

And my eye bursts in a fierce blast of red light.

I lose all control.

I lose myself.

Not into my mind.

But into complete darkness.

I awaken, with the left side of my vision gone, lying wet upon the glass building. Hot breath flows heavy against my skin. Rough fur glides along my body.

I rise to my knees and see him standing near me.

"I can take you away from here," he says in a deep voice that comes from all around me. His blood red eyes stare deep into my being. His fur is darker than the black sky that surrounds him.

"To where?" I ask.

"Anywhere you want," he replies without moving his massive jaws. "I know how alone you are. And I can end that loneliness."

"How?" I ask, still sitting upon my knees. "I am everywhere and everyone. Any other life would be a lie. A masked emptiness."

"But emptiness is what you want, isn't it?" he asks almost compassionately, walking around my body. "After all, you ended up here, in this void."

"I'm here because I know that there is nothing else," I say. "I'm here because—"

"You lost your way," he says angrily, moving his eyes close to mine. "And I can show you the path back to where you belong. I can show you that what you feel is real. That you are separate from this world that you can control."

"Who are you?" I ask as I rise to my feet.

"Do you really need to ask?" he laughs, turning away from me. "I'm a part of you, just as everything here is. I've always been a part of you."

"So I can give myself the answer," I reply, "to why it is that I'm lost? I can give myself the way out of this place?"

"You can give yourself anything you want," he tells me. "You are everything."

"You speak in lies," a voice says from behind me.

I turn to see Vidya standing on the edge of the glass building, his jade eyes burning through the rain as he moves in my direction.

"You are neither nothing nor everything," he says looking towards the red-eyed wolf.

"Don't listen to his meaningless words," the black wolf growls. "He's just another part of you, as everything is. And he's an absurd part of you at that."

"You are not lost," Vidya says, turning his great eyes up to mine, "for there is nowhere to lose."

"Then why am I here?" I ask him. "Why do I live within this chaos?"

"Because you've fallen away from what you are meant to be," the black wolf says furiously. "Because you've left your throne as the one who is all."

"You're not meant to be anything," Vidya tells me, "besides who you are. And that is why you are here. You're adrift within and without. You're not awake, yet not asleep. You're between where you were and where you will be. That is, you are here."

Their words confuse my mind as I become overwhelmed from the collision of meaning and meaninglessness. The disorder of thoughts within my head pulls me in every direction, leaving me stunned within my mind.

"What you need," the black wolf says to me, "Is what you want. Forget truth, for there is no truth."

"There is only truth," Vidya says.

"And it is a lie," the other wolf replies powerfully.

"There is only this," Vidya continues. "Now."

"There is everything," the black wolf says grinding his heavy paws into the glass. "And it is eternal."

My vision.

The sight within my single eye.

Begins to blur from the confusion.

"Be aware of yourself," Vidya speaks quietly into my mind, "and you will see the truth."

"No!" the red-eyed wolf screams out as he lunges forward to Vidya. The two collide and roll across the wet glass surface of the building. I force my only eye to focus.

Their loud roars ring out across the emptiness as they dig at each other's flesh. Vidya gnaws into the black wolf as they spin about and separate. The two wolves stare each other down through the heavy falling rain.

"The words that I speak are indeed empty," Vidya says to me while continuing to stare at the black wolf, "yet they are echoes of what has truth. They come from deep inside you. And they come from far without. His words, however, come from the surface of your thoughts, from what lies between your depths and distances. They have as much meaning as my own, yet they resonate not from truth, but from the lies of attachment."

"Enough talking," the black wolf growls. "He doesn't need to listen to voices inside his head anymore."

"Ignorance must die," Vidya says, "if you are to see what lies beyond words. Only knowledge, through its own sacrifice, can bring the end of ignorance. Only through the death of both can you be free, for neither can exist without the other."

And as Vidya finishes his words, the black wolf dashes forward, digging his jaws deep into the damp fur of Vidya's neck. Blood pours out from his teeth, staining the gray coat of the great wolf.

I watch as the two devour each other.

As blood sprays from both across the glass building.

Cries of pain ring out from their fighting.

Though I cannot tell from which.

And the rain grows stronger

As I stand beside the two of them

Unable to move from the confusion in my mind.

Their words devour my thoughts.

Am I everything? Am I nothing? Or am I neither?

And the questions create a chorus of emptiness in my mind.

For no answers are found.

I snap back into the moment as the large black wolf pins Vidya down, ripping at his face, sending blood across his body.

Vidya goes limp beneath the weight of the red-eyed wolf.

And I watch, unable to help, unable to do anything at all, as he grips Vidya in his fangs and drags him to the edge of the glass. With a heavy force he throws Vidya from the side of the building, down to the Myriad that angrily stirs below.

"You will live again," the black wolf groans, limping in my directions, "upon your throne, where you will have whatever you desire."

"I desire nothing," I tell him.

"You can't lie to yourself," he replies. "If that were true, I would be dead."

"Then you will die," I say stepping forward.

"You won't kill me," he says back. "I can take you away from here. I can make you forget. I know who you are and what you crave. I'm the one who brought you here. And I am the one who will take you away."

"I know who you are," I say to him, stepping even closer. "And what you desire as well. You became a part of me when I tried to stop your existence. And since then you've grown strong inside my mind."

"You cannot end this," he growls, "for you've killed the only thing that can harm me."

"You killed Vidya," I tell him, "not I."

"And I am you, remember?" he laughs back.

I do remember.

That I am everyone.

That I am alone.

And that Vidya still exists.

Within me.

"You cannot exist without him," I say, digging my feet into the glass. "And so he lives within me still."

"It's time to end this," the wolf roars. "Its time for you to be born again."

And the rain stops within the air, as it has before.

But now it stays frozen.

Time ends within this moment.

I stare into my eyes of red as they run in my direction.

And I dissolve into my thoughts.

Where the movement continues through my mind.

The wolf.

Running forward.

His claws.

Ripping me apart.

And I appear, falling backwards, pushing the static droplets of water through the air. I land upon the glass, sending cracks outward across its surface.

"You can't escape me," the wolf says walking over my body, his heavy paws digging into my chest. "I'm within every part of you."

His deep red eyes look down at me as I lie beneath his weight.

I hear the glass crack underneath me.

I feel it begin to crumble.

And as the he lifts his massive claws into the air and sends them back down at my body, the glass beneath me shatters away.

We fall together in the downpour of glistening shards, past walls made of soft pink flesh, as the movement of existence slows to near stillness. Beneath us a light glows upwards through the almost liquid air. I force myself to move through the thickness, spinning my body around until I'm face to face with the wolf.

And I watch as he slowly opens his jaws wide.

And moves towards me.

I let go.

And feel the pain of his existence.

Within myself.

As he rips away.

At my single eye.

My single body.

My single mind.

And in return.

He dies.

As he destroys his opposite.

And thus himself.

And I slowly fall.

Blind to the world around me.

To the pain of my body.

To everything.

Everything but thoughts.

Which are no longer are my own.

And they collide.

Against each other.

Forming sparks within a mind.

That is no one's.

And the light they create.

Is seen.

Not from the place of lost eyes.

But above and in between them.

And deeper into this being.

This life.

Me.

And I become myself again.

I become Cyan.

Fragments of the world begin to appear in this new vision, as wild thoughts spark together into vivid forms of amber and gold. I see the fleshy walls around me as I float downwards toward a sphere of pure light. Before I reach the brilliant shape, I land upon a thin, translucent surface that hangs within the air.

"You haven't died yet?" I ask myself, though the words are not my own. I feel my mouth move as I speak without speaking.

"I'm here, aren't I?" my voice answers back.

"Yes, yes, but it will come soon enough," I tell myself. "You will die just as you have before and you will die just as you will die again and again."

"And why can't this be different?" I ask. "This afterlife, this escape, has shown me the emptiness behind everything. And I want nothing to do with it, the lie of living."

"You think that you've escaped? That this is an end?" I laugh, waving my arms outward towards the world around me. "Your shallow sense of emptiness is nothing. You've been caught since the beginning, since the day your eyes opened wide to the bright blue sky. This is no afterlife. It is a beginning. It is a birth. It is your creation."

"It is nothing more than this," I say, though this time it comes from my own influence.

"Oh?" I reply, turning around to face no one. "You think you know the truth now, do you?"

"Maybe he does," I tell myself, tapping my finger against the side of my head. Specks of white light have begun to drift downwards, like falling snow, to the sphere of light below. The walls, which glow golden in my mind, pulse with a slow rhythm that gently shakes my body.

"Maybe isn't good enough," I say quietly. "He must know for a fact what he really is."

"And what is that?" I ask myself.

"You think that I know the answer?" I reply. "Why would I? I am you after all. Do you know the answer?"

"Maybe there is no answer," I cut in before I can respond.

"Oh please," I scoff back. "I think he's tried that one before. That's what this whole thing has been about!"

"So there is an answer?" I ask as the falling lights grow more abundant.

"I told you I don't know!" I yell back.

"Listen," I say calmly. "Maybe the point isn't the answer."

"Then what is the point?" I ask.

But I don't reply.

Darkness overtakes me.

The falling lights disappear.

The sphere below fades into a faint glow.

As the pounding rhythm grows louder.

And the golden walls crumble away with each great pulse, revealing the eternal world around me within the eye of my mind. The Myriad stretches on below to a distance immeasurable. Above it lies infinite darkness.

"It's beginning," I say quietly.

"What is this?" I ask.

"It's the end," I tell myself.

And in a sudden, violent motion the Myriad flashes upwards and switches its existence with the endless nothing. The contents of the chaos grind about in loud movements. I watch from my mind's eye as above me everything collides with all, as the countless forms of things exist in countless different ways.

The infinite distance of the Myriad crashes inwards in a moment that takes both forever and a single instant.

Now, swimming above, is the Myriad twisted about in a densely formed cylinder. It dances across the endless black sky in powerful movements until it quickly spins itself around and solidifies into a colossal staff that sits straight within the emptiness.

It hovers in place high above the dimly glowing sphere of light that sits below. Gradually the long form of the Myriad begins to move downward, gaining speed until it falls fast through the emptiness.

It strikes against the sphere in a powerful collision, pushing the ball of light downward until it dips into a hidden sea of darkness. The sphere, which now glows immensely bright from the collision, sends light across the waves that shoot infinitely outward through the black sea, forming a thin line of white across the distant horizon. As the

Myriad digs its way into the radiant sphere, the tail end of the tall staff goes loose and shakes violently in all directions.

With the last part of the Myriad forcing its way into the globe of light, a perfect sound rings outward across the now empty space that I exist in. It flows against my senses and eases every part of my being.

In a sudden snap, the noise ends, as cracks of the eternal darkness below shoot across the sphere of light. Gradually, almost too slow to see, the dark veins grow across its surface.

And in the distant horizon
Where the boundless waves of emptiness
Form into a single white line of light
I feel a tranquil sensation grow towards where I stand.

An empathetic consciousness seems to flow from the furthest reaches of my awareness, from the endless horizon around me.

The place between everything and nothing.
Where existence collides with the void.
Where life greats death.
And death greats life.

And suddenly the distant consciousness moves from the horizon and into the center of my being, where it flows throughout my body and my mind. The sphere of light still sits below, slowly mixing with the darkness, as I feel this perfect awareness become a part of my existence. The waves, which travel forever onward, no longer reflect the light of the sphere, for the light now goes directly to my heart. And from my chest it collects into a single strand of blue that grows outward from my body. It flows away from my heart, and with its separation I feel a painful emptiness. I reach for the dancing string of light with arms that don't exist.

The thin blue line swims around my body as it begins to grow in size. Its brightly glowing skin seems to envelop an endless depth of mystery as vague shapes dance in and out of existence within its body. Sharp spikes appear along its spine as it continues to grow larger.

It coils itself into complex loops that move about the air.

And as it dances in captivating movements around where I stand, I move myself closer to its enigmatic body. I stare into its depths, where I see familiar objects, familiar places, familiar people, though all of them seem at the same time completely unknown to me.

Enveloping my mind is the urge to feel the being.

The desire to join with this divine presence engulfs my spirit.

Unable to grace the being with my hands, for they no longer exist, I lean forward, caressing the skin of my forehead against the blue glow of its surface. Where it flows against my body, I feel myself dissolve away, though the parts of me that separate still send sensations to my mind. I feel a small part of myself swimming through an infinite distance, caressing across eternity into the endless depths of a ceaseless existence.

Wordless meaning blends into my thoughts.

And I know.

The unknowable.

And I understand.

What isn't there to understand.

As I step away from the glowing blue body that flows all around me, I look upwards to see his marvelous gaze staring down into my mind. Two brightly shining horns rest atop his head. His mouth, which sits wide open, is lined with enormous white fangs that emit not terror, but refuge from all fear. Two long, slender strands of shining hair grow above his jaws, and on his chin lies a thick, bright mane that grows up and around the entirety of his head.

His eyes shine a spectrum of every color that exists.

Above and in between them lies a single white eye.

Unchanging and eternally pure.

"This can't end," I tell myself. "I'm so close."

"To what?" I ask back.

"To escape," I answer. "To the truth."

"The truth," I reply, "is that there is no escape."

"How do I know this?" I ask.

"Because I am you," I reply.

And I know that it is he who speaks within me.

The divine creature that wraps around my body.

"Never are we separate," he says through my voice, "though never are we attached."

"Who are you?" I ask him, I ask myself.

Loud cracks of thunder ring out from the distance, answering my question. Through the empty spaces that move amongst the divine being's spirals, I see that the sphere of light is almost entirely engulfed by the shadows of the void below. As the last bit of light is swallowed by the darkness, the universe inverts itself into its opposite. The boundless sea below and eternal sky above now glow bright white as one endless dimension. The sphere, however, still remains solid black.

"You must go," I tell myself.

"Why?" I ask, staring into the sacred being's eyes.

"Because," I reply.

The wide mouth ahead of me rests down upon the transparent ground I stand upon, drawing me inward towards his body. I walk forward between his large white fangs. As my feet touch his glowing blue tongue, as I join into him, I feel a familiar caress against my skin.

She touches my body.

My mind.

My soul.

And I know.

That I'll be with her again.

As I melt into everything that is.

And isn't.

I know the truth.

Though it doesn't belong to me.

As I swim through the emptiness.

The endless.

Eternity.

Towards the sphere of nothing.

Where I will exist.

Within a life to be lived.

And I reach out for her.

As she reaches out for me.

And I dissolve.

Into my body.

Into my mind.

Into my soul.